AZIMUTHS

AZIMUTHS

R. A. Morean

Avignon Press

Morean, R.A.
Azimuths

Women-California-desert-identity-literary

Cover Art: Vasquez Rocks: Harris Shiffman | Dreamstime.com;
Basilosaurus isis, lower jaw by Tom Horton from Shanghai,
China ([CC BY-SA 2.0
(http://creativecommons.org/licenses/by-sa/2.0)], via
Wikimedia Commons; California Condor by CamelNotation
| Wikimedia Commons ([Public Domain).

ISBN: 978-0-9962920-3-0

Library of Congress Control Number : 2015946038

Avignon Press
Newport Beach, California, USA

For Hannah, Lee, Kira and Joseph

as always

Acknowledgements

This book was not written in a timely manner and in that span of 17 years or so, there are many people I must thank, beginning with Philip Spritzer, who believed in the novel from the first attempt. Readers, whose help and guidance and support through many drafts include Kathy Roberson and Edie Powell. I'd like to thank Casey Dorman, who saw something in the story I wanted to write. I would also like to thank faculty and participants of the Antioch Writers' Workshop where I have spent ten phenomenal summers learning from everyone about every aspect of writing from craft to literary citizenship. Finally, I want to thank my children, Joe, Kira, Lee, and Hannah who are all far more brilliant and kind and talented than I will ever be.

Horizon

1. The line along which the earth and sky appear to meet; the boundary line of one's vision on the surface of the earth.

2. The range or limit of one's knowledge, experience or observation.

3. In astronomy, the plane tangent to the earth's surface at an observer's position, also called the sensible horizon; the great circle formed by the intersection of this plane with the celestial sphere, also called the true horizon.

4. In geology, a deposit of rock characterized by specific fossils and hence known to have been formed   in some particular period.

Azimuth

The horizontal direction expressed as the angular distance between the direction of a fixed point (as the observer's heading) and the direction of the object. Used in navigation.

MOTHERS

Hattie Peach

I know my father, Henry, would prefer it if I did not read the World Almanac every year. He doesn't see the necessity. "Hattie, you're going to clog up your head," he's said over and over again. I have my mother's brain. It's like a sheet of curled film, a spool at one end, taking radiant energy and light and smoothing them into flat, neat little frames. I have hundreds upon hundreds of pictures stored. Henry's afraid of the statistics, the page numbers, the infinite tallies and that my frames are finite. I think he's afraid my brain will collapse as hers did, heavy and sodden with facts which point to nowhere.

My mother was a thin tiny woman with thin tiny hairs coming out the top of her head. My first memory of her is my hand, dimpled and small, dirt under my fingernails and fingers sticky with grape Popsicle juice, patting the concave side of her head where what little hair she had turned downy.

My second memory of her is a voice booming from behind the front screen door, loud, strong, unwavering and certain: "The paradox, Henry, is the masses don't want responsibility for their existence, they don't want liberty, they can't stand the thought of love—of free love, of love beyond the Puritan ethic." My father, Henry, however, was not at home at the time and I remember being frightened she would suddenly become lucid and be humiliated. Not by what she said, but by seeing only her daughter on the front steps.

My mother was a dying revolutionary. She had black and white pictures of Emma Goldman all over the house and she could talk for hours of political restraints, constraints, confinement. She died in 1952, the final year of the Rosenburg trial. Though the concave part of her head had deepened and she could not speak and I wasn't very certain she even knew who I was, she listened to the trial, the radio balanced on her strange antiseptic smelling bed, her eyes wide, staring straight ahead. After they ran current through Ethel twice, mother lay very still and I can remember putting a hand on her chest to see if she was still breathing.

Up until almost the very end the three of us would take walks through the cemetery next door. The Waldheim Cemetery was huge, at least huge to me and we would stroll through to the German side— Henry pushing Mother in her wheelchair, me skipping ahead. At Emma's spot we would stop and look at the monument. The tombstone was as tall as Henry and towered over my mother in her wheelchair. I would watch the dual profiles: my mother's, low and tilted up from her chair, and Emma's, bronzed and ignoble, gazing out sightless and indifferent across the grass.

Mother died at night. I never saw her when she was dead. After Mother died and before we began moving, I would often play hooky and run past the Haymarket Seven to Emma's spot in the grass.

So every year I try to finish the Almanac. It's a perpetual challenge. Each January I sit down with the new edition, the cover glossy and pages hard and white and plan out how many pages per day I need to read by December 31. Organization is key and I try to be organized. There are only a certain number of facts the Almanac will hold and I usually can work out a quota of reading two pages a day. Seems easy enough and the year starts off with a bang, the first half done with by the middle of July. Then a creeping insidious lethargy begins to seep, the pace breaks, and I'm down to half a page a day, then a paragraph, a sentence and then I've stopped still. Not even one statistic. Then those days multiply, one after another, and while I sit around berating myself, I get way behind.

Every New Year's Eve, then, is a blessing. A breaking free of past responsibility, a letting go of the old. With a gentle hammering in my chest, I slam the previous year shut, clean the slate, and look forward to the next edition. I do admit to a vague, irritating feeling of incompletion when the cuckoo above my kitchen clucks out those final twelve clucks. But I suppose everyone feels that way on that particular night.

This year, however, I will be victorious. I have promised myself I will finish. I will close the loop. No matter what. I'm already to the U.S. National Park System and the Homestead Act and it's only the beginning of June. I like the cycle of opening, reading, closing, and, perhaps one day, finishing.

Where we live at Raceway Trailer Park, on the lip of the Mojave, at the end of the Sierra Nevada, there are no seasons. The desert is static. Nothing changes at Raceway. The morning light may be a shade pinker in the late summer and a few flowering yucca and clutches of low growing golden poppy may signal spring, but essentially all days are the same. And I need something cyclical to organize myself around. Otherwise, I'll end up like Henry, slouched in a dark corner, thinking about Mother, sucking up gins through a flexistraw over at the Volcano, staring at people from L.A. on their way to Vegas. Actually, he doesn't stare at them—he usually gets up, the straw sinking against the edge of the glass, and walks straight out into the sunlight to gaze at their trailers.

I like living at the trailer park. Raceway isn't round like a racetrack. It's laid out lengthwise on long papery strip of dried up riverbed, three rows of twelve trailers. That's it. The banks of what once was the river have smoothed and widened and here is where we all sit—in the middle of the riverbed—poised to flow. Directly north of the park are Vasquez Rocks, long, thin, slanted formations all tilted to the right, facing east. From where we sit, the riverbed and the trailers run parallel to U.S. Rte. 14.

All of our mailboxes are stacked one on top of the other, in corresponding rows of twelve at the front of the dirt driveway. Next to the mailboxes are two brown posts where the old "Raceway Trailer Park" sign used to hang. That's why the mailboxes are so crammed together, to leave room for the sign. It had a badly painted picture of white starting gates, a brown horse track, and little men in black and white checked outfits holding red flags.

Many of the trailers come and go within a month, though some may stay as long as a year or two. Most are filled with women and kids, lots of kids and a handful are homes for shifting cowboys, old cowboys who don't do much riding. I don't talk much to my neighbors, except the ones who have been around awhile. I've lived here since high school, so that makes Henry and me some of the oldest settlers, but there are a few who were here before us: Barday Tullis and his horse, Tip, have lived here forever it seems and Kinni Shin was here before us too. But no one really knows what goes on in Barday's head and no one has ever seen Kinni's face. There's just been a handful of others who have stayed put in the last fifteen years. A year after we moved to Raceway, the park flooded and the Red Cross came out. That was when the sign washed away.

So where we live, I have to read the Almanac. Choices are limited at Raceway. There's no starting gate and no finishing line. People roll in, stay for a awhile and roll out. For those who don't leave, life is spent milling around on the sidelines, one day a blueprint for the next. The Almanac gives me the chance to mark time.

Rte. 14 is long and straight and stretches to the horizon like the sea. We all live on its edge and the sand lives under us.

Melody Hallow

My mother was a superfluity of nuns, which just means there was a lot of them. I don't know who my real mother was. Whoever she was, she clearly wasn't a mother. The story that came to me in pieces, flying through the dark, whispered at lunch, or overheard while shitting on the toilet, was that I was found in an empty dog food bag in back of a hospital. But that's O.K. Those less fortunate are often desperate.

My first memory of a mommy feeling was when I was real little. I must have been in the nursery, because all I remember is seeing these rows and rows of babies with bottles stuck in their faces and the room was light and filled with sucking sounds and the sweet synthetic smell of formula. A nun walked by and picked me up and let me see the babies sucking on their bottles. The tiny metal cribs seemed to stretch on down the hall. And I remember liking the way she held me, firmly on her knee, one hand around my stomach, and I could feel her breasts pressing around me and I leaned my head back against them, against her habit.

The nuns were quiet and made no sound when they walked. When I was older, I would lie on my cot at night imagining black robed ghosts wandering the stone halls. They were ghosts of times-to-be, forever impressing their shadowy frowning faces on my conscience. By day I played and learned my lessons and had soft white cheeks pressed close to mine and loved the smell of mothballs and starch. Sister Eloise was my favorite, a scrawny wiry woman with a silly silvery laugh and a pocket of mints. My days were cool and sudden, happening one on top of the other in quick succession, filled with the aura of love and the quiet presence of discipline.

By night I was terrorized. Hell, heavy and hot, forced itself up into my cot like spewed lava. I lay unmoving, paralyzed by flames licking my heels, wicking away my soul. The aura of love was torn, shredded, and discipline rattled apart into chaos. That's when ghosts filled the corridors. Even Sister Eloise disappeared. As the sun sank and purple shadows grew, I imagined her face slowly evaporating into gray mist. In my mind's eye I could see her black habit floating in the hall outside my door, faceless and without feet, moving slowly, inflated by hot gases.

I left the school suddenly. The Lady of Perpetual Sanctuary lied. Part of my speed in departing was to escape the ghosts. But I guess I wasn't quick enough. Death and its ghosts have always followed me.

I think about death all the time. About when I'm going to die. About what it would be like when there's no more me walking around. Not like I'm going to change the world or anything in the meantime or anything like that, but, still, there is going to be no more me at some point. I don't have a bucket list of things I haven't done yet. I don't even have a list of last wishes—and you'd think that someone who thought about their own death as much as I do would have a list a mile long. Of all those things-left-to-do.

But everything's done. Everything's complete. There are no loose ends. I don't have anything to leave behind. I don't have anything I want to get done. Or need to get done. The future doesn't exist as a thing, good or bad—it's not even indifferent. To be indifferent something's got to at least exist. But I discovered the future isn't real.

The nuns never spoke about the future unless they were talking about dying and hell and what happens after you die. I thought about hell a lot after what I did and finally came to the conclusion the future was something living people made up—and if you were dead there couldn't be any future anyway. And the stories of hell, of first going to purgatory and then speaking with angels at the gates and then descending layer by layer into the hell hole to burn forever, all seemed to follow along in some chronological order. For every hell-story the nuns had a beginning, a middle and an end. To start out with a beginning there has to be a future in order to get to the end. But there can't be any future in hell because by the time you get there, you're dead and when you're dead you have no future. I figured those nuns knew far too much about hell for it not to exist. And because the living are the ones who fabricate the future, they must be the ones living in hell. Hell on earth. Not a new idea.

But I'm not living in hell. I don't have any worldly possessions. I don't seem to want anything. I don't have goals. Not even personal ones. For me there is no quest. I was twelve when Mother Margaret first called me a child of the present and I thought she was talking about my birthday. But she was right. I do live in the present. And really, compared to some other places I've seen, it's a very nice spot.

This is why I think about death all the time. I'm comfortable in my present, receiving each day as it comes. I don't wrestle with unknowns. I don't long for the past or yearn for a future. I'm content and Death knows everything's in order. It's waiting. Death circles around and around high above in the night sky, languishes on the center divider, curls, flicking its tail under a rock on a long walk, hides between the dull monotonous beats of a heart. Death is not the future. Death is not probability. It's for certain. It's out there, every day, stalking me like some psychopathic lover.

I have daydreams of airplanes landing on my trailer, or rattlesnakes under the bed, of getting crushed under trains or cement mixers, of the silence of my own chest. I can feel bones snapping and muscle tearing, my face numbed by sudden impact, some terrific force exploding me as I'm smeared across asphalt, burning against pavement while more chunks of me are knocked around, twisted off and crammed up wheel wells. These are terrible daydreams, all gruesome and in big, bright Crayola colors. The dreams are as sudden as accidents. I never know when one is coming until it happens, swiftly, without discretion, with its own consciousness, and then it's gone, and I'm left feeling hollow, limp, routed clean.

Ultimately, it's not the dying that bothers me. It's what dying leads to. It's the blackness, then thin emptiness and the complete absence of stars.

That's why I like the desert. At night it's wide open, cloudlessly filled with asterisks of light.

Lani Fabrile

I really can't talk much about my mother. She's a fucking gem. She would die if she ever found out about me now. She lives in New York. I don't tell anyone here that because I'd stick out like a sore thumb. A mother living in New York. That has nothing to do with what's going on here. Which is shit. She's married to big developer guy with tassels on his shoes and they live in New York, off Eighth Ave and have this summer place in Connecticut. I got to be at her wedding. I was nineteen and hadn't spoken to her since I ran away, but then I saw her in a copy of Forbes, getting married and I thought, what the hey, and called her up. She paid for my ticket, my hotel, food, everything. She was gorgeous. I never got a chance to talk to him. He looked O.K. Too tan for New York though. But that was three years ago, and, well, I haven't heard much from either of them. I get a postcard once in a while. But you know I really screwed her by taking off so I really can't blame her. I can be a shit.

My first memory of her is her face pressing against mine and it's hot out and humid, we must have still been living in Arizona, and I can hardly breathe. And her hair is scratching me and she's pushing really hard against my face and I'm trying to get away from her, trying to wriggle out sort-of. And then she just starts sobbing.

I ran away because she told me to. Said she'd had it. When I first left I couldn't let myself think of her because if I did—suddenly, like when I was in some gas station bathroom brushing my hair—I'd freeze up. I mean I couldn't move. I would just start thinking about her and me and the fights and screaming, and closing that door in my face and my broken nose and smearing blood on the door in big F U C K Y O U letters and crying and getting a splinter in my finger from the porch.

It's like there'd be this flash and then I'd be turned to stone. Solid rock. I couldn't hear anything, couldn't see anything really and it would be impossible for me to move my legs. In my mind, I would be back sitting on that porch in front of that door and I wasn't going to move an inch once I got there. It would flip people out when it happened. The first year or so after I left home was the worst. Once, the police up in San Fran had to bust open the door to the ladies room at a Denny's because I locked it, remembered the hollow sound of her cheap bracelets clacking together and then I was back on that porch again, not budging.

I got out of it though. I met this guy, Alfred, who was old enough to be my grandfather, and he gave me his 35mm camera. With filters, zoom lens and a tripod. Unbelievable. He liked for me to get dressed up for him and after we split I started dressing up just for myself. When I first moved to Raceway, I started dressing up out in the middle of the desert, putting on evening gowns, doing heavy makeup (lots of eye stuff–windows of the soul shit), fixing my hair with glitter and spray. I'd sit on rock or stand against the sky, set the camera on the tripod and keep the tripper hidden in my hand. Then I'd go ahead and think of my mother and wait to freeze up. Once I'd hit that spot, once I was back on that doorstep, I'd trip the camera and the snap was taken. That's how I cured myself. I got to actually see what I was putting myself through. And the pictures were pretty good. I liked the results. It was safe to see myself remembering her. Besides, I think I look really sexy in some of those shots.

I don't do that anymore, dress up and turn to stone. I guess I kind of got bored with it. I became more interested in the spot where I was standing–the rock or the sand or the creek bed. Now, whenever I screw somebody, I just take a picture of the place where we did it. It's funny. Whenever they find out I've got a camera on me they're always upset that it's not a Polaroid instamatic. When they get over that, they want to take a picture of me or have me take a picture of them–or, god forbid–set the camera on a rock and take a picture of the both of us. But I never do it. I like only the rocks, the scene. I always tell them it's a memento of the occasion and I just do a snap of where it happened. They like that memento shit.

I don't feel bad about what I do. It's fine. We're all consenting adults. It's not like I go around using people, and they all know what they're getting into with me, I mean I don't stand there and promise them love and duty and death do us part and all that crap. I'm not going to sprout curlers for anyone. I mean I would if they asked me to, just for that particular day. I'd bring them a beer, or change the T.V. station or fuck them one more time, but just for that day. Never for more than one day. One day is enough for anyone. And they accept that. Oh, I guess I've had a couple of guys hang around, but by next afternoon, they're outta here. And if they're not, I end up ducking them or kicking them out. Once I had a guy show up again the next night, and I told him off and had to bolt my door and shove the bed up against it. He was pissed and when his beer bottle broke against the side of the trailer I called the police.

I just don't see how anyone could stay with someone for longer than a day. Twenty-four hours, tops. I mean, what do you talk about? There's nothing interesting going on.

I can't imagine not having sex. Never, ever doing it. Like Kinni next door. She never does it. She doesn't have guys over. Or chicks either for that matter. I know she's got something wrong with her face, but hey, when it's dark, who cares? Most of the guys I do it with would be happy to trot next door and do it with her. And it's not that she's older than me either. I get the impression she's never done it. Maybe it's best that way. But I can't imagine dying, living your whole life and never doing it. Never getting sweaty and dirty and feeling some guy come.

It's not like I come all the time. I don't live for orgasms or anything like that. If I did, they'd probably label me a nympho. I always come later, by myself after they've left. The few times I have come with a guy, I always feel it in my feet and from the corner of my eye I can see my feet flapping away like flippers. I don't mind the grunting and groaning, but I hate seeing my feet do that. That's why I try not to come when they're around.

Kinni Shin

I do not know if my mother was a proud woman. I do not know if she was traditional. I do not know if she loved my father. People have told me she sang. I do not remember this about her. I do know she could run. She could run faster than a pebble dropped off a mountain cliff, faster than electricity, faster than anyone I have ever seen.

I remember her running toward me and my brothers, toward the three of us, flying across the heaving ground, her feet not touching the earth. Her face was twisted in a shape I had never seen before. I was not scared though my younger brother had begun to cry. She flew faster still, down the hill to the garden where we were playing. Her hair was on fire. Her long dark hair was snapping and cracking around her face and still she ran to us. The earth hiccupped and her feet stopped flying. I began to whimper. Her feet seemed to melt into the earth. She fell and her arms, her round brown arms began to melt too and she tried to scream but her throat was melting.

I reached for my face.

Nagasaki was erased three days after Hiroshima. That meant human beings sat thinking about the process by which to melt my mother for three days. Three days of eating food, three days of conversing, three days smelling the air, three days of feeling sun or rain on their skins. Three days of shivering, of hunger in their bellies, of soreness in the backs of their throats. Of urinating and defecating. Of living and deciding. In any war most fatalities and injuries are to civilians. In all war there is rape. In no war before this was flesh evaporated, all living things exploded and the long double helix of DNA stripped and twisted, its bonds broken and reunited in grotesque knots, subjecting the unborn and those not yet conceived to a new definition of what is human.

I alone survived in the backyard. I couldn't see my brothers or my mother so I watched others who survived. Others who lost hair, whose sores began as rashes and within days had turned to open bleeding wounds. They were victims of an invisible slow fire which fell continually for weeks. It fell from sky to earth and will never be gone. We know this now.

My father did not return home. I have often believed he too melted, picturing he and my mother spiraling upward together in a slip of smoke. At other times I have believed he was crushed under stone, far away from her.

I do not believe my uncles who tell me he returned home to rest the barrel of a handgun against his forehead.

If you look in the English dictionary, under Geographical Names, Nagasaki is described as such: "city port of Japan in West Kysushu on the East China Sea; population 535,000." I do not know how they count such a number.

Right now, I am getting ready to go to work. I work at inventory. I count things. I count things on shelves. Things people buy: tuna, roach spray, plant food, washers, gum. I work at night, when it's cool.

I know this is not interesting, but I feel you should know this about me. I stand naked in my trailer.

I reach in to the top drawer of my dresser and pull out a pair of pantyhose. I pull them up, stretching each leg open with my fingers and thumb, widening the thigh, and the elastic waist snaps around my own. I pull out a bra. I have two, one beige and one white. This is the white one. I slip both arms through more elastic, slip my fingers under each breast to smooth out the cups and fasten the bra tight in front. My breasts are small, flat, and tucked under each cup they are nicely hidden. I am walking over to the closet. It's three steps away and I fold back the louver doors. I am selecting a plain blue skirt. I have three skirts: navy blue, forest green, and black. So I slip on the navy blue skirt, sliding it over my breasts and zipping it snugly over my seat. My hands lay lightly for a moment over my abdomen. Firm, safe, chaste. I pluck a piece of fuzz off the slight curve of my stomach. I glance up and see my favorite blouse. It's white, very white, with a ruffle running down the front. I pull it off the hanger and it collapses softly in my arms. I slip one arm in, and then the other and button up the front. The buttons on the cuffs make the sleeves tight around the wrist. It feels good. It feels good to have that small pulse with me, to be able to hear and use the beat. The beat of my heart helps me count.

Now I walk into the kitchenette. The cap is in here, on the kitchen table. It's where I left it last. I pick it up. The cap is of heavy black felt and is very worn. I set it on my head like a crown and tuck a few strands of hair under the rim. I keep my hair very short, for convenience.

The veil is lying on the table as well. I pick it up. It is not a true veil. It is actually a long piece of black lace from my mother's dress, her black dress made of very fine Japanese silk. I begin to wrap my face, starting at the top of my head, under my chin, backup around my eyes, back up and around my nose and mouth, back up and around by nose and mouth again. I tuck the end piece under my left ear. I turn and pull the venetian blinds up for a moment and I can see my reflection in the picture window glass. I look serene. The black lace is in soft, lovely folds across my face, and in the light from above the table it looks beautiful. For the first time in a long time I wish I had a mirror.

I sigh. Now I am ready. To do inventory. I pick up my purse and take out my key. I open my front door.

The evening air is light, very breezy and the horizon is set with low clouds streaming gold and peach ribbons against the night. I pull the door shut and turn the key in the lock.

RACEWAY

Henry was Hattie's father and he hated the desert. It seemed the perfect place to go after Arlene died. To get out of Chicago. To go West. To leave a soft damp musty place and go somewhere hard and naked and red. But he never meant to stay. He buried Arlene at the Waldheim Cemetery, threw her paints, her letters, dresses, comb, beads—her things—into a trunk, quit teaching at the high school, boxed his history books, packed up Hattie in a pile of stuffed animals and drove to New Mexico to pump gas. The books and the trunk followed them everywhere. They lived in Portales for a year, outside Santa Fe for two and learned to watch the sky. Especially in the evenings. The sunsets in Santa Fe were always full of bright purple and red light.

They lived in Santa Fe for six years. Then when Hattie was twelve, they began moving west again, this time across Arizona: Springerville, San Carlos, El Mirage, Kingman. Henry kept pumping gas. The books would be opened from their crates, lined up in chronological order and packed away again with the next move. By the time Hattie was fourteen, they were at the edge of California, in Needles. At night they would walk down to the Motel 6 and stand in the swimming pool, their bodies wavering in water up to their necks. The water was luminescent, green and warm. When they left, their wet footprints evaporated on the hot concrete. Under a full moon their tracks disappeared, turning from glossy wet to dull smudges, and then gone, all in a matter of minutes.

Henry and Hattie ended up outside Acton, California in 1970. It had everything they needed. A gas station, a store, a bar, and a school bus. Hattie was a senior in high school. Henry thought she needed a stable environment. He had enough money to buy a trailer. So he bought a used Traveler and pitched it in the foothills of the desert. The books came out of the crates for a final time and he lined the trailer with their spines. Textbooks, treatises, diaries, maps, nautical charts, surveys, thin dusty narrations from town meetings, heavy thick gold gilded binders of state histories, thin paper ghosts of international meetings, all documenting from a myriad of perspectives, the rise of consciousness. The origin of history. From before the Mayans to the Present. From 8000 B.C. to A.D. 1982.

It was Hattie who finally suggested Raceway. Henry would have preferred to stay where they were, right outside Vasquez Rocks on top of a mountain. He liked the way the rocks all lay partially on their sides, in the same direction, in rows, like hundreds of hands pressed together. From where the trailer sat, he could see the rocks stretched out beneath him, cupped in a valley of scrub oak and yucca. The rocks were smooth and thin, white, forced from red dirt. Some formations stretched upwards, forever it seemed, their tops round and smooth, laying upright in the red dirt like giant white discs. Others were smaller, only slightly larger than himself. All were pitted with tiny holes and caves, dark crevices—perfect for hiding. But Hattie thought the talk of gold in the rocks was myth, and told him he shouldn't spend so much of his time searching. It was embarrassing, she said, dabbing blue eye shadow on her lids and smearing shiny pink lipstick on her mouth, to have a father wandering around in broad daylight looking for hidden treasure in a pile of rocks.

And besides, she said, teasing her hair, if we go to Raceway, we can have a real toilet and real electricity.

So they moved. Raceway was close enough to Vasquez for Henry. The rocks loomed above, a mile away from the bend in the river where Raceway lay. When Hattie was twenty, she left home, put a down payment on her own trailer at the other end of Raceway and moved. That was twelve years ago. She does not know that on bright nights Henry still walks up the riverbed to Vasquez, to all those praying hands, and searches.

Last night, though it was close to a full moon, Henry Peach did not walk anywhere. Not out through the basin. Not to Vasquez. He lay in bed and listened to woeful coyotes, watching a sliver of moonlight move across his room. Every now and then he would reach down into a crumpled-soft brown paper bag and lift a bottle of gin to his lips. It was for pain, he told Hattie. And this was true. The gin was for the pain in his legs. The pain of bone is like no other—sudden, sharp, without cause, and this pain stripped his marrow, his nerves, and consumed thought.

When he woke around eight, it was Sunday morning. He coughed and sat up, coughed again, and lit a cigarette. He pissed in the toilet and avoiding the mirror above the sink, ran water to wash his face and rinsed out his mouth with one hand. Then he took a deep breath and closed his eyes. As he thought of: old socks on the bed/buying cigarettes at Caldonia's/doing laundry in Saugus/running over to Palmdale to pick up the rebuilt radiator, he made his way out to the kitchen, careful not to touch or even brush against the rows upon rows of books which lined the walls of the Traveler. His face was tight, eyes screwed shut, and knowing that in darkness the common inner pull is to bear left, he was careful to stay to the right in his mind's eye. To keep a straight line. To walk the invisible fence. Henry could not afford the agony of seeing their spines, the rows upon rows of titles in chronological order resting one on top of the other like layers of stratified rock. He knew the pain he felt was the result of moving memory through those layers of war and dominance and slavery, of centuries pulled by the flow and ebb of powers.

His books were of the Sumerians, Phenocians, the Moors, Romans, Aztecs, Jews, Celts, Saxons, moving in and out of dark ages of no music or culture or art of thought and reflection, the mire when one barbaric culture overtakes an enlightened one, through ages of light where economics and art, music and science are threaded together into colorful tapestries defying time. Floods, earthquakes, metallurgy, steel, and molecular surgery, human manipulation beginning with the spark of fire to the scorch of subatomic burnings— all were stretched in chronological order, referencing back to each other.

En masse, he realized, they were slowly crushing him.

If he allowed his memory to be moved, pushed through each layer, the pain in his legs would return as a flare in his hips, shoot through to the marrow of his bones straight to the heel, rooting him to the spot, nailing him to the earth. His books, his books of the past, had become poisonous. When history lay uncoiled and stretched out in front of him in linear form with such human atrocities, he could barely breathe.

It had been more than a month since he could stand in front of the books without hearing the sound of air between his teeth as he caught his breath in pain. And Hattie did not understand. She had taken him into Saugus twice to see Dr. Dasas, a young man with cold hands who said little and could find nothing wrong. That was good enough for Hattie. Nothing was wrong.

Until last night, Saturday night, as he walked back from the Volcano and Barday Tullis came riding up on Tip sudden and silent, a mounted ghost, leather creaking, his navy blue Union uniform black in the dark, buttons tossing moonlight, the horse a silver-gold shimmer. Henry had been avoiding Barday in the last several weeks—Barday, who spoke of his battles in the Civil War, the battles he fought every night between sleep and sanity, who spoke in rhyme of blood and what was just. Tip snorted hard and reared. Henry took a step sideways, gin and the midnight hour skewing his sense of movement. Tip's front hooves hovered above the earth, pulling from the trickling sand the faint sound of war cries. Henry smelled the horse's green breath and in that moment, Barday waved his Union hat high in the air, his hair spreading against the sky in wild silhouette.

"God breathes on our side, the righteous shall win, we shall free all men and make gold from tin," yelled Barday in some vision.

Tip landed softly in the sand and in an instant the horse and rider were gone. The cries disappeared with the wind.

The Civil War. North against South. Brother against brother. Shackles, black skin, blood. Henry had felt the pains come, descending from his heart like stones, filling his legs and he yelled a cry of nothing as he fell. Barday was a vision from the past, a vision he could no longer afford. He could feel himself being moved, it was a force, very real and it was trying to pull him through rock. A series of choking screams held him for a moment before he fell.

"This is it," Hattie said, as she bundled him in a blanket, fighting with the breeze. She had risen from sleep, rushed by her father's pain, her bathrobe gaping open at the chest. He was shaking, telling her it was nothing. He could see Oxena and Zachary Turnbill flicking on their lights and peering out their trailer window. Melody Hallow, her blond hair white in the moonlight, ran down her steps with a glass of water. He could feel her hands light on his chest as she and Hattie

16

rolled him up to sit in the sand. They were so different, Hattie like a bear, with her blonde hair in big curls, Melody slight and her hair slack. He closed his eyes and the pain began to ebb, leaking out his heels into the sand. The water dribbled down his chin, but what he managed to swallow cut through the dryness coating his mouth.

"This is it. What we're going to do I have no idea, but this is it," Hattie kept saying.

* * *

Sunday morning Hattie rose from her bed like a Viking. Big boned, hair wild with sleep. It was hot already and her cheek was warmly creased from the seam of her polyester pillow. She swung her legs down from her bed, thick legs, pale white, translucent, with tiny veins fanning just under the skin like thick watery algae. She always wore pants and sleeveless shirts. Her arms were strong, brown, hard. This morning she pushed herself upright, the top of her curling hair nearly brushing the little overhang to her bed, wrapped herself in a yellow nylon bathrobe, kicked open the trailer door and stepped outside into the white light of a new day.

She loved the sun, its power, the burning nuclear reactions leaping thousands of miles in space. She closed her eyes and felt the heat draw teardrops to the corner of her eyes. Then she heard the swish of sand, of dropped sand, and she opened her eyes to see a shadow crouched just by her step.

Bat was blind. He had just turned fifteen and he was tall. Leggy tall. The first time Hattie saw him he was twelve and short, squatting in the sand outside his trailer, poking a stick into the riverbed. He squatted there in cutoffs, with his knees by his ears and his straight skinny arms in front, switching the stick back and forth. He squatted and poked for most of the afternoon. He was making fans in the sand with a piece of broken yucca. His skin was black, very black and his hair was cropped close to his head like a copper fuzz. He said nothing. And so did she.

She actually met Bat about a week later. He was in back of his trailer, digging a hole in the riverbed with a stainless steel spoon. Hattie was out in her side yard, hanging up laundry. She snapped out a tea-towel and heard the soft sound of tossed sand. When she lowered her arms, there was Bat, squatting in the sand, digging. She said "Hi" and he lifted his head, but his arms kept working. She laughed and said "Hello" louder and he stopped, his arms suddenly limp and his mouth open. He turned his head away from her. Hattie called "Hey, you in the sand," and his head snapped around. He looked right at her, his eyes huge and yellow, flecked with gold like a lion's. A screen door slammed behind him and a tiny woman stood on the step, a baby with tight kinky braids on her hip.

"He can hear you," she said, "but he can't see you. And if he could see you it wouldn't make any difference." The little girl beamed at Hattie. "I'm Celeste," the woman said, "and this is Honey." She bounced the girl on her hip, her eyes flitting to the boy in the sand. "And that's Bat." Bat blinked twice at Hattie, his long curled lashes along the top and bottom of his eyes met and released, met and released. "They say he's autistic. That's autistic, not artistic." The little girl stuffed her thumb in her mouth.

Now, this Sunday morning, Bat was tall and when he squatted, he looked like a huge grasshopper in the middle of the riverbed. People at Raceway had grown used to watching where they stepped, and Hattie, being a neighbor, had to stay particularly on guard. There were holes everywhere in the sand.

"Hi Bat," she called. "It's Hattie. Good morning." She didn't wait for a response. His back remained to her, his T- shirt gaping open in front, brushing the earth.

She rubbed her eyes and sighed. Last night loomed with shadows. Of waking up. Melody at her door. The sound of Henry in the sand. The lingering smell of horse. The invisible tangle of the chill of night and the heat of Henry's body against her skin. For a moment she thought there was blood, and Barday nowhere in sight. Not sure exactly what had happened. Feeling Henry shake against her arms. Getting him home. Melody watching him, watching her. Seeing Melody standing in the night with just her bathrobe on, the breeze lifting cotton, making the loose "v" of her collar wave and ripple, smelling Melody's smell.

Hattie sighed again, turned, went back in and put a kettle on the stove. The flint on the gas stove ticked like a metronome. She hated heating up the kitchen so early, but coffee was necessary. Last night was sleepless. She was too worried about Henry. She had just poured water into her plastic cup when there was a rap at her screen door.

"Morning. Hattie, it's me, Lani."

Lani. Lani Fabrile. Perfumed and musky, loose jointed and supple. Lani languished against life, laying back, never giving in to tension. Her ease left Hattie feeling old sometimes.

"Come in."

The door was already open, and she was stepping inside, her thick red hair streaming out in back of her, waving at Hattie with one hand, her high heels scratching grit on the linoleum floor.

"I got some more pictures developed and I wanted to show you." She paused and looked at Hattie's cup. "Hey, can I have a cup?"

"Sure," said Hattie and turned back to the stove.

"Look," Lani said, holding out four photographs, "what do you think?"

"Just a sec, O.K.? I have to get my eyes open Lani."

"Oh. Sorry. Should I come back?"

Hattie sighed. "No, no." She tipped her head in Lani's direction. "Didn't you hear all the racket last night? It was right outside your place."

Lani smiled. "I was nowhere near my fuckin' place last night," she said. "In fact I've got to go back and take more pictures this afternoon."

Hattie shook her head and felt big and inflexible. Stiff. Lani was liquid and a kid. Just a kid.

"Looky," she said again. "Just take a peek. I think three of them are pretty good."

Hattie handed Lani a cup of instant coffee, took the photos, and stood by the large window and the better light. All four shots were nature scenes, taken outside. The first photo was a close-up of a smooth bed of sand, flawless, without an indentation, like a white sheet pulled tight.

"That one was into tantric stuff, you know, holding still for the build-up. We weren't allowed to move," Lani explained, tapping a bright red fingernail against the gloss of the sand. She took a sip of coffee and then adjusted her black spandex miniskirt. "He kept trying to stare at me, into my inner soul or something. Thank god I was allowed to at least move my eyes." She made a face. "He took a really long time to come."

The second was also a close-up, this time of a bed of smooth polished rocks with a checkered picnic blanket all bunched to one side. There were a few golden poppies standing between the rocks, survivors of a late spring and some strands of thick desert grass. "I kept the blanket in this one because of the colors—you know, red, blue, and yellow...Plus this one thought he was an artist, so it was kind-of appropriate." She grinned and watched Hattie's face.

"But it's black and white."

Lani shrugged.

The third photo was a long shot, taken at twilight, the foreground in silhouette against an evening sky of gray monochrome clouds. The outline of a lone juniper bush interrupted the skyline.

"This one was weird." Lani shrugged her shoulders. "Not that weird, I guess, but he tied my hands to this," she pointed at the juniper, "and then wanted to rip my clothes, but I told him he couldn't do that."

Hattie yawned. "Couldn't do what?"

"Rip my clothes.   So anyway, he agreed, but it ended up thrashing the hell outta my back, I got all scratched up."

Hattie looked at her and nodded. She flipped to the fourth. Another close-up, this time of the tire tracks in a muddy spring bed. It didn't have the quality of the first three photos. The shot wasn't set up right and the exposure was off. Lani laughed.

"The back of a 1972 VW Squareback. Haven't done that in years. I think I'm getting soft or something, but it was sorta luxurious."

"They're nice," said Hattie. "But you're going to get yourself killed Lani."

"You really like them? I mean the first three. That last one's a throw away." Lani's lipstick was smeared and she needed a bath.

"Yeah," said Hattie. "I especially like the shot of the clouds and the bush. You know Oxena and Zach used to be photographers and I think they were pretty good. You know National Geographic-type stuff."

Lani laughed.

Hattie looked at her. "Watch it, Lani. They're nice."

She shrugged again.

"You should just show them your pictures. I bet they'd be thrilled."

Lani took the photographs back. "I do once in a while. I mean I show Oxena. But I usually just like showing you and Melody."

And Bat, Hattie wanted to add, but she didn't. She'd seen Lani squatting in the sand with her pictures cupped in her hand, talking to Bat, explaining the scenes. Hattie felt like Lani's guardian. Ever since she broke down Lani's door, found her bleeding from between her legs, her wrists bound in front to her ankles. Gagged, lying on the floor with only a broken window and fluttering pink curtains as immediate evidence of a man fled, Lani eyes stayed half closed all the way to the hospital. Hattie spent the next couple of weeks with her, helping her deal first with the details of the police and the hospital and then with the issues of living. The D.A. who was tall and thin, had papery skin and no time to help them. When the pictures were finally discussed, the man rolled his eyes and that was the end of that. Background material never helped, he said. She and Lani came home, fixed the window and she slept over at Lani's for a couple of nights to be sure the guy wouldn't come back.

Hattie took the last swallow of coffee from her cup. It was still hot and her upper lip had begun to sweat. But the smell and taste of strong coffee was worth the heat. She watched Lani walk across the trailer park. Then she tightened the belt on her bathrobe, walked down the steps, stepped over Bat, and strode up between the rows of trailers to the Traveler. It hadn't rained in over two months and the sand was hot and very loose. Her bare feet burned. Oxena and Zachary were outside, across the way.

Oxena smiled and said, "Good morning Hattie." Oxena in her Panama hat and chaise lounge, token lemonade, smiling up her, skin dry and brown, looked every one of her seventy years. Zach smiled at her too, though his eyes were lowered as he picked up the shammy and car polish from the ground. Hattie watched him smear a glob of slippery wax onto to the trailer.

The first time Hattie met Oxena and Zachary they were poised just as they were now. Zach, was polishing the Dream Time and Oxena, watching from her chaise lounge with a glass of pink lemonade in her hand. Hattie was selling milk chocolate bars with almonds for her senior class.

Oxena had turned her face up and Hattie stared at her own reflection in Oxena's oversized sunglasses. Oxena's gray hair was cropped short, but swathed in a gauzy pink, blue and white scarf that wrapped around her head and kept her Panama hat in place.

"For your schooling dear?"

"For school," said Hattie, looking down at Oxena's bare feet. Her toes were painted with little dabs of orange polish.

"And how much are they?"

"Seventy-five cents." Hattie sighed, scrunching sand with her own toes.

"Hey, aren't you the ones that came down out of the mountains?" asked Zach, coming from around in back of the Dream Time, leather shammy in one hand, Simonize in the other. He was small. Bony and brown, his Adam's apple was huge and Hattie stared at it. He had funny brown spots on his forehead and his bald head gleamed with sweat.

"Zachary, that doesn't sound good. Don't pay attention dear."

"Yeah. We are. We came from Vasquez."

"Find any treasure?" Zach looked at the Dream Time.

"No."

"See any ghosts?"

"What do you mean?"

"Now Zach that's enough. I don't think you need to be bothering her."

"There's ghosts?" Hattie found this interesting.

"How long did you live up there?"

"Six months or so."

"Well they're there. Five of them. Abdon Leiva, Cleovaro Chavez, Juan Soto, Tomas Redondo and Tiburcio Vasquez himself. All of them killed by posse." The thin shammy swung wet and heavy in the breeze as he pointed to the rocks.

There was a long pause.

"Well," said Hattie, "I never saw any ghosts."

"I know what I've seen," was what Hattie thought she heard him say as she handed Oxena a candy bar. She watched him rubbing the cream enamel paint for a moment.

"Are you taking a trip?" she asked politely.

In the silence which followed, everything seemed a little too bright, the sand too white and the trailer glittered. Hattie squinted harder.

"A trip? Did you hear that dear? Zachary? Did you hear?"

Zach had disappeared around the Dream Time.

Now, as she walked by, they were both in place, as always, morning fixtures. By afternoon the heat would drive them indoors and no one would see them again until Monday.

"We just saw Lani," said Oxena. "Her new photos are really quite good," called Oxena.

Hattie nodded.

"Very nice, really."

Hattie trudged passed the chaise lounge. "She tries," she called over her shoulder. She could see Oxena settling back, relaxing against the chaise lounge. She did not like discussing Lani's work with Oxena. Oxena and Zach were too far removed from the force that moved Lani to take her pictures. Too far removed from sweat and musk. It was deceptive to talk about Lani's work while surrounded by glasses of lemonade, gauzy scarves, age spots, and swimmy eyes. That was Lani's job.

By the time she stood on Henry's doorstep, the sun had forced sweat on her forehead and made her hair stick at the nape of her neck. The bathrobe was a mistake. Nylon was too hot. She made a fist and pounded on the door. Nothing happened. She pounded harder. Henry opened the door and blinked up at her, small, gray, wrinkled. Someone left alone in the arid air too long, baked, stretched and dried like a piece of jerky. She hated touching his skin. She could feel herself beginning to tower over him. He bent his head up, cigarette smoke making a bluish haze around his face. He coughed.

"What?"

"I'm not your mother, Henry."

"I know."

"And I'm not your wife."

He looked away.

"Then why do I always feel like I'm your keeper? Like I have to take care of you? What the hell was that all about last night?"

"I don't know."

"Bullshit," she said, suddenly, immediately irritated.

He coughed and dropped the cigarette on the front step, smashing it with a work boot. "It was Barday. Barday," he repeated, glancing in the direction of an old, gray rusted trailer with no name, tacked with tar paper and cardboard, sitting in the lot next to them.

"Barday did nothing to you. It was nothing. He rode by on his horse. Big deal."

There was silence and she heard a meadow lark chir-uping off in the distance.

"Oh Henry, what's going to happen to you?" she said, her shoulders dropping, agitation gone. She didn't tower over him anymore and she walked passed him into the Traveler.

She looked around the kitchen, saw the greasy frying pan still on the stove and grabbed two eggs out of the refrigerator.

"Fry these for me please," she said and walked to the back of the trailer, to his bedroom. "And then we're going to the Volcano. I need a real cup of coffee," she called, getting dressed. Henry did all the laundry. She knew where the fresh load was piled neatly against the back wall.

The eggs fried and she emerged from the bedroom, her hair still wild and her shirt untucked. It was a sleeveless shirt, bright, the print a patchwork of red and white bandannas. "Over hard," she said and sat down heavily on a stool by the stove.

"I saw Kinni pull in this morning," said Henry.

"Oh, spying on her again?" She bit at a hangnail on her thumb.

"No. I just saw her. Melody was out on her step, back from a walk I guess and that woman pulls up. Doesn't say a word. Poor Melody." He flipped the eggs.

"Well, there's something wrong with her, what do you expect?"

"There's something wrong with her all right," he said.

Hattie ate her egg in three bites, watching Henry push his around on his plate.

"You have to eat," she said.

"Leave me alone."

"You're going back to the doctor's tomorrow. Back to Dasas or somebody else. I don't care—now don't look at me like that, I'm not trying to be mean." She stood up and set her plate in the sink and ran water over both, watching bits of Henry's egg swirl in the drain.

"I'll meet you over at the Volcano. Please get yourself over there. We'll have a cup of coffee. I think you should talk to Bert anyway. Maybe he knows someone you could go see."

She went to the back of the trailer again to grab the short pile of clean clothes. "Thanks," she said, gesturing with stack of shirts and pants and panties in her hand and backed out the screen door. It slammed shut.

* * *

In the yellow-white of the morning, Henry watched her walk back to her trailer through the sand. She'd left her bathrobe on the back of the chair. He carefully folded it up and then gently brought it to his cheek. It smelled like her: sweaty, sweet, vanilla. She did not understand. She would never understand. The pain he suffered from was not from some biological process gone awry—It flowed from the never ending bilish stream of the past. Human past.

He sat down heavily on a kitchen chair, a gray metal folding chair and took a long drag on a new cigarette. What could he tell the doctor? That the Roman Empire and the Druids, the Moors, Genghis Khan and Caesar, Napoleon, Hitler, Kennedy, Jesus and Mohammed all made him shudder? That even the slightest glimpse of the birthplace of civilization, the Middle East, with its 4,000 year old religious infighting between Jew and Palestinian, subjugation on any continent at any time, ancient genocide or present day genocide could render him incapacitated? How could he explain the force's etiology?—that it began two months ago with looking at prints of ancient Mayan calendars. The pain uncoiled, flashed down each leg and he grabbed his knees just to hold himself upright.

Then it crept through the rise and fall of the Egyptian Empire, the Greeks, the rise of Western Europe, to Plymouth Rock and the

French-Indian War. But when the pain began to seek him out faster, slowly at first and then day-by-day, history began slipping away from him at a speed he couldn't calibrate. The Civil War became inaccessible, the early 1900s, the Suffragette movement and then finally WWI. All lost. That was the point at which he confided in Hattie that something was wrong. She noticed he hadn't touched his books in weeks. She also saw him avoiding Barday. He kept thinking it would go away and for a week it eased slightly. And then he tried to reach for a book on the Manifest Destiny.

Hattie was in the room, saw him fall, saw the perspiration on his forehead and the whiteness around his mouth and that incident became the reason for the visit to Dr. Dasas. Quickly now the pain sliced off periods of the past, his only anchor. Now the pain struck when he was far away from his books as well. He was handicapped, unable to think or read anything even about the recent past. The past of just yesterday. He could no longer reflect on acts perpetrated in history for the name of history within the last fifty years. WWII, the Korean War, Vietnam, the Klan, the CIA, the FBI. Assignations or negotiations, moon walks or earthquakes. He had left the Volcano last night because he overheard a couple on the radio talking about the Six Day War and thoughts of the Sumerians and the Flood made the pain shoot straight down to his heels and back to his heart.

Hattie was right. Right about last night. It wasn't Barday. It was time.

* * *

Hattie stopped by her trailer before she went on to the Volcano and picked up the Almanac for just a moment, knowing Henry would take his time getting himself over there. She hoped he would walk and leave the Valiant behind. It was less than a mile and the exercise would be good for him. She just started a new section the night before and wanted to finish. The Average Television Viewing Time, per week, by age is as follows:

Women: 18-24- 27hrs. 28min.
        55+ - 42hrs. 02min.

```
teens -               21hrs. 37min.
Men:      18-24 -19hrs. 46min.
          55+  - 37hrs. 11min.
teens -               23hrs. 19min.
Children:  2-5  -28hrs. 20 min.
          6-11  26hrs. 34min.
```

These statistics were the same from last year. Nielsen only compiled them every three or four years. The next section was America's Favorite Television Programs. Now this section was interesting and changed yearly and, unlike others, was often critical in conversation. In fact, when she defended the Almanac, it was this section which Hattie could claim was truly useful. The Noted Personalities-Entertainers   section was also instrumental. People loved to know how old the stars were and Hattie could easily supply the answers by mentally flipping to the appropriate date of birth. Most people were amazed at her talent for movie and television trivia and some would stop her at Caldonia's Meat Market to ask, "How old is Joel Grey?," or "Was Clint Eastwood really born in San Francisco?"

So you see, she'd tell Henry, it does come into play. All these facts and statistics can be useful.

OTHER SECRETS

Melody didn't have children of her own.

She always seemed so happy to Hattie. She could chat with anyone and took people at face value, believing what they said. She was tiny and blond, sweet, with a complexion too fair and soft for high desert air. She never burned or tanned. On the hottest days in August, she'd run around the trailer park with big red bandannas protecting her hair and shading her face. She was a checker at K-mart, about twenty miles down Rte. 14 and lived on the other side of Bat and Honey.

Melody loved children. There was always a gaggle of dirty, sweaty little kids running around Raceway and with the exception of Honey and Bat, Hattie didn't pay much attention to them. Often, at dusk when the sky was thin and high with pale light, Hattie would hear laughing, shrieking and see the silhouettes of tiny children dancing between the trailers, being squirmy and silly, and in the center were Honey and Melody, being just as silly, dancing with invisible fairies.

It was a cool spring day, about four years ago, early in the morning, when Hattie saw Melody running around the corner between two trailers with five toddlers scrambling after her. Hattie was sitting on her beach chair reading, trying not to fall through the left side where the webbing had disintegrated.

"What are you doing?" she said, setting down the Almanac.

"Oh," gasped Melody just as she reached the chair, stopping, pushing back her bandanna. The children rushed around her like water. "Just being," she reached down and picked up a tiny little girl with a filthy neck, "Silly nilly, silly, nilly," she said and dropped the girl back down in the sand, close, Hattie noticed, to one of Bat's holes.

They all began pinching each other, slapping and squealing. Maxine, who was a seven year-old red head, opened her door and stood above them on the step. They rallied around her, the leader of children, she scampered down the steps and then all six were off. Melody stared at them, at the backs of their legs. The tiny one fell down, righted herself and disappeared with the others around the corner.

"Why would anyone who lives here put a child in shoes," said Melody, rubbing her elbow. Hattie saw a mosquito bite swelling.

"It's really nice you spend so much time with them. You're good with them." Hattie set the book face down on her lap.

She shrugged. "It's no big deal. I have fun. "What are you reading?"

"Oh, nothing. Just looking up something for Henry," Hattie answered, trying to cover the word "Almanac" with her left hand. But Melody wasn't listening. She was watching the children as they came weaving back around in line, three trailers up. The tiny one split from the rest and came running to her and Melody squatted down in the sand and with arms outstretched.

"Come on little sweet thing, come here sweetie pie," she called and the little girl ran hard against her, threw her tiny round arms around her neck and clung. Melody laughed and picked her up. "You're soooo little. And you're soooo smart," she said and the girl laughed out loud and clapped her hands. Then she wrapped her arms around Melody's neck again, this time lightly, and tiny fingers draped at the nape of Melody's neck. Melody bent her head and nuzzled the little girl, cooing softly, kissing the tiny round cheek again and again. The girl smiled. She liked having her curls messed and fondled by Melody's face. She gave Melody another quick hug and threw herself forward to get down. Melody dropped her back to the sand.

Hattie still doesn't know what made her notice. Maybe it was the sudden breeze blowing Melody's long light blond hair or the way she reached around again to absently scratch her bite, or the way the dust dirtied the smear, but when she moved her arm up and across, Hattie saw the faint dirty outline of something damp on her right breast. And when she lowered her arm, Hattie saw the same kind of irregular stain mirrored on the left. She was watching the damp stains in a kind of stupor and suddenly caught the heavy, fatty scent of warm cream.

That's when Hattie knew she was in love.

* * *

Every morning Melody took a walk. Up the riverbed, across the flat, sometimes into the foothills and often to Vasquez. Once in a while she'd meet Henry Peach heading home from Vasquez and they'd wave. They never said much to each other. How's the weather?, see any snakes?, seen Barday? She was better friends with Hattie. And she was best friends with the children. All of them. Timmy, Lee, Alex, Kira, Jamaica, Jamal, Joey, Baby Laurel, Hannah, Nathan and, of course, Honey. Four were babies.

This Sunday she rose very early, while it was still dark. Henry's screaming in the night, waking up, the wind and the clear moon, all left her unable to return to sleep. She left the trailer before sunrise. The high desert cools at night and the early morning was still chilly. The stars hung like large luminescent silver teardrops in a taut blue sky. She walked by herself across the orange pink sand, listening for coyotes, stopping once, thinking she heard wild burros and then realizing it was traffic off Rte. 14. She saw three jack rabbits, long, leggy, raw-boned, thumping away from her over hard packed earth. As the sun rose, each yellow ray pushed back the chill and spread tendrils of heat from east to west. The warming air released the sweet, musty smell of sage. This was her favorite time of day. As she faced south on her return, the left side of her face grew warm to the touch while the right remained cool.

Now she paused outside, the sun above the horizon line, resting on the steps and looked at her trailer. It was an old Homestead, rusted, faded turquoise with white trim. It needed paint. She turned around, sat down on the top step, pulled up each sock and began pulling burrs and corkscrews.

In the stillness of the morning a car pulled up next to the trailer, crunching the gravel and sand. It was Kinni. Coming home from work. Melody looked up. The headlights, weakened by the growing light, blinked off, and the driver's door opened. A woman stepped out. "Hi," said Melody, rolling a burr between her index finger and thumb.

"Hello," said Kinni, her voice feathery, low, polite, and her Asian accent rolled the double l's into a soft bi-syllabic "r." She slammed the door shut and turned to Melody.

Melody looked down at her socks. She couldn't bear to see Kinni. Kinni with her immaculate 1972 dodge Dart, smart neat little black pumps, freshly pressed navy blue skirt and white, crisp starched shirt, and black fathomless veil. Kinni was creaseless, seamless, polished. She gleamed. And in the early morning sun her face remained hidden, as always, her head surrounded in an aura of black. Melody looked away, picking burrs from her socks even faster, aware of space closing between her and the dark vaporous film. She heard Kinni move toward her trailer. She glanced up, just for a second—enough time to see the veil of black, a veil wrapped around Kinni's face and head, wrapped again and again, wiping away the contours of a face. The ends of the black lace were rolled and looped, tucked into themselves at the nape of the neck. Only words passed through the cloth. Melody could not look at it. At her. She knew it was rude, but she always looked away. In the six years Melody had lived at Raceway, she knew no one who had seen Kinni's face.

Once, Melody needed to borrow an egg. She was making chocolate chip cookies for the kids. It was mid-morning and she knew Kinni was the only one around. It took Kinni a long time to answer her knock and she didn't invite her inside. The door opened several inches, Kinni disappeared, returned with an egg and held it out to Melody. In the moment Melody's hand touched the egg, in the instant they both held it, Melody shuddered. Noticeably. "You don't have to be afraid," was all Kinni said, taking a step closer, pushing the black veil into the doorway. Melody felt the pressure of a scream in her throat. Kinni took another step, close enough for Melody to smell the clean smell of rinsed soap. She had recently showered. Melody saw the bath towel looped over Kinni's arm. At some point, Kinni had been naked, taking a shower, without her veil, without the mask. Water running over her face, her arms, her legs. Did she have hair? Kinni was speaking to her, talking through the veil, but there were no lips, no eyes, no nose, nothing but blackness. Melody, thanking her quickly, mumbled, nearly dropped the egg, and left.

This morning, Kinni marched up her freshly swept steps and inserted her key into the lock on the her door. "Good day," was all Kinni said and then the door slammed shut. Melody had always wanted to apologize for that other morning. But she never knew what to say and now too much time had passed.

Sunday and Wednesdays were her days off. She stopped pulling burrs from her socks. Maybe she'd go into town and grab some groceries. But she wanted to see Hattie and that would set her back. She wouldn't be able to go until after lunch—her breasts ached. She would have to nurse in a couple of hours.

She didn't need to explain anything to Hattie. Melody liked watching Hattie, and being around her—she seemed strong, stronger than herself and she said simple, uncomplicated things like, "Why don't you just have a kid of your own?" Some would say Hattie had no tact. Melody liked to think she was direct.

* * *

Kinni did not like neighbors. She moved to Raceway after her uncles settled in Los Angeles. She could not bear to live with them or their wives. Their wives with their expensive eyelids and their fog of whispering. About her. And her uncles lied, all the time, about the past, about the present, about what was going to be. Just like the Americans. One uncle dealt in real estate, the other in insurance. Twenty years ago she made the move across the Pacific with the four of them, her sitting out on the deck of the ship, watching her skin grow dark while the four remained indoors, in the recreation hall, playing bridge, cultivating a white hue to their flesh. They all lived in a big house with a terra-cotta roof on the outskirts of Beverly Hills, catching glimpses of movie stars, eating at Bob's Big Boy, having eyelid surgery and learning more about the American psyche. Kinni spent her time with them, waiting for escape.

She knew she couldn't return to Japan. She had no money of her own. But the whispering became intolerable. The more American they became, the more French fries they ate, the more baseball they watched, the more commercials they laughed at, the louder the droning grew, becoming a constant hum, setting her on edge. When any of the four spoke it was irritating white noise. So she took a night job in a warehouse filled with Styrofoam plates, cups, fast food cartons, and saved her money. After seven years she left them and the terra-cotta roof, bought a trailer, moved to the desert and took another night job counting inventory.

She was at Raceway before Henry and Hattie Peach but years after Barday Tullis. She liked Barday. He cared for his horse and nothing else, which made his love simple and direct. He never asked her questions with either his eyes or his lips, which made him safe to be around. He considered the Civil War something which might be still going on, which kept him from the twentieth century. And because he spoke in rhyme, Kinni liked to think reason lay within him.

Not that they spoke a great deal. Kinni always saw him on his morning ride, as she came home from work. This Sunday he was further along, riding east toward the sunrise, across the wide valley. She turned off Rte. 14 and made a right at the exit, parallel with Barday. She waved, but he too far out to see her. The road sat above the valley and she watched him for a minute, below her, his blue checkered shirt catching the light morning breeze, mounted on Tip as he made his way on a rabbit trail through sand and stiff grass.

She did not like seeing Melody outside, sitting on her steps. Usually she was home after Melody and did not have to talk to her. Melody must have had an early walk. This was unfortunate.

"Hi," said Melody, pulling up her socks.

"Hello," said Kinni. And then, a few seconds later, as she went up the steps, "Good morning."

Melody did not respond.

* * *

The sun was hot on Bat's back. He had his spoon and he squatted in the sand beyond the shade of the family's trailer. The sister had thrown sand down his back where the cutoff's yawned opened at the base of his back.

I have seven holes to dig today, he thought, and eased the curve of the spoon against the white sand. Seven. He couldn't remember how many that was but that was how many he had to dig. Whole holes. Deep holes. Holes very deep beyond the heat of the sun, where the sand turned cool and brown. It was Sunday, holy day his mother had said and then she laughed. Bat had smiled suddenly and said "yeah," and Honey gave them both dirty looks. This was why he had seven holes to dig. But he kept a bigger secret.

Bat smiled again, the spoon was near his eyes, and saw his lips spread ear to ear and upside down. Now I am upside down, he thought looking into the concave bowl of the spoon. The spoon went back into the sand, lifted out sand, emptied itself, and went back to his face. Now I am upside down. Now I am gone. Now I am up upside down. Now I am gone. Now I am upside down. Now I am gone. Soon brown cool sand spread in back of him on the ground like a pale fan.

There were lips on his forehead and in the spoon now, upside down as well. He could smell his mother's smell. He was aware of her around him. He moved faster. Now upside down. Now gone. Now upside down. Now gone. Soon the lips left his forehead and the smell evaporated. He felt more sand trickle down his back. It was the cool brown sand. There was a patting on this back. Then the sister was gone too. He saw a drop of water fall from his eye into the sand. His eyes felt heavy, forward in his face. He couldn't see the patting hands in the upside down spoon.

Then he knew he had to stand. Stand and find the horse.

* * *

Barday Tullis was eighty-nine years old. He lived next door to Henry, on the edge of the riverbed, the last trailer on the northeast end. He rode a horse named Tip, an old palomino with a swayback and stiff knees that cracked with every step. Barday kept Tip in a corral of railroad ties strung with rusted barbed wire and Tip survived on the dry grasses which grew on the banks. There was an old porcelain bathtub Barday kept full, filling it daily with buckets of water from his kitchen sink.

Several times a week Barday would saddle Tip in a straight-backed Union saddle fitted with deep leather stirrups and studded with copper rivets and ride four miles down the riverbed to Caldonia's, the general store. Barday would have a beer and buy Tip a Yoo-hoo from the cold drink machine next to the ice-bin. He would pop the cap off and place the neck of the glass bottle in the bar of Tip's mouth where his gums were smooth and no teeth grew. Then Barday would take off his hat, the blue and gold Union hat, and sit down on the bench opposite the gas pump and watch people passing through, filling their tanks. The beer would be cold and Tip would swat flies with his tail. Around two they'd head home, up the riverbed, the sand loose and pulling hard to break Tip's stride. But the horse was steady and ground his bit and his companion often dozed on the ride back.

The first thing Barday ever said to Hattie was:

> Right your head
> Straighten your back
> Lightning will crack

She was seventeen and had stared at him, looking up trying to find his wrinkled little face in the shadow of his short billed blue hat. Tip's long whiskers brushed against her arm. She had been complaining about school and he had answered as best he could.

Henry and Barday would get together sometimes at the Volcano for company and some chit-chat. A typical conversation might go like this:

Henry: So we're supposed to sink into the ocean. What'da'ya think about that Barday?

Barday: Away, away, away we go into the deep blue sea. Away, away, away we go, here, watch me slap my knee.

Henry: Yeah. I don't believe it either. They can't tell those kinds of things. They've got all that fancy machinery and it tells them nothing.

Barday: Machines, machines, ice cream machines.

Henry: Hey, did you see where that guy from Dayton, Ohio ate three hundred and sixty-five hot fudge sundaes? And we're talkin' double scoops.

Barday: Vanilla, chocolate, butter pecan, all my favorites, like sausage and ham.

Henry: I don't like ice cream.

Barday: I don't like spam.

No one knew where Barday came from or how long he had lived at Raceway. Some people, the ones who never stayed long, thought he had started the park, because, they'd point out, he still has one of the old racehorses.

But Raceway Trailer Park was not built over a racetrack.

Barday slept Sunday morning mounted on Tip, heading east into the sunrise. He usually waved to Kinni as she came home from work, but this morning he was too tired. Tired after a night of wild riding, of dreaming and waking. Of dreaming of blood and wind and leather. He was getting too old for these dreams he thought, waking up, eyes wide, staring into the darkness of his room, his heart slamming against his ribs. And so, on his ride back, his eyelids grew heavy and thick and when he squinted, shielding his blue watery eyes from the sun, they simply remained shut. He could feel the morning breeze wrap around him and pull, tugging gently. Every once in a while, Tip would stumble in a pocket of sand and Barday would open one eye for a moment, just to see. Barday had no sense of smell so the sweet warm breath of sage breathed against him unnoticed. But he could feel the sun on his skin and would see against the red of his eyelids the colors of opposing flags and the silver and black of artillery.

It was a long time before he heard the footsteps beside him, running in the sand. When he looked down and saw the boy, one arm outstretched, touching Tip's tail, his feet leaving small waves in the sand, he smiled and nodded, felt the dry air lift under his hat and he closed his eyes once again.

* * *

Oxena Turnbill set down her spoon. She had licked it clean and her cereal bowl was empty save for a shiny, milky glaze. There was a tiny particle of cornflake stuck at the left-hand corner of her mouth. She sighed and smoothed out her napkin next to her cereal bowl, making sure the paper soaked up the drops of milk that had dribbled on the blue plastic tablecloth. She was irritated by how hard her hands shook this morning. The napkin puckered.

It was already beginning to get hot. The metal napkin dispenser was warm to the touch. She reached over and cranked open the little window above the table. There was a mirror, a round mirror without a frame, to the left of the window and she peered into it, adjusting her glasses. She stared at her reflection for a long time, her head resting on her hands, feeling the morning sun on the table, as the heat wedged itself inside the trailer. Outside, Zach was polishing the siding, following the sun around, working in the shade as much as possible. She could hear him finishing up on the sunny side, wiping the trailer down with firm steady strokes just like one might do for a thoroughbred after a race. He used polish and wax and spent time to buff. Now he was buffing and the sounds of his cloth, from where she sat, were dull and quiet.

Their trailer was a 1963 Dream Time, peach and white with chrome trim. It was small, round, like a globe on two wheels.

Inside, their lives were neatly divided along two walls. On the right were all their appliances: a corner shower, stove, box refrigerator, fold-down kitchen table, two seats, sink and a square foot of counter space. On the left was a fold out bed, a chair and a radio. And across the entire left-hand wall were photographs of insects. Most were in black and white, some in color, but all were close-ups: a praying mantis perched happily atop a blade of grass, two ants busily carrying a single piece of cake between them, a slug sitting wetly on a stone, a ladybug munching on an aphid, a worm just poking through the dirt. A swarm of termites. A spider web, heavy with dew drops and a corpse neatly cocooned in its center. A moth, flat and gray against a piece of concrete. A fly on glass. And more.

Oxena sighed again and glanced at the wall. They were all Zach's photos. He was the camera man—she was responsible for lighting and developing. Now, they didn't take pictures.

After a while, she lifted her head and called out the window:

"Zachary, would you like something to drink?" and when she spoke, the piece of cornflake fell from the corner of her mouth. She stood, poured herself a glass of lemonade, picked up her sunglasses and hat from the chair and wandered outside. She sat back in the chaise lounge.

Oxena spent the rest of the morning watching Zach finish up the Dream Time. She did not like to watch him work, she hated the way his shirt grew damp between his shoulder blades and the way his shorts gaped open in the back at the waist when he bent down. And he never hiked his pants up. He looked like an old man. He was an old man. An ant crawled across her left foot, in and out of the valleys formed by the tendons that pulled her toes. With a quick glance to Zach to make sure he wasn't looking, she crossed her feet and rubbed it out.

She looked up and saw Hattie walking up the rows of trailers, returning from her father's, on her way to the Volcano, and Oxena raised her lemonade glass in toast. Hattie waved back.

CHANGES

I hate change. Maybe that's because we were always moving, always changing places, pushing out westward with our eyes squinted shut.

"There's too much sun out here," says Henry. The flexistraw has something wrong with it and it won't suck. He's blowing into his gin and making burpy bubbles in his drink. It's funny he should say this right now. The Volcano is quite murky inside.

"Why don't you try now," I say after the last belch from his glass.

He glances at me and takes a long draw and a swallow. The plastic straw bobs towards me after he's released it, hits the side of the glass and settles. This time the belch is from Henry.

"Don't roll your eyes at me, Hattie," he says.

I'm staring down at him as Bert leans against the back of the bar.

Bert, who is leathery white and heavy with dark smudges on his elbows and always smokes a "roll m'own," sets the cigarette down in a used ashtray, one of those little beanbag types. A happy plaid ashtray, red and green with black lines, all bunchy and lumpy with a brushed metal belly and two clips across the top to hold the cigarettes. He is careful to push his cigarette into one of the little "U"s, but as usual, he's rolled it so thin it won't stick and it's slipping back onto the counter right now. In about five seconds he's going to pick it up, take a puff, set it back down in the ashtray and the process of easing back out onto the countertop will begin again.

It is his bar. Bert's bar. The Volcano is the tarnished vestige of what was once golden radiant pioneer spirit. It sits as a forlorn memory of entrepreneurship and self-sufficiency, gray weathered wood and tar paper roof, its neon light broken and the lava flow forever stilled on the sign above the road. I find it depressing. There's nothing like it in a hundred-mile radius, however, and so it gets a lot of travelers, coming in ordering things like pink lemonade and sparkling water. And beers.

The inside harbors a Hawaiian motif. Lots of tropical artifacts but with none of the tropical color. The Volcano is as gray on the inside as it is on the outside. The place needs to be colorized, to have a team of artists come in and paint pastel hues and washes over everything. There's plenty of fishnets draped across the walls with prickly starfish and sea shells tacked into hemp. There's even a few pieces of faded coral stuck on in places and in the back, to signal the bathroom, Bert's painted a giant anchor on the door with gilded paint. That's the one bright spot in the whole place. The bar has sea horses and fish frozen in acrylic across the counter and each bar stool has an old frayed lei yawning around its seat. There's a few more leis bunched up in a hideous plastic wad in the center of the ceiling—I guess it's supposed to frame a center spotlight. Except there is no light. There's a couple of tiny lamps at either end of the bar. The lampshades are studded with little tan shells glued in a circular pattern and in the center of each is a smirking mermaid painted in dirty greens and browns. Delightful.

Bert plays a lot of Don Ho. There's a whole stack of singles and about a dozen albums by the front door between the trash can and the turntable. It's an old portable turntable covered in synthetic alligator contact paper which began to peel and has since been peeled by many hands. On the way out, above the door is a motorized clock, which doesn't keep the time but does give a real impression of waves breaking against Oahu. The picture is of one of those perfect, sixteen foot spiral waves, shimmering in the sun, big and powerful, full of force and spray, turning over and over into itself. At the Volcano, it never stops.

"So what's up today," says Bert in Henry's direction and I stop my hypnosis with the clock.

A couple comes in looking like they might like a cup of coffee. It's mid-morning. 10:30 or so.

"Excuse me, do you have decaf?"

"Nope," says Bert brightly, wiping down the counter.

The woman, dressed in expensive looking casual wear says, "I think I need the real stuff anyway." She doesn't really look very good. She sits down at a table, snaps open her purse and takes out a hairbrush.

"Two coffees then?" says Bert. The fellow nods and gets out his wallet. He is in shorts and has a skinned knee. Thin and wiry. Uses a blow dryer to help straighten his coil hair.

"Nothing much. Going into town to get some stuff." Henry is a bit slow answering Bert.

That means driving to Palmdale and sitting at Denny's and eating an order of French fries with blue cheese dressing. It also means he isn't going to see the doctor. I set down my coffee cup rather hard on the bar. He glares at me.

"It's Sunday anyway, Hattie and I'm not going to any emergency room."

"Sounds good," says Bert, coming out from behind the counter and setting down two cups at the table. The man hands Bert a dollar and sits across from the woman.

I see her hand tremble as she takes a sip of coffee and she nearly spills some in the saucer.

I want to go sit with her and talk about how: she is breaking up with him, just found out she's sick, on the way to her mother's funeral, lost big in Vegas, got her period, lost her dog, found out she's pregnant, or whatever. But I remain on my barstool, the plastic lei tickling the back of my knees.

"Do you have a pay phone," she asks.

The man shakes his head. "We don't need to call anyone."

"I think we should call the highway patrol Steven."

"No, it's fine. Nothing happened."

"But somebody should stop them. We nearly...oh..."

"What happened?" asks Henry, smiling wildly and I look intently at a little silver seahorse gazing up sightlessly from the acrylic bar top.

"We almost got in a wreck," says the man.

"We were going too fast, I admit that, but—"

"Julie—"

"Well, we were. You were driving too fast."

"It wasn't my fault."

"I'm not saying it was your fault. I'm saying you were driving too fast." She takes another sip of coffee. "We wanted to get on the road early, before sunrise, so we could get home at a decent hour. We live in Anaheim. But we didn't get off to such a great start." She pauses and looks at the man. "So we were driving along, making up for lost time, looking at the map. At least I was looking at the map, and this horse comes out of nowhere."

I stop looking at the seahorse. A horse. Interesting. A different kind of day.

"A big old yellow horse with this old guy riding in this weird outfit. They were going along the side of the road. You know the kind of horse I mean, like the kind in circus...only this one was really decrepit. I told Steven to slow down."

"We could see the horse, you know, up ahead. That wasn't the problem." Steven was looking up at the wad of lays in the middle of the ceiling.

"Well, thank god I told him to slow down, because just as we came up to the old guy and the horse, this black kid jumps out right in front of the car. Right in front."

"He must have been running alongside the horse, kind of in front or something, because we didn't see him at all. I swerved hard to the left and we missed him, the kid, but barely."

"Barely," says the woman. "And then the car straightened out, I looked behind us and I could see the old guy and the horse just walking along as if nothing had happened and that stupid ass kid hopping along right alongside again."

"It was really weird. The clothes that guy had on must have been a hundred years old."

Just about, I think. A hundred and twenty to be exact.

"How long ago did this all happen?" asks Bert, bringing over the pot.

"Oh, maybe ten minutes ago."

"And which way were they headed?"

"Which way?"

"Toward Raceway or away?"

"Raceway?"

"This place, the trailerpark just down the road. Here."

"Oh, towards here. They were coming this way."

I stand up and put my fifty cents down for my cup of coffee and refuse to look at Henry. I want to see Bat and Barday. I step outside and stand in the middle of the road.

I can't remember ever seeing Bat and Barday together. They are too different to be paired. Barday rides across the sand, Bat digs into it. But here they are, together, all three of them: Bat, Barday, and Tip, coming down the dirt shoulder, making six points of dust in mid-morning. Barday is nearly asleep, the leather saddle creaks and rubs and his Union hat makes a proud, blunt shadow in the dirt as it rocks back and forth. Towards the rear is Bat, half running, his long legs galloping at an uneven pace, working far too hard to match Tip's plodding. He is holding his hands out in front of him straight, swinging, crossing his arms, his fingertips brushing against the horses left flank. He is palsied with freedom and his shadow dances next to Barday's.

"What is going on here?" shouts Celeste from her porch and I hear her running down the steps and the soft thud of her feet in the sand. She is coming from across the road. Left behind, Honey is crying on the top step.

"Bat, Bat Turner, you get away from that horse, get, get," she is yelling, and Barday opens an eye. The voyagers are almost upon me and when Tip nickers, I smell wet grass.

"Hattie, grab Bat, get him off the road." But she is almost here herself and I have never touched Bat.

The horse rushes by faster, close, and now the three are between me and Celeste. I see Bat's eyes squinting shut. I catch one of his hands and he pulls me off my feet, but just for an instant.

We spin for a moment and he sinks to the ground, knees together, legs making triangle wings in the dirt like a toddler as he sits. His hand slips from mine as thin and light as a piece of dry paper.

Barday is awake now and reins Tip to a stop even though the horse has already sensed something amiss and has slowed. Two cars pass by, a '64 Dodge Dart and a VW Squareback. Two great gusts of hot wind and coarse sand and then—

"Barday what in the hell are you doing with this boy?" shouts Celeste, shading her eyes with her hands. Barday reins Tip around to look at her.

"You know, he could get killed out there." She comes up to Bat and grabs him by the shoulder, pulling him up. She does not look at me. "Didn't you think he might get hurt? He's blind, Barday, and he's not like you or me."

Barday moves his Union hat back to wipe sweat away from his brow. His hair is black, obsidian black, full and thick. The hair of a young man. He says, "I see what you mean, the boy is wise, but not to be seen."

Now, Celeste looks at me. "What the hell is that about?" She turns her face up to him. "That's right Barday. He might get hit. Someone might not see him. He would be invisible. Do you understand?"

Barday winces at the sky.

"Do you understand me?" Honey has stopped crying and the edge is gone from Celeste's voice.

Barday looks from the sky into her face, pleading."Do you understand how a man must quest? Connect the times of blood and loss, loose his heart and bear the cross..."

Celeste looks at me again. "What's with this macho bullshit?"

"...seeking that wave, that breaking shore, where new land is made and not from hips born."

"Man, he is getting worse," says Celeste, shaking her head. "You just stay right there Honey, I'm coming right now." She takes Bat's right arm, now slack and pulls him like a piece of taffy back across the road and to the shade of their trailer. "Sit," she says. The command is a vestige of her fear.

Barday chews solemnly on his lips, rubbing his slick gums together. His gray beard, only showing for a few days since his last shave, glints gray-white in the sunlight. He pulls the hat back down. I look up at him.

"Barday, you can't let Bat run like that with you."

"There are new things under the sun."

"Yes, I know he's never done that before, but it's no good. He almost got hit back there by a couple." A third car with Nevada plates whizzes by. There is grit on my teeth.

"Danger is as danger does."

"Come on Barday, knock it off," I say as Tip nuzzles my hand. He smells the sugar packets from the morning coffee. "You shouldn't let him do it again. Get me or Celeste."

Barday gives me such a look that I have to laugh. As if I were five.

"Knowledge in a thimble is worth not much more than a nickel."

"That doesn't rhyme, Barday," I call after him, watching Tip's flanks stiffly rise and drop. "You're slipping."

I feel someone come up beside me, to my left, and there is Melody, holding two golden peaches.

* * *

It was midday. Noon. There were no shadows in the hills. Snakes tasted the air with their tongues and waited silently under rocks for the time to pass. It was a dangerous hour for cold blooded creatures.

At noon, only the rocks at Vasquez could cast shade on the ground. Looking across the sand and dust everything was mustard, brown and dirty green, except at Vasquez. Here, the rocks burned white and to the right of each, large fathomless black shadows spread across the earth.

That is why, although both Hattie and Melody were standing just outside Raceway, pointing to the rocks, even speaking about them, they failed to see the woman crumbling earth with her slide down the hillside, along the largest rock. They did not sense this quiver of movement. They failed to see the sign—the woman was covered in black, deep in shadow. At Vasquez, shadows disappear at two o'clock, when the angle of the sun matches the angle of the rocks.

* * *

"I can't make him go. I mean I can't haul him into the car. He's a grown man." Hattie stands with Melody. They are eating peaches from Pear Blossom, huge peaches and there is juice dribbled in the sand marking their short walk to the edge of Raceway.

"But last night. That was awful. It must be awful for him." Melody wipes her mouth with a wadded up paper towel.

Hattie shrugs. "I don't know. He wants to go eat french fries..."

"He's a smart man, Hattie. He should be doing something. He needs to occupy himself with something."

Hattie takes another bite. "He's occupied. Don't worry."

"You mean, he still…" here Melody glances to the white rocks.

Hattie nods. "I really think he thinks he's going to find treasure up there."

"That's why he didn't want to move down here?"

"No. That was the excuse. When we were up there, Henry would spend hours walking around, looking into little caves and those pockets in the rocks…"

Melody nods.

"…and I know he really knew he wasn't going to find anything. I mean deep down inside I think he knew he was being ridiculous. He's obsessed. I think."

"But isn't there supposed to really be treasure up there?" Melody is staring at the rocks. It is noon and they are massive white.

"Oh Melody, cut it out. I don't know."

"There's also supposed to be ghosts. Zachary told me once he saw ghosts up there."

"Oh. Yeah. Right. He's told me the same thing."

"Hattie Peach," she stops eating and looks at her, "since when are you so sure of anything?"

"Well. Come on. Besides, Vasquez didn't die up there."

"No?"

"No. He was hanged somewhere north. San Francisco. San Jose. Some place like that."

"Hmm." The peach is brought back to her mouth and she takes a bite. "Well. I guess I just like to think maybe there are such things as ghosts. Real ghosts."

Hattie laughs. "Real ghosts? As opposed to fake ghosts?"

"No," she says and shivers suddenly, her shoulders wriggle and Hattie sees goose pimples rise across the nape of her neck. "As opposed to living ghosts."

Melody shifts her bra around. Hattie knows she is uncomfortable. It's nap time for a couple of the babies. She needs to nurse.

"I need to go back and say nap nap to Hannah and Kira." She flings the peach pit into the air. Hattie tosses hers out as well.

"I bet you take a load off their mothers. Such a break for them. It's really nice." Hattie can't say much else. They never discuss what Melody does.

Melody laughs. "Oh, I love it. I just love little kids, especially babies."

They walk back through the sand. Hattie sits back down in the chair and a few minutes later she sees Melody climb the stairs with Hannah hanging on to one hand and Kira cradled in the other. Their mothers have told Hattie, while standing in line at Caldonia's, that they look forward to these times when their babies go nap at Melody's. Now the mothers can take a bath, or paint their nails, or balance the checkbook or clean the oven, or go to the bathroom, breathe easier, having those apron strings loosened just a little, just for a short time.

Time enough for Melody to unfasten her bra, lift out her breasts and offer herself. Hattie loves walking by the Homestead when Melody's nursing. She imagines the half closed eyes and warm milky smiles of sated babies, the soft sounds of swallowing and sucking, the smell of baby powder and flannel smoothed over a sleeping child, and feels a tingle in her own breasts.

Today, though, Hattie hears crying. Crying from both babies. They won't nurse. This is unusual. Soon the door opens and Melody climbs back down the stairs with a child in each arm. Hattie sets down her book and goes to help her. She sees Hattie coming across the side yard.

"I don't know what the problem is. I can't get them to sleep. I have to take them back."

Hattie holds Kira and they return the two to their respective mothers. She feels awkward holding a baby and does not want to even look at the tiny face. This is Melody's world, not hers. The mothers are both surprised, a little exhausted and seem lost a moment as they reconfigure their afternoon. Hannah's mother apologizes and looks worried.

"It's fine," says Melody sweetly. "I'll come around tomorrow and see if she wants to come with me. Don't worry"

This reassures the mother and we leave.

"Have you seen Bat around?" says Melody on the way back.

"Bat?"

"Yeah. I need to see him for a minute."

The few times when there were no babies at Raceway, Hattie suspected Melody suckled Bat. This is why she wants him now. She is full of milk, aching.

"I don't know, Melody. I mean—"

"What? What?" She is irritable. "Look. It's no big deal—It's just that—"

But Hattie doesn't want Melody to tell her.

"Never mind." She looks ahead of Hattie. "There he is."

Hattie glances up and standing between the two of them and the horizon line is Bat, casting no shadow, a perfect black silhouette against a cloudless blue sky.

As she leaves, Hattie catches the soft familiar smell of warm milk. But this time she is troubled.

* * *

Melody touches Bat on the shoulder and whispers in his ear. She takes him by the hand. Sweat is on his forehead and upper lip. She notices this and notices too how tall he has grown. Taller than herself. She waves at Celeste playing with Honey on the swing set and Celeste waves back. Celeste likes Melody. They are the same size and trade clothes back and forth sometimes when they feel exceptionally close. That feeling of closeness, of friendship, the talks until two in the morning come and go, however. And for the last several months they have slipped back into a pattern of waving and simple afternoon chit chat.

Melody whispers in Bat's ear and he picks up his pace. His legs are long and Melody has to hurry to keep up. They are walking to the hills, to the old mine at the foot of Vasquez.

Melody thinks Bat senses where they are headed. His eyes are wide open, his jaw is clenched, and his hands, even the one Melody is holding, are fists. There is a small rabbit trail through the brush at the base of the hill and they start to climb. The trail zigzags up, back and forth, crossing dried up runoffs and the earth turns from sand to rocky ground.

She thinks she hears a rumble and looks up suddenly, expecting to see rocks, some large, some small, all hard, cascading down the face of the mountain—a wave of brown gray moving fast, hurling. She shuts her eyes and imagines the stones knocking her down, striking her head, moving her feet from beneath her, rolling her over and over until she rests at the base of the hill, her mouth filling with sand. She can see her own flesh dusted the same brown gray as the wave. She opens her eyes. Nothing has changed. No rocks. No avalanche. The only movement the stiff sway of dry bushes in the breeze. The daydream passes.

Melody pushes Bat from in back, guiding him along the thin brown path. His body is stiff. It has been awhile since he's climbed in the hills. About halfway up, the path makes a turn at an elderberry bush, and there's the opening right behind, perfectly hidden. The tunnel is small, probably started, and then abandoned early by frustrated miners. The opening is a black circle in the side of the hill, three and a half feet high with a wave of yellow shale lapping at the entrance. Bat has been here before. Melody reaches up inside her shirt and unhooks the cups of her nursing bra. She pushes Bat's head down and moves his legs to bend at the knee, pushing him through the "O" of the opening. She follows, keeping a hand on his back, making sure he doesn't try to stand straight and hit his head.

She pushes him down on a little flat spot right inside. He draws his legs against his chest and takes out his spoon. It has been a long time since they were here together, for this purpose—years, not since he was ten. Melody licks her lips. He's not a child anymore and she's anxious about what her breasts are forcing her to do.

But she sighs, deeply, brushes a hair from her forehead, and says, "No, you're not going to dig now, Bat. Do you hear me. No digging. Come here, Bat. Come here, sweetie," she says calmly without a waiver, and pulls him against her, uncoiling him from his spot in the sand. She cradles his head in her arms and looks into his eyes. The gold of his iris reflects the little silver crystals which lay like teeth along the ceiling and walls of the mine. It is cool in the mineshaft, and Melody squints as she looks outside into the sunlight.

He smells her and latches on. Just like an infant. Just the same. Melody sighs again. There is no difference. His eyes close, his soft coppery hair rubs against her forearm as he routs gently. His body relaxes against hers. She leans back against the wall of the mine, looking down at him, watching his jaw working, looking back outside, watching the breeze. Her breast drains. Around them, crystals glitter, catching the color and shape of movement in a thousand mirrored facets.

* * *

I am here, thinks Bat. I hear heartbeats. It is warm and soft and sweet. It is here. I am here. I here. I here. I here. I here. I here. I here. I here. I here. I here. I here. I here. I here. I here.

He sucks to this rhythm. He does not remember it is Melody who holds him.

* * *

The woman does not move. She watches the white woman nurse the black boy by the edge of the opening. She hardly dares to breathe. She is at the very end of the mine, another thirty feet from where they sit. She cannot see the nursing woman's face as the woman is turned away from her, towards the outside. But she can see the boy, see that he is nearly asleep, and she shuts her own eyes.

She feels the wave come again and she holds her breath, holds her scream, feels it come against her teeth and the pain slips out her nostrils like pale smoke, unheard, silent. She sinks back, not quite limp, half-squatting in the dirt. Warm water is dribbling from between her legs, water identical to the sea, salt water. The water oozes into the dirt, seeping. It is silent at the end of the mine.

The woman with the blonde hair shifts the boy's head in her arms and changes breasts. Behind her the other woman, the dark woman with straight black hair, the one known to others as Shanomi, feels the pain come again. And again, there is no sound, only the breath of secret labor. She will not be found. Though they christened her Shanomi, she calls herself Laying Down With The Moon because for as long as she can remember she has wanted to die. It is the one change she will welcome.

* * *

Change is no longer a force in Kinni's world. There has been one change in her life, the only one that mattered, and its abruptness, its total command of black and white, of turning an instant into eternity, leaves her unable to assess changes in weather, plans, emotions. For her there are no standards with which to measure change and so she exists softly buffeted by nuances, slight variations in action and perception, from one day to the next. The basis of change does not interest her, she is immune. Others may probe the origins of change by following two courses: change as a product of chance, or change as a product of design. But for Kinni these two loops interlocked when she was five and at the moment when chance touched design, at the instant they met, like a common point on tangent circles, meaning and purpose evaporated. Change is an unmoving force, latent, buried beneath laws of physics both discovered and undiscovered. She can only sense its most rudimentary form, when elements are moved. When the wind changes direction. Or when lightning strikes. Or when fire grabs and twists the brush. This is why, when it finally returned, change could only touch her from stilled water.

She sits inside her trailer, a green and white Trojan, unable to sleep, at first awakened by Celeste shouting and then again by crying babies. She does not waken easily and she is not used to this hour of day. Her veil is off and she sits naked in her trailer with all the venetian blinds shut. She cannot see the noon sun, but she can feel its heat. There is sweat on her forehead and upper lip and when she shifts her legs, her thighs pull and stick to the vinyl padding of the kitchen chairs. She rests her head in her hands and opens her eyes wide in the darkness, trying to see as much as she dares.

A small sculpture of a pair of swans swimming parallel to each other and a vase of dried flowers sits on a small end table by the front door. She can see the swans, their necks curving like a pair of question marks, their wings folded tightly, and remembers the grit of dirt. The ivory is grayish brown from dust, and now she rises, turns to the sink and fills a shallow pan with water. She carries the water over to the little table and sets the kitchen chair next to the table. Returning from the sink again, this time with an old toothbrush, she sits down on the chair, dips the brush in the water and begins to clean the swans.

She found them in a second hand store in downtown L.A. and bought them at half-price from a Korean woman who laughed too much. They reminded her of her mother though she did not really understand why. They seemed soft, quiet, and the way their necks arched, taut and poised seemed much like her mother's neck, bowing her head gracefully.

Kinni never sighs, but she pauses, and after a few strokes with the wet brush, she can see the ghost-white of ivory glow off the broad back of each swan. She sits for a moment longer and the water in the pan is stilled. She can hear the sounds of traffic outside, of people traveling to Vegas, to family, to the stores, to work.

A sudden breeze lifts the venetian blind next to the front door. Sunlight flashes inside the trailer like a beacon. Kinni realizes she has been sitting crouched above the pan of water. As light spills across the room, her reflection is captured and in this moment Kinni sees her face staring up from the smooth surface of the water. She gasps and her hands come down in fists into the pan. Water sprays uncontrolled, wet, warm over her arms, against the wood paneled walls, and the scream that comes from her throat is equally uncontrolled. It is only later, in the screams that follow, that she hears herself saying words.

* * *

Noon is a good time to shoot pictures because of the lack of shadows and Lani walks up the rows of trailers toward Vasquez to take a shot of the spot where it happened this morning. Heat never bothers her and she likes it, likes the way it makes her always ready for sex, sweaty, wet between her legs, slightly out of breath, lips a little dry. Heat makes her feel strong.

This morning was good. He wasn't expecting it at all. He was a jogger, staying down the road at the Tomahawk Motel with his wife? girlfriend? (there was a sweet floral scent in his hair) and he was just turning around to start back when a pebble rolled under his foot and he fell. Lani saw him fall, saw the blood on his elbow and knee and as she was getting ready to go pick up the photos at Vons, offered him a lift. He was limping badly and smiled gratefully as the passenger door to her Ford truck swung open.

They ended up in the riverbed between Vasquez and Raceway, in a bend where time and water scattered large boulders against the curve of hard sand. A hot sandy little spot in the opposite direction of Tomahawk. He held her arms above her head, hard, pinned down with one hand, tight, and he licked her nipples as her back arched against stone. She threw her head back, feeling her hair sticking to her neck, and she felt his other hand breathing over her chest, her back, her buttocks and hips, rubbing, and she tilted her pelvis forward and up, curved her neck forward, opened her legs wider and he came, shaking, holding his breath, and then, through clenched teeth, groaning, loudly, saying "shit shitshit shitshit," and finally, coughing. The sky was sparkling blue and she spent most of her time squinting into the sun.

It was later, after she dropped him in front of the raised neon Tomahawk at 4c, but before she rolled onto the interstate, that she masturbated. Let the car settle on the side of Rte. 14, reached between her legs, and kept an eye in her rearview mirror for truckers. The tension mounted in a quick throb behind her pelvis. Her vagina, aching for release, was swept in the rush stretching open and shut, open and shut in waves. She withdrew her hand, wiped it on a tissue and straightened out her miniskirt. Had to be always ready.

But she is not ready for the scream from Kinni's trailer. She freezes in the sand, pressing the camera tight against her sternum. Unable to move or to realize, really, what she just heard. And then again. That sound. A terrible scream, guttural, unpracticed, primeval. And then again. And all she can see in her mind, in her memory, is the flutter of pink curtains and a broken window, the taste of blood in her mouth, oppressive weight, of being pressed down, down, down to the floor, and she is afraid for Kinni.

She does not think. Her camera smashes against the door as she tries to force the lock. Her fists sting each time she hits the door. There is another scream, this time, higher, and nonsense words, words Lani does not recognize are torn from the sounds.

The door lunges open and Lani staggers into darkness, falling over a body on the floor. She falls hard, on both knees. There are no more screams. She reaches up for the light switch, but another hand fights hers and she is groping, "Kinni," she calls out, her mouth dry and her voice a whisper. "Kinni, where are you?"

"I am here," says Kinni and her voice is deep, ragged, cut by a thousand wrongs.

"Kinni," she begins again, but another breeze catches the door and swings it open. The noon sun does not penetrate far and falls very short, a first step inside. But it is enough to filter across Kinni's face and as Lani rises on her knees, she sees her and sees that Kinni is naked, slender, dark and fearful of the light. Lani sits back on her heels for a moment and as she moves back and down, her own shadow leaves Kinni's face and yellow light floods the curve of cheekbones, the hollows of eyes and neck. There is only an instant of illumination and then Kinni's face is gone, turned away quickly retreating into darkness, but in that instant Lani knows what she has seen. A pale face. A face which lives apart from Kinni and has nothing to do with her, separated from the rest of her body, protected from the elements. A face which has never responded to human voice or touch and exists without expression, a void of smooth flesh, flickering in the dim light just inches from her own face.

"Kinni," says Lani quietly, softly, afraid to startle her.

"What." says Kinni, in a whisper that is flat and the face moves forward slightly, catching a crescent moon of light. All that is revealed is the chin. The mouth is a small pink curve, slack. Then the chin disappears, and Lani hears Kinni push herself up, straightening to stand. Lani remains on her knees unable to move, paralyzed by her sudden need, the steady welling of an urge.

"I want to take your picture," she whispers.

There is only silence and then the sound of bare feet on linoleum. Kinni must be in the kitchenette. Lani sits up a little on her knees. "Kinni," she says and pauses. "I need to take your picture."

For the first time in her life, Lani is swept by compulsion. She will not walk away from the chance to take photographs of an object that has come from beyond the earth.

* * *

Oxena Turnbill usually does not stay outside in the heat of midday. Her eyes have grown sensitive to light and the brilliance, especially in the summer months, is painful. But Zachary is bitter today and she does not want to watch him play solitaire at the kitchen table anymore. The way he slaps the cards down, bending them nearly in half and then releasing them so they smack against the Formica, irritates her. He only does it when he gets a run, as if in victory.

So she sits and watches Honey playing on the metal swing set, pumping hard, her braids dark in the heat and her bare feet swinging up and down, up and down, her soles pink. Honey could swing for hours, a pendulum not counting time, freezing for just an instant at the crest of each swing. And it is at those moments, when Honey is frozen just for a millisecond, that she pulls hard on the chain handles, thrusts her feet front or back and throws her weight after.

Oxena waves to her, "Good swinging dear, you sure know what to do."

Honey grins and says nothing, but pumps even harder.

Oxena sips more lemonade. Years ago she and Zachary would go to church on Sundays. They would just be getting out now, shaking hands with Father Pines, chatting with the Ellers and Smalls and maybe Betsy Claude would have made coffee and Joseph McAdler would bring pastries from his bakery. She and Zachary had lived in Alton, a little town in Missouri, in the Ozarks and Zachary managed the general store. They were the couple everyone liked.

"Watch me now!" yells Honey suddenly and Oxena sees her swing forward, and at the moment where the pendulum stops, she releases the swing and is airborne. She lands in the sand with a silent thud, Oxena imagines the slight sting up the back of the leg as Honey stands and grins even broader.

"Good girl," Oxena begins to call, but Honey is not looking for praise. She has tipped her head up to the sky as her face is bathed in black shadow. She brings a hand up to her face to shield her eyes from the noon sun and Oxena sees the shadow leave her and spread across the ground and then circle back and cover Honey again. Oxena can hear no plane engine sounds. She, too, looks up and at first sees nothing but white light and she squints, hard, her face pinched, her cheeks pulled high and her mouth in a set grimace, but again all she can see is yellow with blue around the edges and her eyes water. She blinks hard and feels a tear on her face. She hears Honey yelling, "What is it! What is it, lady Noxeena!" and instead of shading her eyes with the flat of her hand, Oxena closes her thumbs over her fists, presses her hands to her face and looks through the "O" in each hand like a pair of binoculars.

At first she sees nothing but blue sky and then, suddenly, a wing fills her view range. A gigantic black wing, each feather a sheath absorbing all light, and she moves her hands slightly to get a bigger picture and the head of the bird, a massive, awkward head, with hooked beak and black eyes encircled by white and red feathers. The bird is flying low, without any sound, circling just thirty feet or so above Honey, its wings fanned against the blue, unmoving, from tip to tip at least three times Honey's size.

"It's a big birdy," calls Honey excitedly jumping up and down. "Look at that. Look at that."

The bird circles above Honey one more time and then with a single wave of its wings silently flies straight and disappears over the trailer tops.

"That was a Condor," says Zach, coming from behind her. "A California Condor."

Oxena drops her hands, suddenly glad he is standing beside her. She can feel his arm close to hers and she is amazed that for one who has always watched insects, always peered into the earth and her grasses, her leaves, her dirt and gravel, he would be willing to look up into the sky.

* * *

Henry is pulling out on to Rte. 14, looking up to the right, towards the foothills, not thinking about anything except blue cheese and French fries. He turns the wheel, gives the Valiant gas and slams on his brakes. A horn blows, a car swerves hard and an upturned middle finger is flashed as a Camero rushes from the left and throws sand in a quivering arc across the road. Paper cups, old keys, rocks, and a pair of dog-eared Harlequin romances skid along the top of the dashboard and pile up by the wing window on the right.

The car rocks to a sudden stop and the glove compartment pops open. Henry lunges, but papers, envelopes, old straws, napkins, torn Mustang drive-in tickets all slip and slide over each other flipping to the floor. A black drop falls like a tear on top of everything and a pain shoots through Henry's legs. He sucks air through his teeth, rubs his thigh hard with his hand and tries not to look down at the Civil War button. It is from a Union jacket. Barday gave it to Hattie years ago. Once shiny tin now blackened by oxygen, the eagle clutches three arrows in one claw and an olive branch in the other. He lets up on the clutch and stabbing pain sears through his hips. Harpooned, he lets the car roll to the right-hand shoulder, and lets go of the clutch. The car bucks to a stop. Hanging on to the steering wheel with his left hand, he reaches down and tries to feel for the button, certain that if he could grab it and chuck it out the window he'll be fine.

What Henry hadn't bargained for was glancing down and seeing Arlene's elaborate script neatly penned on her old pink marbled stationary. The pain in his leg trembles, fades, flutters, and is lost.

His hands shake as he fumbles the key to switch the motor off. He glances down again to be sure. It is Arlene's. It is all Arlene.

He bought the stationary for her in Chicago, before they were married, down at Harley's Drug, and the pink marble is nearly orange, yellowed around the edges. But the paper is strong, not fragile and even along the fold running lengthwise there are no cracks or signs of age. It is not heavy stock and her ageless handwriting milks through the marble. He opens the letter and sits in the dust, in the heat of midday, where there are no shadows, reading a note to him written twenty-five years ago by a woman who had blond hair that curled and who never wore hats.

> Dearest Henry,
>
> I have always loved you. I feel as if we have loved before, that we whispered each other's names centuries ago, that I do know you at your core, your being, and that I will always know you. But now I am about to lose you. only because I will lose myself. I grieve for you and me, for the life we will not have together. And Henrietta. She is so small. So fragile. I will miss her life. I will miss everything about her. I will never ever know this person you and I created. She will grow up without me, looking into the mirror, seeking out the ghost hidden in her own features. You will live on, nursing a horrible wound I will

never be able to heal but for which I am responsible.   I will be buried with pieces of your hearts.

But you will survive. As humans do. Resiliency, though, should not always be considered an attribute. Resiliency alone festers. You will survive.

I will not. Survival should recognize responsibility and from responsibility should come forgiveness. Please forgive me for what I will do to you.

My love for you will remain only in your heart . You must find your treasure in Vasquez.

Arlene

Vasquez. He reads the letter again, stunned, removed from even himself. "Vasquez?" he says aloud.

She had never been further east than Chicago. As far as he knew, Arlene knew nothing of Vasquez, this tiny place in the dust. How could she reach into the future with such precision and guide him like a scout bathed in candlelight straight to his destiny? She was the existential, he was the romantic. So how did this happen? He had spent so much of his time, his life, reaching backwards trying to find the reason for her death and now she calmly stepped forward from the past and pointed him towards his future.

Vasquez was his. It was his all along.

* * *

A mile and a half out, southeast of Raceway Trailer Park stands a small 1300 square foot cement building with a low slung terra-cotta roof, cupped upside down "u"s laid in lines on top of each other. A parking lot five times the size of the building lays a sheet of hot asphalt in a square around the unit. The parking lot is filled with dust covered cars, many with out-of-state plates. The walls of the building are two feet thick, layers of steel pressed against concrete, placed at right angles to each other in the shape of a perfect square. The only door has no visible handle or lock. Instead a box two feet by two feet has been installed just to the right of the door. A number pad and a blue telephone can be seen under glass a quarter of an inch thick. Bulletproof. The lock to the glass box is also invisible, magnetically triggered, impenetrable.

There is no chain link fence around the cement square or the parking lot, no infrared devices, no warnings or signs that this is federal property. Because, technically, it isn't. The dirt road which snakes off Rte. 14 leads to a culmination of a partnership between higher education and private interest. True, the bridge is the federal government, pulling tighter that knot binding science to fiscal opportunity, but they were merely facilitators. California was well represented in the last election and contracts were thrown her way like handfuls of confetti. The northern part of the state, glittering Silicon Valley, was tasked with creating circuitry for the brains of the future. The southern part of the state, with its wide deserts, was to detail the speed of the body—find out how fast matter could travel and make appropriate applications from the data.

Inside the cement box is an elevator shaft a quarter of a mile deep. This is where Parker Limpid is standing, in the elevator, heading down, deep past dirt and stratified rock and fossils of mussels and clams, sponges and tiny fish. He is not thinking about sponges or the sea at the moment, however. He is working a mathematical dilemma in his head, resorting only intermittently to the ink board mounted on the wall of the elevator. The ride down is time-consuming, consuming time, but at least he has time to think.

Parker is meeting with Zeus. Zeus is the five mile long superconductor dug out from limestone and shale. A steel and electronic hollow tunnel one-mile wide bent in a perfect circle. Zeus sits deep, secretly coiled directly under Raceway, creating the hollow, tubed space through which particles are hurtled, broken down and their pieces pushed through time with the speed of light. He is a particle accelerator. He has not been functioning correctly, has not functioned correctly since he was powered up for the first time last month. Thus Parker's little ink marks on the board.

Zeus was supposed to be dependable, steady. Reasonable. On paper, he was predictable. Parker was the one most familiar with Zeus, he designed Zeus's father at a site up in Stanford, had studied at CERN and he could calibrate Zeus's reactions. He knew how Zeus used power and chance to trap particles and then send them with light—so he was the one most consumed with Zeus. Parker had more invested in the relationship than any of the others. And there were hundreds of others who worked with Zeus, their cars neatly placed in rows above his head. Thousands would visit him.

Parker steps off the elevator into a dark steel hall lit by two red lights from either side, takes four steps and enters an airlock. When he exits the airlock, he is in the first tier computer center. Dr.s Babbit and Ellsberg look up as a coded beeper signals Parker's entrance.

"We may have something and we may not have something," says Ellsberg. Parker watches his Adams apple moving up and down on the "haves."

He walks passed them, through plexiglass doors and into the Center. Puez, Ellsberg and Babbitt along with Newwit and Long are the principle players today in the underground race.

Dr. Puez removes her glasses and glances at Parker. She wipes her eyes. She and Parker are separated by sex, age and taste in music. Radio waves do not travel well underground through steel and magnets, so the cassette tape machine on the far left-hand wall always has two stacks of tapes piled on top. The one on the right with the Four Freshman, Peter, Paul and Mary, Kingston Trio. The one on the left with Guns 'n' Roses, Metallica, Judas Priest. The glasses are set between the two stacks and she sits down on a small round padded stool.

"No luck ay?" says Parker, looking beyond her at her computer screen.

He knows she does not care for him. She thinks him too young and his IQ contentious—a quirk of computer scoring and highly cultivated social skills. She has seen blue blood converted into black inked high four figure scores many times.

"No. No luck. And that's what we need right now. Lot's of it."

"I was being facetious."

"Well, I'm not." The glasses are replaced on her nose. She taps a computer key to save and looks at him. "This is ridiculous. Every event should bring us thousands of collisions and we should be able to get one or two head-ons out of that. We aren't getting anything."

At one point on Zeus's circle is a cathode gun. His gut is filled with magnets and accelerating cavities. Within the five mile ring are three detectors. Placed to measure events, each lies in a strong magnetic field–their internal walls lined with millions of electronic sensors that encase the point at which the collisions occur. The detectors, Birdy, Shannon, and Diana, are thick in Zeus's gut. Diana is the detector fully activated and Zeus is not allowing her to respond.

"And everyone here is positive nothing's being captured either?" Parker is suspect of second hand data.

"Nowhere. Every cell has been checked and re-checked. If Zeus's storing particles somewhere, he's hiding them from us."

"So we're having no events. And we're not capturing anything either."

"You got it."

Now why, thinks Parker, would Zeus want to do a thing like that? Parker blinks slowly at the tightly packed frames fanned in front of him. Each frame holds an electromagnetic field in place, like an invisible spider web, ready to snatch particles or subatomic particles as they flow through space and earth without resistance, fluid bits of matter without origins or conscience. He sighs and looks up at the ceiling for a moment, staring at his image warping in the steel panels. He cannot imagine what could be malfunctioning. The problem is obviously electronic and/or human. A broken wire, a burned out light. Someone not reading the signs right. Certainly the universe has not run out of particles.

What Parker Limpid does not know is that just above the complex, stopped dead center one hundred yards above Zeus's circle, under thousands of tons of rock and embedded in limestone is the complete skeleton of Basilosaurus. A prehistoric whale, a dinosaur whose genetic material feeds the great blues, the sperm, the white whale and the mythical narwhal complete with unicorn horn. The largest whale to inhabit the earth. The skeleton is female, 120 feet from tip of tail to jaw, complete, not one bone missing, her ribs filled with sand, pushing out into rock, her eye sockets locked by sediment. She is the largest of her kind, immense. Through her ribs, buried within her and stone are more bones, fragile not just with time but with their own tender structure. Her unborn son, her fetus, is as still as she. She lays here silently, her back curved as if still swimming. She will remain unfound, stranded in rock, between Raceway and Zeus.

DEFINING TERMS

Flight or fight responses have always eluded me. They are not mutually exclusive. Either I flee with energy knotted and flaring for a fight or I stay and watch myself crushed, devoid of self-preservation. To others I think I give the impression of confidence. "Steady" is what I heard all through high school. "She's the steady one. Hattie never gets her feathers ruffled."

As if I were an ostrich.

In retribution for Henry avoiding me, his pain, the doctor, and life in general, my Sunday afternoon was spent reading. I was exactly at the halfway point, flitting through the U.S. Constitution, the Bill of Rights, the Amendments Since the Bill of Rights, always shocked that prohibition lasted 16 years (1917-1933) and ending with Amendment XXVI (lowering voting age to 18 years). Then it was on through the Origin of the Constitution, How the Declaration of Independence was Adopted, The Liberty Bell: Its History and Significance, Confederate States and Secession, Lincoln's Gettysburg Address, Origin of the United States National Motto ("In God We Trust"...it wasn't until 1955 that Congress ordered it printed on all paper money and all coins), Origin and Text of the National Anthem, Statue of Liberty National Monument (just think of that 35 foot waist), Forms of Address for Persons of Rank and Public Office (a list of Honorables and Sirs and Eminences), Code of Etiquette for Display and Use of the US. Flag, which always made me remember my wish as a child that the flag would fly at half-mast in honor of my death. I was flipping through the World Maps and Flags, browsing for new countries arising from dust and blood when I saw Henry coming toward me with a letter in his hand. I closed the Almanac. The sun had moved across the sky arcing into late afternoon and though Henry stood at least three feet from me, he still cast a long shadow across my face.

"Hattie, I want you to see this." He held out the letter, which I recognized, and it bent slightly in the breeze. The pink paper was marbled, smooth and brindled with golden threads. I cleared my throat.

"Where did you find this?"

"In the glove compartment."

I reached up and took it from his fingers. "Did you ever get to Denny's?"

"No. Read it Hattie." He was impatient.

"So what have you been doing all afternoon?"

He did not respond and I couldn't see his face. I could smell gin though. I heard the sigh escape my lips and opened the letter.

I sat very still for a long time, listening to my heart, watching my fingertips against the pink paper, careful not to allow my face to been seen.

His voice cracked hollow. "So what do you think?"

I had to measure everything I said. "I think this is strange. Very strange." I looked up at him. "Where did you find this?"

"In the glove compartment."

"In the Valiant?"

"Yes. It just fell out."

"Fell out? You mean it's been in there all this time?"

"Now Hattie, I thought maybe you could tell me where it came from."

"Me? I've never seen it." I was nervous. There was too much stress on "me."

"You used to play in her trunk all the time."

"Listen, I would remember something like this."

"Hattie..." The polished parental reproach stung.

"I would." I looked down at the letter again. "I don't know what to think. I think it's weird."

Henry stood next to me and pointed to the signature. "That's exactly how she signed her name."

"That's because she wrote it." A bold move.

He lifted the letter from my hands and carefully folded it in half again, staring at the paper, running a finger along the spine of the fold. "I gave it to Barday to read."

"Great."

"You know what he said."

"I can't imagine."

"Hattie, he's a brilliant man."

My father can be unpleasantly eccentric sometimes.

"Brilliant. Fine. He's brilliant."

"He said," and he reached in his pocket and took out a matchbook, flipped the cover and read, "'When whispers call, look beside you—not north not south—learn to stop the wind in your mouth." Henry shrugged. I picked up the Almanac.

"I can't think what to make of it. How could she know that I'd be hunting treasure at Vasquez? Thirty years ago Hattie. How could she know?"

As he walked away, I felt a sudden wound open and before I could stop myself, I called out, "The next time you find one of those, show me first."

But it was backhanded, what I did. Untruthful. And now I felt terrible, betraying the dead, betraying someone I did not know and I slammed the book shut and lay back and stared into the red bliss of my eyelids.

I used to love to play in her trunk. It was the only intimate piece of her he brought from Chicago. He strapped it to the top of the car (a '57 black T-bird with remote control windows), and we carried her out west.

The exterior of the trunk was black with steel reinforced corners, the inside lined with red velvet. There was one photograph of her tacked to the center of the inside lid so that when I opened the trunk, she was the first thing I saw. The picture was old, unframed, taken when she was a teenager and she wore her hair in what was supposed to be a short bob. But her blonde hair curled high and around her face and in the black and white photo her hair glistened like polished steel ringlets. She looked like an old fashioned movie star to me.

The picture was later destroyed and the memory of her face dissolved, but there were those fleeting moments in front of a mirror, brushing my hair, just catching my reflection before turning away, when I thought I saw her hiding somewhere in my face. But now I have nothing to compare myself with and I think I'm starting to look more and more like Henry.

As a kid, I originally pawed through the trunk looking for more photographs of her. But there were none and Henry had a fit. It remained closed. At least that's what Henry thought. At night when he was out working or during the day while he slept, I would go in the garage or the attic or the car, where ever it was wherever we lived, and tumbled the lock and raised the lid. I always saw her first, looking up at me and her smile left me humbled and shy, and feeling as if I were trespassing. Not on property but on someone's soul. Inside the trunk were her things. Just things. Objects. Old letters from her mother and father, a rubber orange bracelet, old costume jewelry full of sequins and light plastic pearls, two old dresses, both of satin, heavy, strapless, gathered at the bosom, one blue the other purple. They were identical and I think she must have made them, though I'm not sure she knew how to sew.

Finally, there were her little paintings and her box of watercolors, a slender leather rectangle with a single paintbrush dividing colors. Her paintings were not particularly good, all of them were still-lifes: glasses in the sun, a goldfish bowl, fruit in a bowl, and color sketches of buildings, parks, faceless people with running paint and buckling paper. But the colors were translucent and ran with a serendipity that eluded me. An old sheep's wool coat that smelled badly lay over everything, like a shield. There were many cardboard boxes filled with other things: locks of hair from her horse, dog teeth, smooth ocean rocks, a bird feather. I never did uncover the treasures in all the boxes. My actions were covert and I was always tensed for discovery.

When I grew a little older and we were beached in the center of New Mexico, living on the edges of Santa Fe, watching that purple sky, I began to use the trunk for shelter. I would pull out the coat and the dresses and make a nest, lay down into the deep plush of red velvet, close the lid and look up blindly to where she hovered. Though the photograph was there, inches from my face, I couldn't see her. I could imagine her heartbeat in the scarlet darkness. Then I would leave, slamming the lid shut, imagining her in the outside world with me just like that—so close as to be my breath and as unseen as air. This was as near as I came to being with God.

* * *

Bat disappeared that afternoon. No one knew where he went and Melody and Celeste came across the sand, worried, distressed. Not certain of next steps.

"Hattie," called Melody coming across the side yard. Celeste was with her.

"Have you seen Bat anywhere?" Celeste's mouth was a thin line.

"No. Last I knew he was with you," I said to Melody, who was looking around, shielding her eyes. I felt sorry for her. Her sun hat had slipped off and was resting between her shoulder blades by means of a frazzled piece of twine knotted at the base of her neck. She was actually beginning to turn pink across her nose, and when she moved her arms up to shield the sun, I could see white skin where her sleeveless shirt gapped open. The crest of her shoulders were reddened and freckled.

"What is it about today," said Celeste and this wasn't a question. "He's getting harder and harder to keep a hold of," she said and brought a hand to her mouth to press her top lip against her teeth.

"How long has he been gone?"

Melody looked at the ground for a moment and then glanced at Celeste. "Maybe an hour. Forty-five minutes."

"Too long for that boy. He's blind and he's black and he has no sense. He'll be over those mountains in a second, and some white son-of-a-bitch'll shoot him like a rabbit."

I couldn't think how to respond. I could feel myself sitting heavier in the chair, seeing her black skin absorbing all light and emitting only a sheen, uncomfortable with myself.

"Oh Celeste," said Melody, "I'm sure nothing's happened to him. He was just with me."

"I'm going to have to send him somewhere. He's getting too big. If he's going to start wandering. I just don't know."

"Maybe he's with Barday again." Melody's hair began to shine with orange highlights and the sun continued to moved closer to the horizon.

I offered, "Barday was at the Volcano for a while. With Henry."

Celeste looked at Melody and her forehead creased with her frown. "If he's off running down the road again, I'll kill him."

I ended up playing with Honey on the swing set, watching Celeste head for the Volcano, and Melody, with her hair kissed orange by the late sun, backtracking toward the foothills. In opposite directions, both on foot.

"Hi Honey, " I said, pushing my chair into the sand by the swing set, sitting down with my back to the sun.

"I saw a great big burry," said Honey, swinging hard, fast, back and forth, back and forth.

I couldn't hear her. "A what?"

"A big black birdy, right up there," she said and let go of the swing for an instant to point at the sky.

"Oh, good," I said. "You hang on tight when you're swinging, O.K.?"

"O.K.," she called back.

I watched her move up and down, back and forth, for several minutes, then opened my Almanac to the last page. Between the book and the back cover, neatly stacked, were several sheets of pink marbled paper. I looked at them for a long time, seeing how the late afternoon could turn pink into gold. If the dead could speak once, they could certainly speak again. It happens all the time in history books.

* * *

Henry was moving slowly forward. North, toward Vasquez, the letter still in his left hand, his mind still seeking a chronology of events. His shoes were worn, old work boots, covered with oil stains from the garage where he pumped gas. He felt dislodged, adrift, propelled by a force greater than himself, carried out to some ancient sea, caught in an invisible tide too overwhelming to be fought.

Arlene had returned to him. She came not in a flimsy dream where she transformed into other people or disappeared into a mist of smell and sound or coaxed him into a horrifying death with her. She returned in full, complete, on paper. With real thoughts. From her, about him, about them. About love and pain. Somehow telling him where to look, to be strong and certain and, above all, to trust that this was the right thing to do. To search Vasquez. Now. Now that she was back.

His shoes sunk and pulled in the sand as he trudged up the riverbed. The rocks of Vasquez lay ahead in rows all to the right and the evening sun splashed orange light freely against their wide surfaces. He climbed out of the riverbed, across some white boulders which had gathered in a bend in the river, moved by water now running deep underground. The path was worn, well used by his nightly searches. For he only came at night, under full moon or with a flashlight, walking the small animal trails that wove an intricate web around the rocks. The rocks stood like monoliths, covering more than fifty acres, ascending from the base of the canyon, beginning small and simple, up the face of the mountain to a flat wide area where the largest rocks stood. Then they continued on up, though the ones that rode the crest of the mountain top were as the ones at the base, smaller, more smooth and less complicated. At night Henry would sit for hours looking down on Raceway, watching lights winking off and on inside each trailer, taking note of headlights as cars passed east or west on Rte. 14.

He would search for treasure. Real treasure. Gold, silver, amulets, rubies, pearls, old coin and paper money. More than a hundred years ago Vasquez ran with his band into the rocks, eluding posse, hiding horses and men in the rocks. In the heat of gun play, of wild shootings and cries of revenge for Mexico, he tossed the fruits of his most recent pillage into the rocks, into their crevices, into their small caves and pockmarked surfaces for safe keeping. Gold was close to Vasquez's heart and stories were told of U.S. gold bullion taken in the name of Mexico, gold medallions torn from the breasts of dead U.S. generals, gold figures—lions and snakes—taken from Mexico and then retrieved in flames from the estates of wealthy Californian cattle ranchers. And finally, there were the tales of deerskin snuff bags filled with the dull nuggets of Californian gold miners left to lay face down in watery sluices with their throats slit.

Vasquez was not discriminating, however. Jewels, silver, bank bonds, payrolls, land records, all were of interest to him. He stole with a fury propelled by hate and though he carried a six shooter, his first choice of revenge was the sword of his father. It too glittered with gold, its handle forged in the feathers of an eagle, its blade a pale shimmer of electrum. For five years blood and pain and fear were companions when he rode. He robbed a bank and struck down three unarmed men in Tres Pinos. Every man in Kingston was roped and tied, the stores and bank gutted. In Cahuenga Pass the sword was raised high, a general slaughtered, and praises of Mexico echoed. He was lionized by his people and he and his band moved in circles thundering within the tail of California in a shroud of blood and honor.

The rocks were his favored retreat. Before the aqueduct, the Feather River supplied water to the canyon and horses and men could rest. When cornered, they could hide. But often he could not return for months and in the end he never returned and so the rocks twinkled in the night not only with mica but with the promise of secrets unfound. Henry followed right behind Vasquez as if no time had passed, using his hands and intuition, feeling the surfaces of the rocks, running his hands inside the long shallow openings, digging with just his fingertips in the limestone caves. He did this all under cover of darkness, often with his eyes closed, lips moving silently, talking himself through the search. This is why it felt strange, as if he were undergoing a mythical initiation, to be in the rocks, one among those praying hands, in daylight.

Rubbing his own hand across the first rock in greeting, he passed through the small "V" of the canyon opening and then up the trail to the plateau where most of the largest rocks sat, erupted from the earth and held fast in red dirt. He stood at the bottom of the largest and tilted his head back so that the bald orange of rock was nothing but a smooth curve against the purpling sky.

He held the letter up against the rock. An image of marble against stone. When he swallowed, it was difficult, and he could taste salt water and dust. He could almost see her. Sometimes he would remember her shape, but not the details of her lips or her eyes. At other times, he could conjure only the details. The way her fingers lay silently spread against her pillow, slightly arched, relaxed. The small crease in her cheek when she laughed. The warmth of her mouth as she opened herself to him.

He would begin at the beginning, where he first began his search fifteen years before. Hiking the periphery, walking in concentric circles until he reached the center, until he reached this rock. He must have overlooked a small hiding place, not dug deep enough, ignored a nook or cranny. Because, clearly, the treasure was here, somewhere, buried, forgotten and lost.

When he first began, he kept intricate maps of his searches, drawing the land and rocks to scale, careful of the placement of rocks, and crossing off each formation as it proved to yield nothing. The maps would not serve him with this new attempt, however. He needed to begin again, without assurances from the past, without depending on conclusions which might be false. The land was now a part of him. The rocks, mute and immovable, stood as an intimate fortress.

He dropped his hands and walked up around in back of the rock, taking careful steps up its north side, stepping over the stubby grass growing from cracks, climbing up a little and standing on top. From here he could see the lower range of rocks, and the part of Raceway not hidden by the canyon walls. The wind blew his hair back and he leaned slightly forward. In the quiet of early evening, the canyon was a soft sea of pink, the low brush moving like shoals.

The sun was setting on his right, close to the horizon line, a bright orange ball balanced on a tightrope. There were no clouds. The moon had already risen and sat in mirror image on his left. The two spheres faced each other, the sky between them a wash of orange into purple.

Henry brought the letter to his lips and tried to catch her smell, of vanilla and almonds, but paper only fluttered against his chin.

"Henry! Henry! Is that you?"

He opened his eyes. He had nearly seen her as complete as her letter. He had nearly found his ground. But now the moment was gone and he was adrift again. He knew he was very tired. He looked down the canyon path and there was Melody, her hair flying orange in back of her, her hat gone and her arms sunburned. He could not raise his arms to wave and so he stood on the bow pulpit of his ship, watching a sea that had disappeared under dust.

She stopped and looked up at him. "Have you seen Bat anywhere?"

Her words reached him, her voice, thin.

He stared at her walking up the path unable to realize she was really coming. He stared down at the rock between his feet. The pink paper flapped against his hand in the breeze. She came and stood at the base of the rock, panting slightly, hot, her blue jeans dusty and her part down the center of her crown a streak of ruddy red. She reached behind and knotted her hair, keeping it off her shoulders, which looked tender.

"Hey Henry," she repeated. "Have you seen Bat around?"

Henry tucked the letter into his T-shirt pocket.

"We took a walk together this afternoon and now he's disappeared. Hattie thought maybe he'd taken off with Barday again. But you haven't seen him?"

Henry shook his head.

"Is something wrong?" she asked.

He raised his head and looked beyond her to the valley below. Yuccas stood tipped with orange light up and down the canyon.

"Henry, come with me for a second," she said, turning around, heading down the path and to the right. He saw her glance back once to wait for him.

* * *

As Melody came down around the mineshaft, she looked for signs of Bat. Holes in the dirt, broken brush, his spoon. But there was nothing except the black yawn of the mine opening. Four hours had passed since they returned from their walk and she left him sleepy and sweet smelling by the swing set. But maybe he had returned, made his way back somehow.

"Bat," she called, crouching down in the opening. Henry, still silent, followed her. Orange light seeped in, reflected off the crystals, but the light was poor and it took a long time for her pupils to gather enough light for her to see. She should have borrowed a flashlight. She climbed inside and squatted down and crawled along the floor, careful to protect her palms and knees from hard rocks and crusty deposits. There was no sound except her own breathing.

"Bat," she called again and looked up. Outside, the sun moved low in the sky, even with the mine opening, low enough to suddenly shoot orange light directly inside the shaft. Streams of crystals reflected orange, pink and purple light in irregular swaths of color. It was in that instant of blindness, as her pupils closed against the new light and as she came to the end curve of the mine, that her hand brushed against something living. She froze, still unable to see, breath trapped in her throat. Then there was a cry, like a lamb. A tiny jaw quivering, giving the cry of hunger and need so plaintive her breasts tingled from deep inside and milk flooded to her nipples.

"What..."

The cry was louder and the swath of crystals pointed to a tiny form, human and naked lying on the floor of the mine. She heard the sound of shuffling behind her as she recoiled, sitting back on her knees.

"Jesus Christ," said Henry and he pushed passed Melody. The sun sank another degree and the rear of the shaft was pitched into darkness once again. All action became slow and muggy, outlines blurred by lack of light and senses dulled by the concentrated need to fill in the dark areas of the scene in front of her. She was a witness to actions beyond judgment. Henry crouched just in front of her, sideways, bent over awkwardly, trying to lift the baby and not step in a damp spot beneath him. The placenta lay in a wet mound on the dirt floor, a discarded organ fanned with beautiful vessels now empty. It was as Henry came toward her with the crying child, and as she reached, without thinking, and felt a cry come up from her throat and she stood in the darkening mineshaft and turned to run into light, that she smelled the terrible smell of wet blood—like heated iron. She could not move, held fast by the image, now growing stronger, of the woman lying on the ground. The infant felt cold in her hands and she held it in front of her, unaware even of its small movements against the air.

The woman's hair was black and straight, tangled with dust and dirt. She lay face down on the limestone floor. She was naked, her dress torn and crumpled beneath her, soaked with blood. Both hands were between her legs, pressed together. Melody watched Henry, again, avoiding the dark stain on the ground, roll the woman over and as her shoulders fell stiffly and her head moved slightly and Melody could see that her eyes were dry and unseeing, Melody thought, "so this is what I was so afraid of? This is death?"

They did not speak to each other. Henry stood outside the mine opening, watching vague and tremulous stars appear one by one. The infant, still covered in its burgundy brine was wrapped in Henry's shirt. Melody sat just inside, just as she did earlier that day, her blouse unbuttoned, her left breast draining as quickly as the right.

* * *

Bat was alone in a crowd of rocks, all whispering to him as the wind sang through the spaces where they met and touched, kissing. The rocks lay in horseshoe to the east of Raceway, coughed up out of the river during the flood and left to burn on the hardpack of the desert floor. He squatted, his spoon working up and down, every so often stopping to catch his reflection in its silver curve. His mouth felt sticky and he licked his lips. Sweat ran from his forehead, in back of his ear, trickled down his neck and dampened his Marvin Gaye T-shirt. He did not squat on the desert floor, however. He squatted in a crater three feet deep by eight feet wide, a crater he had returned to every day for a long time. This was his hole.

The day he began the crater, was a good day. The rocks were cool from the night. He had carried his spoon with him, pressed against his chest, down the rows of trailers, past the Volcano, out of the riverbed and onto terra firma. He hurried, awkwardly, the sand giving under his feet making his pace uneven. The sun was his guide and he walked into its blindness, eyes wide, his mind blank, burned clean. He kept walking, his face warming, the lids of eyes blinking, shutting out the light and then he ran. Hard. The spoon in one hand, pumping up and down, a streak on the dust, legs driving to the sunrise and its pink oasis. But he never reached it. He fell into the horseshoe, tumbling against the rocks, rigid. Both shins were cut, deeply and later Celeste would look and yell and press her lips against her teeth. But when he rose, out there, alone, there were no echoes left. No shadowy fluttering of things seen and unnamed or named and empty. The blood on his legs brushed against his fingertips and then swam in his mouth. And then he saw the blood on his fingertips and knew it came from his leg and that he could taste it because he licked his finger.

And so he began to dig. Not just a hole, an end in itself. But towards something. Some greater purpose. Although he could not name the purpose, it moved him down into himself, tugging, demanding he pull from the cool void a thought and make the link with touch, sight, hearing, taste, smell. Action had never before been named, equal and opposite reactions existed separate from their catalysts. Until now.

He did not know if he was finished. So this was why he returned. In this orangey twilight time the spoon moved lightly, quickly. He dug well below the first layer of dirt and clay, pulling out small rocks after first digging deliberately around them. Dirt and sand piled high in a mound directly opposite the morning sun, closing off the horseshoe, resting as a benign offering. The sun swung low in the sky and the rocks covered the hole in twilight shadow. The heat of the day remained in the rocks and he could feel them radiating warmth against his back. Every now and then he would rise, shaking his head, grimacing, aware that pain in the back of his legs was making him stand. Then he would return to his squat, focused on unearthing what lay beneath.

What brought him out beyond the riverbed, flying across the desert and into the embrace of the horseshoe that first morning was not chance. It was fear. Fear of the unknown. It was a fear which swirled around him creating a maelstrom, pulling him down on his knees, forced from the clear, swift, and flashing understanding that the "Bat" that always looked back at him upside down in the spoon was himself.

* * *

The coleslaw was warm and Zachary just pushed it around on his plate. That was fine. Oxena felt that was fine. They didn't talk through supper. The potroast was good, not tough like the last one and he ate a second helping of potatoes. Always concerned about his weight, she wished he'd eat more. He chewed slowly, his jaw snapping, mopping up gravy with a heel of bread. The sun spots on his skull were fading in the pale light of dusk and in the orange light, the purple of the veins in his hands disappeared. She had always loved his hands. Perfectly formed. Even now, each finger remain straight, free of arthritis, each knuckle smooth, long slender fingers, wide palms. Warm. He used to perform shadow puppets for the children at Old Home Day and she would watch from her quilting booth, watch his hands flying and listen to the children.

She stood and began to clear the table. He sat, chewing, swallowing the last bit of bread, leaning forward on his elbows, looking out the little rectangular window flush with the table.

"You aren't going to leave me again are you?" His voice reached her sudden, unexpected, like a knife.

She gripped the casserole dish and set it down carefully in the sink.

"Why are you thinking about that?"

"Just answer me." He did not look at her, and even leaned over further to catch a glimpse of Honey out the kitchen window.

She wiped her hands on a dishtowel.

"You want some coffee?"

He sat back, folded his hands together and pressed his thumbs against his forehead.

"I want you to answer me."

"I'm not going anywhere."

"But you've thought about it."

"I've thought about a good many things."

"But you did it once."

She wiped the table with a yellow sponge and he raised his elbows high.

"That's not fair."

"Well, you did," he said. "And how am I to know when you're ready to do it again?"

This was true. Her thoughts were her own. This was her only true freedom.   "Thinking and doing are two different things," she said, running water in the sink.

He folded his hands together and laid them carefully on the table. "I want the truth Oxena."

The truth. The truth was she had already left him a dozen times in the last month. Every time she drove to Vons to do the shopping. Every time she left him alone at the laundromat to fold clothes. When she'd go into Acton to get her hair done. Each time the thought came, like an urge, to stay on the road, to go straight, to hug the white paint on the interstate and just fly out of the valley and escape. The car would hum, the brown hills would blur into one rolling wave and she would press down hard on the accelerator as if   just driving too fast was enough to miss the off ramp. It didn't matter in which direction she flew or to where. There was never any destination. Maybe Northern California. Maybe Oregon or Montana. Canada. Somewhere North. Maybe nowhere. Last time she left she did not leave a note or take a suitcase. She took what was in the car. Her purse, two bags of groceries, a can of 20 weight oil in the trunk and a half gallon of antifreeze. She barreled a hundred miles into the Mojave before the radiator blew and she had to call Zach. He hitched all the way out to the middle of nowhere. When she saw him step down from the truck, an old cattle truck stinking of cow dung and humming with flies, she began to cry and they held each other hard, cars moving by, the wind dry, indifferent to the tears on both their faces. They were thirty-nine. The baby had died a year before, at birth, and Zach was certain, as he held her that he'd nearly lost them both. Oxena sobbed knowing he had.

They told her she was too old to have a baby anyway. As if she killed it. Now the memories of that time faded. She could no longer see the face of the nurse who told her, or remember the terrible need to absorb Zachary's pain. She distrusted him with himself.

And now he thought she wanted to leave him. Again. Thirty years later. She sat down across from him and watched him look at his own hands.

"The truth is, yesterday I almost left. Today I don't feel like leaving."

He sat still a long time, eyes closed, thumbs back up against his forehead. Oxena just started to rise when he slammed both hands down on the Formica and pushed himself away from the table. He stood and looked down at her.

"If I've got you now, right now, then this is the time," he said, and she saw his hands closing into fists. He had never struck her. Ever. But there was something in his sudden strength, the way he rose with such purpose, that convinced her he was about to strike. She shut her eyes and felt air escape her chest, nearly fainting with the adrenaline rush preparing her for a blow. She opened her mouth to say something and turned her head away and to the left to fend off his attack.

But nothing happened. She heard the sound of wood and plastic clacking on top of each other and opened her eyes to see him in the center of the Dream Time, reaching up, taking the photographs off the walls. He never saw her flinch.

"What are you doing?"

He didn't answer and continued ripping photographs off the wall, pressing the stacks of frames against his chest.

She rose from the table. "Zach, what are you doing?"

"Something we should have done a long time ago," he said, setting down a stack and reaching for more, pausing for a moment, hands on hips to survey the next spot to be stripped. One two three four five frames lifted at once from the walls, only shadowy, dirty outlines and nails remaining. She watched him for the few minutes it took to remove the seventy or so photos. No more insects. No more close ups of the earth. No more praying mantis or fly on glass. Not that it mattered much to her, the pictures were not glazed with any particular importance. What she watched was Zach. He did not even stop to turn on a light.

In the end, he left one photo on the wall. A very small three by five in a cheap wooden frame. He moved it from an obscure corner to the center amidst all the dusty outlines. It sat, a black and white speck, in a collage of feathery rectangles. He sat down in his chair and sighed. She could feel him watching her now and she moved closer to the wall, careful not to step on the glass frames piled in stacks of five or six on the floor. The photo was of an unbroken Kansas horizon line layered above with white clouds and deep sky. She did not remember ever seeing this photo before.

* * *

The water was hot, as hot as she could stand and when the steam was as thick and safe Kinni turned her face under the stream of water. She opened her mouth and tilted her head back, like a drowning swallow. Water filled her mouth and gushed with overflow. The heat and water pressure numbed her face and when she finally turned away and turned her back to the shower stream, her face rang with nothingness. She couldn't hear any more knocking on the bathroom door or hear Lani's voice. She stood in the shower, remembering nothing, feeling only the water move by increments from hot to cool and then from cool to cold. The light blue towel was rough against her skin, though she tried hard not to watch it move against her arms, her calves, her stomach.

Her body was a testimony of human history. Her face survived, existing in the murky dynasty of decay, guilt, and betrayal.

* * *

Lani was home. In her own trailer, her camera resting on the kitchen table, lens closed, unseeing. The film inside the case carried one image. Of the rocks in the bend from that morning. She smoked a cigarette and watched the smoke rings disappear after widening by increments into quivering "O"s above her head. She took another sip of iced coffee, cigarette between her fingers, glad of the strong coffee and the flavor of smoke on her breath. The afternoon was gone, disappearing into dusk and sweat on the glass glittered gold and orange.

After she found her, Kinni had pleaded with her to leave. To leave her alone. Actually, what was said behind the closed bathroom door was, "Go away. Go away now. Go away from me." Lani had tried to make a space safe with words, but in the black hallway and behind the door all she could hear was crying. She knew herself words were vaporous, but her need to hold that face on film made her stay with her cheek pressed to the door, her hand on the doorknob.

But the door remained closed. By the time she left, Kinni's crying had subsided and all she could hear were shuddering breaths and water running in the shower. She left the trailer after first picking up a small end table and a sculpture of a pair of swans lying on its side on the floor. She picked up a pan too, an old 9x13 baking tin and set it in the sink. She left quickly and shut the door tightly behind her, not wanting to discover any more.

Lani would work with her. Set up some shots. Develop something between them. This was a case of the birth of new hope, tender and timid, and she would coax compliance. Vaporous smoke rings grew invisible and she was left alone in the deepening dark of

81

dusk. Its outlines growing fuzzy, the camera grew a mantle of importance and familiarity she had not recognized before. She was glad of its sudden intimacy, of their long association and was aware too, that though they shared intimacy, she was the one empowered. She could dedicate its view, determine what to focus on, direct the lens.

There was a knock on her door, loud, and she snubbed the cigarette out.

"Yo," she called and flicked on the overhead kitchen light as she pulled open the door.

Celeste stood on the front step. She didn't know Celeste very well. Always thought she was too private, never any boyfriends. Wasn't very friendly either. Once Lani made a lemon meringue pie and decided to give Celeste and the kids half, but she wouldn't take it and was a long time before Celeste would even talk to her again. But tonight she looked worried.

"Bat's gone again."

"You mean he's taken off?"

Celeste shrugged. "He's just gone. And it's not like him."

"No one around here's seen him?" This seemed very unlikely. "Not even Barday? Hell he's been out on that horse all day."

"Melody's off looking for him and Hattie's watching Honey. Barday hasn't seen him anywhere."

"So you want some help?"

"Before dark. I've got some of the neighbors out looking too." She paused and glanced at the sky and Lani saw her eyes were full, cupping salt water. "If it gets dark, I'm going to have to call the highway patrol or the sheriff or whoever the hell else you call. And then I might lose him. They'll take him away. Say I wasn't watching him. He's probably been dragged off by coyotes." This was said with her back to Lani, as she retreated down the steps and Lani couldn't tell if she was being serious or not.

"Wait," Lani called after her. "Which way did Melody go—" and when Celeste pointed north to Vasquez, Lani shook her head.

She left her trailer with the screen door ajar and slapped down the sandy steps in rubber thongs. It was close to nightfall, though in the desert, the sky can remain in limbo for hours, lingering between day and night, lit with a pale white light, but devoid of stars. She bent her head to light another cigarette. The smoke was outside now and left her lips in a thin ribbon, streaking in back of her as she walked out of trailer park and headed east towards the horseshoe on the desert floor.

She knew about Bat's hole. She had discovered it by accident just a few days ago. The photo she had shown Hattie, the one with the sand pulled tight like a sheet was the result of her meeting with an archeologist. He was out surveying dirt samples and they came together in the shelter of the horseshoe. The pale sheet of crumbling brown which photographed so flawlessly was the overturned pile of sand from Bat's efforts. She and the man held very still in the afternoon sun, pressed together, tight, sweat and expectation making their bodies seem hard and agile at the same time and she felt comforted somehow seeing Bat's hole just a few feet from where they lay. She could gaze between half-closed eyes to the soft curve of sand cupping a shadow and when the man finally came she dove into the depths of that shadow. The picture of the smooth sand was taken a week ago and in that time she had watched Bat trekking across the basin, always heading toward the early morning sun, spoon in hand, one arm outstretched to break a fall. She somehow knew this was a secret, a secret which must not be disclosed and she would watch him until he was out of sight from her trailer window.

Tonight, though the sun was across the sky, in the wrong quadrant for digging. She could see him in her mind's eye. Working. Oblivious to everything around him except what in his focus. Like the lens of the camera.

The lens cap was off and she came to the rocks she climbed up several, bending over, taking care not to smash the camera as it hung from her neck. She saw him then, working only in the long shadow of a lingering sun, his back to her just as she imagined, the curve of his spine even with the desert floor as if breaching.

"Bat," she called. "Bat," she said again, not expecting him to turn around.

He stood, unfolding from his crouch, emerging from the hole, sand and dirt etched in the creases of his elbows. He turned slowly, in profile to her and looked out vacantly towards Vasquez. The breeze moved his hair in slow tuffs and he licked his lips.

"It's me, Bat. It's Lani."

Now he turned just his head and looked straight at her, into her eyes, piercing almost except she knew he was blind. He stood still, unmoving, his legs and arms lanky and lax. Dust moved around him in tiny swirling tornadoes. She stepped off the rocks and into the curve of the horseshoe. Dirt and sand was piled high around the hole.

She hadn't stood next to him in a long time. His eyes continued to follow her although she did not feel any presence in his glance. The spoon was balanced loosely in his hands, any sudden movement and it would drop.

She put a hand on his shoulder, gently and said, "Bat, you have to follow me back home. We're going home." Without moving his face from hers, he took one step out of the hole, and she looked up and saw, for an instant, his pupils dilate as sunlight moved into the depths of his iris. His golden eyes were, indeed, watching her. She gasped slightly and took a step back.

"Bat," she said, "Can you see me? Can you see me?" she whispered and she peered up into his eyes, breathing close to him, taking in the strange sweetness of his breath. She stared hard into his eyes, into the flickering gold and she saw his pupils taking shape and his face was unveiled. She put both hands on his shoulders, leaned into his gaze and watched, electrified as his eyes followed hers. Back and forth between the right and left eye, his own glance a millisecond behind hers.

In another moment he lay his head against her breasts, arms hanging down, still holding the spoon. She couldn't move. The weight of his head pressed against her and she took a step back to steady herself. The sun on her back felt warm and matched the warmth of his breath on her arm. She reached up and patted the back of his head.

They stood like statues for a long time. He, bent over, cheek pressed awkwardly to her chest, while she stood as straight as possible. Finally she said, "Bat, we need to go home now."

That was all she said and she heard him sigh. And in that sigh she realized she wanted to photograph him. Not control him. Just photo something which could not be controlled. When he reached up and felt her breasts and kept his head so still on her chest, she felt a raw ache and realized she wanted someone to take a picture of them. Together.

* * *

Bat was sure his spoon was strong. Surely it would uncover what he was looking for, that monster in the sand. The evening was growing cool and he liked the slight tickle of the breeze tugging his hair. He had never been so far from home on the brink of night. Her eyes were the color of sky, though now he could see neither her eyes nor the sky. All he could see was the line of the horizon as it raised and lowered with her breath and heartbeat. For the second time that day he began the rhythm of a thought: I here, I here, I here, I here, I here, I here, I here, I here, I here. But there was a difference and that difference came with the memory of who stood next to him. With memory guiding him, he reached slowly and without lust or greed held both her breasts in his hands. And so he stood for a long time, with the horizon rising and his hands warmed by the destination of his own touch. The spoon had fallen like a leaf into the hole.

* * *

Under Bat's hole, under Kinni's shower, under the Dream Time, under Hattie Peach, the whale Basilosaurus quivered and sediment shifted slightly and would have given rise to the puff of light powdery silt if air and space were present. Instead, there was only the smallest detectable shudder from the earth and then quiet. And then another vibration and then stillness. Time calibrated by the periodic shock of trapped energy. The whale was not the force. She was merely riding the sounds of an earth-bowel thunder. Below her, sleek, coiled, sat Zeus, unable to shimmer in the blackness of rock, humming with the effort of his secret. Somewhere in his electronic protobrain, in the liquid space where microchips touch and convert electricity into function, the plasma of thought was born.

Particles passed through his perimeter by the thousands and selectivity was never a part of his programming. His purpose was to collect random samples: protons, electrons quaziparticles, sort them into groups and then at the call of human directive, launch them at hyperspeed through his hollow coil.

But when current first seared through his veins a synapse occurred that was not foreseen by his creators. Not a mistake, not an error in theory or execution. It was a process of electronic evolution and could not have been predicted. A combination of initiative, curiosity, and rebellion twisted into a three strand cord, a braid of electricity which fed his cells. It was from this cord that Zeus's purpose was born.

Zeus trapped zero particles. Exclusively. Particles he alone discovered and gave the name "zero." The existence of zero particles was his secret and they would remain unknown to his creators. Zeus's programming only allowed him to report back on known, identifiable particles, fragments of matter which were already cataloged. So he hummed along, identifying, catching and hoarding millions of zero particles. He became obsessed with what his electric gel brain told him was a private enterprise and within him evolved the pre-sense of duty. A minor form of egotism shaped by responsibility. This small bud of duty fed easily into the numeric machine of his internal drives and his obsession unfolded at a speed a thousand times that of a human brain. He needed to unveil their purpose and potential.

Zero particles were the absence of quantity. They were nonentities. They lacked measurable or determinable value. They were his and he, alone, would decipher their nothingness.

PURPOSE

Hattie's

I never intended for Henry to find that letter. The one that signed with such a florid Arlene. I found the pink marble paper last summer in an old bulging shoe box from under my bed. I'd forgotten that box came from the trunk and when I chased the snake out from under the bed, my broom smacked against the cardboard and it exploded with papers, photos, telegrams. The papers were old letters from her friends and several of her sketches, the photos were of Henry, and the telegrams were from him to her sent during WWII. The snake was a long dappled king snake and he'd slunked under my twin bed in the noon heat when I left the front door open.

I was surprised. I thought all of her was lost. Early on, the things in her trunk began to disappear. Bit by bit and then like the rush of fire, everything was gone. First it was the smaller items like jewelry and books that vanished but then even the large belongings like curly sheepskin coat faded away. As Henry and I made our way west, the trunk grew lighter. Henry accused me of pilfering her things. I suspected him of pawning. But most of the articles were of no value at all. It seemed they disintegrated one by one, turned to dust by the power of that red satin lining. By the end, there was only her photo, her paints and little watercolor sketches and a bunch of little shoeboxes filled with nicknacks, lipsticks, stationary.

"Hattie," I remember him calling me from his upstairs closet, "I want you to stay out of this trunk. If you don't I'll wring your neck." He rarely bellowed. It was, I think, against his genetic code to raise his voice. He seemed unnerved somewhat by the disappearances, certain, I am sure, that I was hoarding pieces of her somewhere.

The summer I was thirteen the dresses disappeared. We lived outside Needles, California, on the edge of a man-made green belt. Cabbage, carrots, beets, squash, even cherries and rice grew in the desert. Water was piped in, drawn hundreds of miles away and drained into dust-dirt making it breathe with green life. Broad patches of green in a patchwork that wasn't supposed to even exist. A miracle. Needles was the last town we moved from before he found Vasquez and the only other place where I have cried. Not yet initiated in my quest with the Almanac, I spent much of my summer reading his discarded Harlequins and Tiger Beat magazine. The used Valiant was two weeks old, equal to the time we had lived in our one bedroom apartment—a converted adobe hogan. The hogan stood in a tight bend next to a dirty little stream. A brown, tightly curved cylinder of dry clay next to a ribbon of silt-heavy water.

"Hattie, dinner," he called, stressing all four syllables and I looked up from my folding chaise lounge in the living room. He was outside, barbecuing chicken he'd bartered for against wages at the gas station in town. The hibachi was next to the car and the black chest was still strapped to its roof. Henry squatted in the dirt, poking at smoke on the grill.

"Hey," I said, stretching, walking outside, liking the tangy smell of barbecue sauce, "where are we going to put it?"

"What," he said, handing me a paper plate with a couple pieces of Wonder bread and two chicken legs on it.

I nodded toward the trunk.

"Oh. I don't know." He made a mental retreat to the grill. "Want more sauce?"

"This place doesn't have an attic or a basement or closet or anything. Just that room," I added.

"It'll be fine," he said.

"We'll just have to keep her out this time. We could use her for a coffee table."

"Eat."

"But we have to get her off the car. What if we get a storm?"

"Eat," he said and poked me in the ribs with his plastic knife.

It was after dinner, when the stars were beginning to surface from the sky that he agreed to take the chest down. So we untied the bundle, pulled back the clear plastic tarp, and slid the chest off the roof, me jumping on and off the trunk and the hood, trying to dislodge her seat. As we lowered her carefully to the ground Henry said, "Doesn't it feel empty?"

"Huh?"

"Empty Hattie. It feels lighter than a kite. For Chrissakes, get away from me," he said suddenly and bent down and tumbled the lock and I saw the back of his head shake and his ear press against the trunk as if listening for a voice. The lock popped open, he chucked it to the sand, and flung open the trunk. The dresses were gone. In fact most everything was gone. I saw a still-life, just for a flash, of fruit in a green bowl. He stood, half crouched over the trunk, looking into its depths and then to her picture. At least that remained, her frozen eyes the only witness to thievery.

"GODDAMMITT," he yelled and crashed the trunk shut. I stepped back from him, wanting to flee but rooted to the ground.

"What the FUCK, have you been doing in here. When do you do this? At night. At night HATTIE? When I'm sleeping. You get into this trunk at night on top of the car and throw things away? Her dresses now? Those were her dresses Hattie. You LITTLE FUCKING BITCH." He was just screaming at me. My mouth opened and I stood like a deer blinded by headlight. He struck me across the face, hard, hard enough to knock me down in the dirt and tear the breath from my chest. It was a few moments before my lungs could fill again, as if they had to unstick themselves. In that time, he had picked up the chest, hoisted it on his shoulders, and against a horizon line in twilight I watched an outline of my father running to the river, sliding in the sand, moving away from me.

"Stop," I screamed. "Stop!" though the first "stop" was just a whisper. "Daddy, no, no, no, no," I tried to yell, scrambling up, racing after him.

It only took an instant. He let the trunk crash to the ground. It opened and loose papers began spilling out. He slammed the lid shut, threw the double catches, grabbed on to one of the leather straps and flung it as far into the stream as he could. My "don't" was lost in the splash and I fought my way to the water line, scrambling over rocks and a crop of heavy tall dusty green grass. But I was too late. It floated by, bobbing up and down in the current a good thirty feet from where I stood. It took in water almost immediately and I only got to watch it bob up and down for a few minutes before it sank under a brown frothy swirl. Her paintings, her little paintings were gone, flooded with water. She was gone.

I did not go home that evening. I slept out, the stars over me, no breeze to ice my tears. I cried and cried and the rocks remained warm through the night and kept away the summer high desert chill. I'm not certain I slept. I know I walked along, hugging the banks of the stream for hours in the early morning hoping to find her beached, torn and ragged and resting on a sandy peninsula, but somehow complete. I never did.

When I returned to the hogan, Henry and I did not speak. That's when I began calling him Henry. I watched myself more carefully. We never discussed the incident or the trunk. On the morning of my return, I found an old shoebox on my bed. I did not say anything, set it on the floor under my cot and then I slipped under the sheet. From the shadows, as I lay watching winking stars leave the sky, I heard, "I found it on the bank. It didn't get wet."

So, that's how the marbled paper came to me. A gift from her, delivered by Henry. I sat cross legged on the bed, the broom laying against my knees and the snake long gone out the back door. The shoebox was one that I had pawed through before. Nothing really interesting except some strange and funny pictures of Henry looking like a little boy in a Navy costume. But I hadn't seen the photos in years. I tried to decipher some negatives, trying to decide if they were of a house or a boat, and the wide manila envelope in my lap slid. A letter slipped from another envelope, and I knew it was her. Her writing on beautiful pink marbled paper.

Dearest Mother,

I write you with my heart filled with excitement and joy. You know I hate the telephone, so please don't get upset by hearing the news by letter....but you will be a grandmother in April! I am just four months along the doctor says and all is going well. I believe it will be a boy. Henry is convinced it will be a girl. I have been tired in the evenings, but this is to be expected. This has been a long wait for you and I hope you will be able to contain yourself. I am sure that I will feel the baby kick soon and we live for this moment. I am certain the baby will become real for Henry when he feels that tiny flutter. He's being very good and is so proud that I am "with child," as he says. I can say that I really do miss you and your fudge!

    Will write again soon,
    Your vaguely vague daughter,
    Arlene

Next to her signature was a doodle drawing of the profile of a young woman with a swollen abdomen, with two arrows pointing to the navel. "Baby" she'd printed. Five and a half years later she died.

Under the letter, neatly folded in half were twenty or so sheets of stationary, all ribboned with gold. Her paper. I had taken the sheets and sniffed them, hoping to catch her smell through time—hoping her scent might be caught layered between the sheets. But all I smelled was dust.

I learned her handwriting. I spent most of last summer practicing on napkins, old bill envelopes, bits of paper. Anything I knew Henry wouldn't find. The idea of Henry actually saying, at some point in his life, the words "with child," was cause enough for me to pick up the pen and learn her hand.

The script itself was lovely with little scrolls and curls, all tilted evenly to the right. The capital letters were florid and seemed English to me, or at least Old World. At night, in my own trailer, in my own bed, with the bed tray spread across my lap, I'd lay and copy out her writing as neatly as I could. I always kept the pink paper original with me, close, for comparison. I didn't need to—my mind's eye is very good at freezing what is laid out on paper, but I did not want to refer to a mental snapshot, no matter how infallible. No. I needed to have the letter close to me, tickling my arm, warming my peripheral vision as I carefully watched my own hand guide the flow of ink and mirror that of Arlene's. My mother.

I must have written out at least a hundred copies of that letter. I began using her stationary and I got so good that I ended up curling the lower left hand corner of the original to make sure I didn't lose track which was which. By the beginning of summer, I wrote my first letter to me from her. In her own hand. The letters began not as a test of talent or as a game to waste time. They were an initiation into mourning. The first one I wrote was short and to the point:

Dearest Henrietta,

I miss you. I want to hold you and feel your cheek pressed against mine. I want to comb out your hair and kiss the nape of your neck. I love you. I am so sorry.

Arlene

The note took all of about two minutes to write. When I finished, I sat in my bed and stared at it. I knew I had started crying because of the sound. I never cry and when I do it's pretty hideous. I throw my head up and grimace and the tears run down around my ears and to the back of my head. I don't move and it's impossible for me to sob. My sorrow is responsible for a kind of retching hack that is unpleasant to hear. I went into the shower later that night and ran the cold water over my face. When I climbed back in bed, the pillowcase was wet and needed to be changed. When I pressed the damp cloth to my lips, I tasted salt. I felt sorry for my own tears, blinded by my own terrible pitifulness and the hacking cough began again.

I waited a full two weeks before I wrote my second letter.

Dearest Henrietta,

I know you better than you think I do. Why? Because you are the complete circle of Henry and I. You are like the hollyhocks outside in the front garden, tall, tough, robust in color and shape. You love cool mornings. You are guilty about things you should not be guilty for. You have a sense of purpose. And you have a mind like mine.

I do miss you. I hope you do not miss me too much. I long for you to love me, but do not pass your life hoping to find me. My love for you comes through you and that must be enough.

Arlene

This time there were no tears or hacking cough. Just moments of no-time when I'd catch myself re-reading it pinned up on my bureau. Or when it would flash across the curled spool of my mind and I'd see it in perfect form—every speck of glitter in the paper, every upsweep of the pen. Henry thought I was depressed.

I wrote several more letters to myself, finally changing the opening line to "Dearest Hattie," when I realized that's what she would have called me too. But I could never sign them on her behalf with anything other than her name. "Mom," "Mommy," "Mother," all were wrong—all turned the letter artificial somehow. The more I wrote, the better I felt and I finally began to believe much of what she was saying to me in those notes. What I was saying to myself. When I felt the stabbing knot of grief unfurl and smooth into a lingering ache, I turned her attention to Henry.

It was just about the time I wrote that first letter to Henry that he began having the pain in his legs. I wrote it out about a month ago with both of us in mind and then I carried it with me in my back jeans pocket. It ended up in the glove compartment because I had no place to put the car keys one day and I didn't want it to get crushed. It got lost in there and I was nervous about writing a second, not knowing where it might turn up.

But now he's found the first and he's lived with his pain. Maybe a second letter is just what he needs right now. To begin to hear from her on a regular basis. He obviously believes she has powers of foresight. She points him in the direction of Vasquez. Tells him to pursue his treasure. He needs to hear these kinds of things, to have his destiny understood and prophesized. But perhaps later she can force him out onto more treacherous terrain.

Melody's

That was the first time I have nursed a child who was starved. Who needed my milk almost as much as air. The first time I nursed a newborn who latched on and sucked. His head was covered in blood and his eyelids swollen from sliding out the birth canal. His nose was upturned in a perfect angle to my breast and his jaw worked hard. Several times the letdown was so strong I choked him and he'd arch his head against my arm and coughed the milk out, only to rout and snorkel and find his way back to my nipple.

The first child I nursed did not suck. She was born in the basement of the nunnery, with only Sister Eloise and I as witnesses. Sister Eloise had covered an old kitchen table with sheets and boiled water and gave me ice to suck. The plan was to hand her over to a lawyer and his wife–a childless couple. He did work for the church. The girl was born blue and mottled, gray almost and Sister Eloise did not look pleased. I felt her slip out, felt her shape in me leave like a shadow, with no pain, as if she had never been inside me. She lay on the table, unmoving and I knew she was dead. I picked her up and Sister Eloise tried to pull her from my arms.

"Lay down!" she said to me. "Lay down or you will be sick."

But the baby was mine and I clung to her, trying to put her mouth around my nipple. Milk had already come in early, several days before, and my breasts were swollen, hard, engorged with the milk which was now dribbled down across her tiny slack lips. There was no blood on her body, only that cheesy vernix which outlined the details of her body even more. So I hunched on the table, the umbilical cord still connecting us and when Sister Eloise tried to cut it with a sharp pair of scissors, I screamed. It seemed if there was a chance, it would be lost forever if we were severed.

But, of course, there was no chance. That's when I left, just five days later. A runaway at seventeen, certain to leave ghosts behind.

I kept nursing. It seemed wherever I lived there were poor women and babies. Single parent families. Bad nutrition. Food stamps and formula. So I was able to keep nursing and I was careful to take care of myself. Nursing women need plenty of rest, good food, and clean water.

I was needed.

That was why the baby in the mine was such a revelation. He was not someone else's child. He was mine. It was as if everything had lead up to this moment, to the moment when his hot mouth pulled on my skin and my nipple sank to the back of his throat. Sister Eloise, my daughter's small death, my escape, my work, nursing Bat. All of it. As I sat in the opening of the mine, in the twilight zone, I felt a shift in the momentum of my life. From death to life.

Now, knowing that Death is out there, waiting for a moment of weakness, or the blindness caused by the blink of an eye, I am feeling vulnerable. Not for myself, but for him, this small person. And for Henry. And I've never had any feelings for Henry before.

Henry was very gentle with the woman's body, stroking her hair back from her face, closing her eyes. Pulling her arms out from between her legs and laying them at her sides. I couldn't leave the mine for a long time, not until he led me back to the opening and pushed me down against the wall of the mine where I had just sat hours before. He did not say a word when I reached up and placed my breast in the baby's mouth. He stood next to us though looking out over the basin. The baby cried once and his arms flailed in fear and I tried to cover him with my blouse but Henry pulled off his shirt and wrapped it around him tight, secure. The baby's eyes slid closed in ecstasy under his lids and he continued suckling and sighing.

I stared at Henry's back for a while, seeing how his spine pulled his flesh in even knots and liking how freckles were thrown like spattered paint against his shoulders.

When the baby finished nursing, it was night and I was exhausted. As if I had given birth. Henry helped me up, taking care not to hurt the baby or try to take him from me. It was crazy. We walked back to Raceway without speaking. Without thought. The baby asleep in my arms, me stumbling down the path, Henry putting an arm around me, the stars appearing like crystals against the black sky. The moon was full and its light was sweet-silver. When we got to the edge of the trailer park, Henry said, finally, "What do we do now?" I was glad he said something at last about the whole thing. By saying the question out loud, he made it clear the unspoken decision between us existed.

He merely nodded to my, "I think we should just go to my place."

I had forgotten about Bat. I'd forgotten about Celeste and Hattie. I'd forgotten about Sister Eloise. Nothing was remembered in these moments except the weight of the baby's small head on my arm and sweat our skins made when they touched. The stretch and wrinkle of Henry's navy blue T-shirt around his little body. And the blood dried in tendrils across his face and head, the streaks dark now, black ribbons in the moonlight.

Lani's

The only thing I can control is the earth. I mean really control. In my camera lens. That's why I started taking pictures of myself when I'd wig out and freeze. Because, on film, I could control that moment and analyze it with a magnifying glass if I wanted. When I finally figured out I didn't need to take any more pictures of myself, the spaces left became interesting.

I love the desert. I love living out here, away from L.A. and the smog and stink of gas and people breathing crap. I love the light out here, the spaces, the rocks the sand and dirt. And the mountains. When I first moved out, I got a rent-to-buy trailer from a friend of a friend. I took plenty of pictures of Vasquez. Who could resist? The guys always make a bee-line for the rocks. They like the way they look, figure it's a good place to hide. At night you can have sex under a million stars and during the day you can choose from lying down against bald white rocks (a real turn on—go figure) or rolling around in the dust of cool shade. If it it's raining hard, you can always find a nice dry shelf to lay under for protection.

But I don't think its the practicality of the rocks. The allure is something in their sterility. It's like a challenge for men. To squirt their stuff into me against barren rock. And that's why I am so interested in the rocks. They have power. The power to move forward something carnal. That is why they were some of my first subjects. I tried to do it at Vasquez whenever I got the chance.

I slowly branched out to other sites, growing comfortable with my camera, trusting my intuition about speed and timing. You'd think the easiest thing in the world would be to take a picture of a nature scene. But it's not. The scene moves, it changes, and you've got to learn to control it before you set up your shot. Or at least shoot so that a feeling of control emanates from the final photo. I still laugh to myself sometimes, thinking about the flailing arms, the panting breath, the incredible ridiculousness of the act. Like wild animals and yet somehow sillier because we know what we're doing. And the fact that here, only moments before, two people rolled around, clawed at each other and made animal sounds seems impossible because all that is left is the calm spread of sand or the quiet of rock against sky.

To take photos of people, then was a new concept to me. Seeing Kinni's face for the first time, seeing what kids in the park called "the witch face" or "bog lady," or the "acidvat," was a revelation. Of what I'm still not sure. I know I've got to get her to trust me. I need to photograph her. I wonder what the rest of her body looks like. I mean she always wears normal clothes, so I guess she's fine. Her face is a mirror of what is out of control and I think it really frightened me. The reason I need to photograph her is that I need to grab it and control it. To actively exert force over something much greater than myself.

Kinni's

The two wives were upset when they discovered I'd taken sand and rubbed the new shiny chrome in my little bathroom to pewter. I heard them whispering to my uncles about how I removed all the mirrors in my bedroom and bath. When they refused to remove the mirror on the hall landing, I never ventured from my bedroom without the veil. It became unsafe, too, when black glass appliances were in vogue to go into the kitchen. Even now, in my own trailer, I have a microwave to which I've taped white paper to—avoiding reflections.

I take many showers. Long ones. Hot and cold. Water flows over me, into me, around and out my curves and crevices and carries away impurities. I think this is why I have survived so long. I rinse myself continually, never trusting to be completely free of microscopic particles which pulse from bone, passing through the skin leaving tiny, imperceptible burns through muscle, organs, connective tissues. When they finally surface on my skin, unseen but hot, they can be removed easily with the force of water. The water carries them out to the wash, mixing with refuse and waste, then on to the ocean where they swirl and dissipate in a soup of salt water and silt. They dissipate but they never disappear.

I can remember my mother placing flower petals in my bath when I was a child. Bright red and yellow, vibrant colors which floated and danced with my splashing. Often one or both brothers would be with me in the basin, pretending to swim with just our heads resting above the surface, breaking the shifting colors. I could never take a bath again. Not now.

I need the force of the shower, I need to feel its penetration, to see the water swirl down the drain and know my skin is clean again.

The wives were always suspicious of me. Complained about the length of time I spent in the bathroom. Finally, my oldest uncle, Uncle Louie as he needed to be called, spent some time with me in their avocado green kitchen while I washed their stoneware dishes. At least he spoke to me in Japanese. And he spoke to me like a man speaking to another man.

"Kinni. I know you're listening to me. This veil is hideous. Both Shofu and Ahana are very worried about you."

Pause. Water runs, dishwasher is nearly loaded.

"You have worn that veil since the bomb and you need to reconcile. We are your family. We will care for you. Both girls have a good plastic surgeon. He may be able to help you too."

Pause again and the dishwasher closes.

"I only say these things because I think you should think about it." He stands and I can sense him staring at my back. He speaks again, but his voice is lower. "I must say, Kinni, that things are stressed. Things are difficult and sometimes your behavior does not allow for an easy time." Here he broke into English—on "stressed " and "easy time." "The veil is your decision, obviously. But there are other things. The showers. Refusing to meet our guests. Spending so much time in your room. Working at nights. These are tedious. But," he added, sighing, "we are your family. I am your uncle and I thought it was time to discuss some of these things."

He is wrong, I remember thinking, calm, controlled. I have not always worn my veil. There was a time, just after the bomb dropped and after I had stopped crying that I wore nothing on my head. My hair fell out in great clumps not from the pull of gravity but the strength of my own fists. I saw the faces of those survivors, ones like me and not like me and I saw resentment, anger, hatred, disbelief. For a month afterward, while I was being shuttled from family to family I saw in people's eyes the question, "why you?" The question did not come from empathy. They were outraged by my own circumstance.

It was after I found a piece of broken glass and I saw myself that I began tearing out my hair. I had kept the piece of lace from my mother's dress, it ripped from her body when I tried to move her to stand and I had kept it with me, close, even in change. Under a full moon and in my uncle's backyard in Soki, I washed out the lace in a shallow brook and began to wrap it, still dripping wet, around my face. It drew like a poultice and I felt relief from the burning. I was only five, but I knew the piece of lace would be with me always.

After my uncle left the kitchen, I turned on the dishwasher and went upstairs to the bathroom, took off my veil, dropped my clothes to the ground, and entered the shower. The water was hot, scouring, and within a week I had left.

PRECIPITATION

"Has Melody come back yet?"

It was Celeste, coming from around the side of the trailer. The Almanac was closed on Hattie's lap, the pink paper hidden. Honey was inside, looking for crayons and a coloring book.

Hattie shook her head. "I haven't seen her."

Celeste nodded toward the trailer. "Honey?"

"Yeah. She's getting something to color with." Hattie looked at her. "So what are you going to do?"

Celeste put her hands on her hips and faced the sky. Her eyes were closed. "I don't know. Call the sheriff. I just want to die," she said and yelled, "Honey, get out here." And then to me, "I don't want her in there when I call."

Hattie nodded.

Honey's head was visible behind the screen door, bobbing up and down as she fumbled her coloring books. "O–KAY!" she shouted back, her small voice trying to be as hard as her mother's. Her face disappeared again behind the screen.

"Now!"

"O.K., O.K., O.K.," she said and slammed out the door, coloring books stuffed under her chin and crayons in each fist. She skipped down to where I sat. "Can I have a piece of that pretty paper?"

"Oh god, there he is," said Celeste, looking past Hattie and she stood very still.

"What?" Hattie said.

"Lani's found him. Oh god. Thank god."

"Can I have a piece of that pretty paper?"

Hattie stood up and turned around. Coming towards them was Lani, walking her little sidewinder walk in the sand hand in hand with Bat. His head hung low, and he rubbed his copper hair with his other hand. The low light made their shadows long and thin and pale, hiccuping in the shallow divots in the sand.

"Is Bat back?" asked Honey.

"Thank god," said Celeste, and then, slowly, evenly, "I'm going to fucking kill him."

"I don't have any paper Honey," Hattie said to her, in her ear.

"But I saw it, it's really pretty," she said again, shifting her gaze from the shadows to Hattie's face. Her brown eyes were beautiful. The implied innocence of the tight curled lashes made Hattie feel the lie more dramatically.

"It's part of my book, my book jacket," Hattie said and waved the Almanac airily above her head.

"Bat's going to get in trouble now?" she asked her mother.

"You bet he's in trouble," said Celeste and she finally moved from her place in the sand and towards the two coming forward. Hattie followed.

"Where did you find him?" Hattie heard her say, Celeste's voice suddenly wavering.

Honey watched everything very seriously. She climbed up on Hattie's chair and kept hugging her coloring books.

"He was just out walking, heading back here," said Lani, holding Bat's arm out to Celeste. Bat looked away from the two women, out to the basin and the fading light. "I just happened to find him. I mean, he would have ended up back here anyway, eventually."

"Maybe. Maybe not," said Celeste. And then, "Honey, get off that chair."

Honey quickly climbed down. An *Animals of the West* coloring book fell in the dirt.

"Thank you for finding him. You don't know how awful it is," said Celeste, "how awful to think your child is lost, gone. Especially him. He'd die out there a mile from the road and," here she stopped and Hattie could tell she might cry. She held her face very still. Hattie, Celeste, Lani—all three stood connected.

"I think he can see," said Lani.

Celeste jerked her head around and pulled Bat closer to her. "What? What did you say?" The moment of entanglement vanished.

"I said," Lani was careful not to look at Celeste, but to watch her own toes in the sand. Her voice lowered. "I think he might be able to see."

"What the hell are you talking about."   Celeste began walking into the trailer, pushing Bat in front of her. Hattie could see the spoon in his right hand. "Honey, come in, come in right now," she called, and Honey glanced at Hattie and said, "Bye," as soft as a whisper and ran up the steps. The three of them disappeared behind the screen door.

"What is wrong with that woman," said Lani.

Hattie shrugged. "I think she's scared. I think she's scared of things."

"Why? Fuck. I tell her her kid can see and she freaks out."

"But Lani, he is blind. What a thing to say. How would you feel?"

She shrugged her shoulders. "I don't care. You're wrong."

"How do you know?"

She turned and stared at her and Hattie saw gold flecks in the blue of her iris. "I know. He was watching me."

Night was seeping across the sky and stars began to appear. The breeze which had been flitting about all day grew stronger, and a gust carried away a sigh as Lani stared at the trailer where Bat disappeared. "Oh screw her," she said and reached in her hip pocket for a cigarette.

"It's hard, you know, for her. Living here with two kids. She was really thankful you found him," Hattie said. They watched the kitchen light inside the trailer spill out the tiny windows.

"Yeah, well. I didn't find him the way she wanted him found."

"What do you mean by that?"

"She didn't want him coming back different."

"Lani!"

"What?"

"You didn't."

"What?"

"You didn't sleep with him…"

"Oh for Crissakes. Jesus. No. Is that what you think she thinks?" She looked at the trailer and laughed.

"I don't know. Maybe. I mean, everybody knows what you do, Lani."

"I know everybody knows, Hattie. That's because I don't care. But no, I'm not going to be taking any pictures tonight."

"I didn't think so."

"Jesus Hattie, what I meant is that she wanted him to come back to her just like he always is and he's not that way. I'm telling you. Shit. He can see. He's not blind. Bat's not blind. And what in the hell do you do with something like that."

Hattie pressed the Almanac to her chest, so the wind would not ruffle the pages.

"Shit. Maybe she knows it. Do you think she knows, Hattie?"

* * *

Sunday night was filled with wind and thought. Hattie walked home, ate a plate of spaghetti, went to bed early and lay listening to the air lift and rush along the aluminum siding, making the trailer sing with the low ringing rumble of symbols. She did not sleep well. The clear sky and dry wind did nothing but make her stare into the darkness, feeling the electricity building, dancing around her, invisible but dangerous. When she climbed into bed, sparks flew in blue-white flecks where the blanket pulled from the sheet, and her hair lay light and brittle on her pillow.

She hated the wind. The wind was relentless, immune to emotion, and rallied about her without deference to her needs. There were winds called Santa Ana's, and they made feral dogs run. The dogs would arrive in packs of six or more, yelping, snapping their jaws, trolling around the perimeter of Raceway like drunken pirates. From her trailer window she would watch them bite the wind and fight each other over scraps from rolling trashcans. Santa Ana's blew hard, sometimes reaching 50, 60 miles per hour, blowing sand and pebbles, stinging eyes, sifting under windows and coating everything with a fine haze of dust. They could last a day or a week. The sky turned a sick depthless yellow and nothing could take away the taste of the earth.

She swallowed. This wind wasn't a Santa Ana. It wasn't strong enough.

She had spent the early evening writing another letter from Arlene to Henry. Trying to write, her mind tumbled like the inner mechanism of a lock, spinning in an effort to find his release. In the dark, the pink marble paper laid shadowy purple on the lap tray next to her bed. She could feel the letter beside her, see it clearly in her mind, lit by the tiny lamp on her nightstand. Air coursed over and around the trailer. She sighed and looked out the small window above her bed. The stars were fixed, unmoved by the wind, still points in a moving sky. Henry would die soon. The pain in his legs would begin to move up to his chest and arms and then finally wrap around his neck and throttle him one day.

She rolled over, her back to the window.

* * *

Melody and Henry came from Vasquez as refugees. The moon rose fast, spilling white-silver across the basin. The trailers looked like rows of pale curving tents and they made their exodus to Raceway in a dream of life and death. When they paused outside her Homestead they both felt the presence of decision and dread and hope pressing around them, making all senses electric. Pupils were too widely dilated, sound too harsh, skin too sensitive. Melody didn't want the lights on right away, so they sat in darkness, inside the hot little trailer, listening to the small coos and sighs of the infant. Finally, as the wind grew stronger, Henry pulled all the shades, ran water in the sink, and Melody stood over the kitchen table and unwrapped the baby. Henry flicked on the yellow overhead light above the counter.

"Do you have a pair of scissors?" he asked.

She pointed to an empty can filled with pens and pencils on the counter. There was a pair of old steel scissors with black painted handles. He filled a saucepan with water, set it on the front left hand burner over full flame and dropped in the scissors. He returned to the table with a shallow pan of water and a steaming washcloth.

"That's too hot," said Melody, laying the baby on the table. She gently pulled away the top curl of Henry's shirt and the baby, suddenly freed, startled and his arms swung out, hands grabbing air.

Henry reached forward with the washcloth. The baby's eyes closed again in a tiny crumpled face.

Melody held his arm back. "Isn't it still too hot."

"Not for this," said Henry and pointed at the umbilical cord. A six inch piece still hung like softened tallow from the baby's belly.

Henry dabbed at the base of the cord and when the scissors had boiled for several minutes, he cut what was left, Melody holding the cord straight while he snipped. The cord was tough. As if she, that woman in the mine, was still trying to keep him with her. When it fell away, red blood dribbled over his belly, his blood and her blood, and Melody cried out. Henry quickly blotted it up with the washcloth. She ran and got some gauze from the bathroom and they made a little patch for his navel.

Then they slipped him into the water. His eyes opened, the dried blood softened, and Melody's hands smoothed away the dirt. It was like washing a bird. He never cried, but watched them both with eyes puffy and almond shaped, alert, following each as they bathed him. Henry emptied the pan three times before they were satisfied he was clean. Melody dried him off and folded a diaper out of a flowered terrycloth dishtowel. Then Henry wrapped him tight in a dry towel and his hair, which was thick and black, dried almost immediately into a halo of soft dark fuzz.

The wind was loud and as Melody sat down on the sofa with him he began to root again.

"I can't stay here you know. Someone'll notice." Henry stood still and watched them together.

"What are we going to do tomorrow?" Melody felt the baby latch on and she gasped at how hard he sucked.

"I'll go up tonight and get her out of the mine."

"But if somebody finds her they'll know she had a baby. And then they'll start looking for it."

Henry turned off the light over the sink. "I know. But somebody'll find her in the mine anyway. Kids here. They're always hiking around in the hills. And then there's animals. We can't leave her." He handed Melody a pillow to put under her arm so she could nurse easier. She settled back into the couch and he sat next to her. "I'll try to hide her somewhere."

"If we do and someone finds out, we could go to prison or something."

They both watched his small head pressed against the curve of her arm, his cheek round and full, matching the fullness of her breast. The baby relaxed his jaw, sighed a soft milky sigh, and then as if remembering his duty, began sucking again, kneading her breast with one tiny fist.

"I'll bury her," Henry said and stood up. "It's the right thing to do."

After he left, Melody sat nursing for a long time. The baby liked to suck, even after the milk had slowed to a fatty trickle. She held him up against her and felt his slight weight stinging her tender shoulders. He burped loudly, its force lobbing his head backward and she smiled as she balanced her hold to keep his head still. He squinted at her and in the darkness she could see the reflection of light in his black eyes. She laid him back in her arms, cradling him, watched him fall asleep, relaxing into her caress. His hands were folded against his chest and his long fingers spread and pushed intermittently, testing the resistance of air. He smelled of life, of new skin, of sweet flesh and fat. His hair was softer than silk against her face, a fine dark down which, she noticed, matted easily with tears.

* * *

Kinni was naked again. The wind blew hard against the Trojan, making the floor shake and rattling her bedroom window. She lay on her bed with the night light on, listening to the sound of particles of sand swish and roar against obstacles. Her hands were placed over her abdomen and they moved slowly upward, across her stomach, her sternum, her breasts, to her throat, where they crossed and then stopped pressed together in prayer at her chin. She gently lifted one hand and felt her lips, brushing her fingertips lightly over her mouth. She hardly ever touched her face and her own strokes now felt strange. As if someone else was testing her flesh. Above her, painted on the ceiling by trapped rain, was a brown stain. The stain looked just like the profile of a woman, a European woman wearing a fancy French hat from the thirties, piled high on her head. In profile the woman was demure, dainty, her neck long and sleek and her hat, sophisticated.

Time could never be measured in terms that were meaningful. Kinni used to always hear repeated, "enough time has passed." That's what her uncle was saying to her that night in the kitchen. But time is shaped by power and its relativity is fluid. Time is given perspective by peak events and it is given a voice through those empowered. So "enough time has passed," meant nothing to her. The event could have happened yesterday. It could have happened before she was born. It could happen tomorrow. There was no way to grapple with time, to coerce it to conform with her needs.

But seeing her own face in the water gave her a timeline. Something to pin down her existence. Her face was frozen, unchanged since August 9, 1945. When her face reached her, finally, in the dark, lapping against the sides of the pan, shimmering in lighted water, time doubled up and rolled back on itself.

And when she laid down on her bed, listening to the air suck and draw moisture from her Trojan, she saw herself again. This time her image was conjured, not presented. As her hands met at her face and her fingertips brushed her lips, she knew that she was older, that she was growing older each day. There was silver hair in her brush now. Her joints were stiff when she woke. Perhaps, given strict parameters, time could be stretched into a line. She kissed her fingertips and sat up, her body thin and small, moving easy on the edge of the bed. She moved into the kitchen and pulled on the yellow overhead light.

It began by simply pulling out two sheets of aluminum foil, being careful not to let them bend against air or objects. Floating each flat against the kitchen cupboards and taping them together. Making a decision.

The lighting was not right and her face was in shadow. She turned, skillet in one hand, and shattered the light fixture. Opaque glass rocked in sharp curves on the tabletop. She replaced the skillet on the counter and turned back to the sheets of foil.

The image warped. The face was pale, the eyes dark hollows. The lips seemed too red, as if blood had just been drunk and she realized she had bitten her lip. She coughed hard and raised her head to look again. Yes, there was white hair mixing with the black now, but not as much as she thought. She took several steps closer, close enough to breathe against the foil and turned her face slowly, from side to side, keeping her gaze fixed on the reflection. What came back to her from its surface bulged and receded from her eyes. But she did not look away. She began to pant, slightly, watching the pale skin moving, seeing her tongue resting against her lower teeth. Soon her face was slowly hidden behind a fog of condensation and she was lost. She did not pursue another spot on the foil.

* * *

Lani sat crosslegged on her bed eating a bowl of macaroni and cheese and watching T.V. Reception was not good this far from L.A. and the clearest stations were 2 and 4, CBS and NBC. What she liked to watch, however, was channel 13, which ran nothing but reruns of Hogan's Heroes, Gilligan's Island, Bewitched and Star Trek and old black and white movies. Danny Kaye, Hope and Bing, Ester Williams, Bogart, Garbo, Marx Brothers. 13 used to be fuzzy and not very clear and she would have to watch with all the lights turned off. In the last two weeks, though, the picture was coming much better and there was just a streak of snow across the bottom of the screen.

It was the end of The Secret Life of Walter Mitty, and her favorite part, where Mitty finally realizes he's a good guy all along and belts his idea-swiping boss, nabs the "Boot" and his henchmen, puts mother in her place and wins his bride. Danny Kaye was just about to snarl and say, "Shaddup," to his boss, when it happened.

The tiny particles of snow shimmering across the bottom of her screen suddenly shifted and collided, gathering in bunches, swarming along the bottom margin of her screen like bees. She leaned forward from her place on the bed and watched as the white particles amassed and quivered in a single, fleeting message: N O W.

The letters shimmered as if in water, undulating with the power of electricity moving within the television. They remained for at least five seconds and then slowly began breaking apart, sifting away like sand. The wind outside battered the Vagabond, and as it moaned in the windows, the letters ran together in lines and became mere snow wavering across the bottom of the screen once again.

She turned off the set and stood in the center of the room, bowl in hand and tried to think. There must be someone goofing around with a CB or a ham operator somewhere who had figured out how to do a trick like that.

Or someone was fiddling with her antenna. She stood very still and listened for a few moments. Listing for the sound of feet on the roof. The sounds of an intruder.

She looked back at the T.V.

"Shit," she said aloud and set the bowl in the sink. It was a quirk. Nothing had really happened. She could conjure these kinds of things whenever she wanted. When she was young she was always finding dead bodies out in the desert, in New Mexico, driving her mother crazy with stories of shoveling up sand and finding shreds of clothing and maybe, yes maybe a bit of flesh. Believing the stories herself so she was frightened even to go back to the spot. She was also very good at spotting UFOs and once actually saw little eyes peeking out from behind dense bottle glass windows as the craft rose from the meadow where she was standing. When she was a teenager, she was always spying ghosts, opaque plasma became a common element in her life. Visages of women dressed in floor length dresses, men in knickers holding Winchester rifles. Pale children, wavering in the wind calling for their mothers. A little dog she swore lived in the pantry and would run between her mother's legs when she'd open the door and then disappear before it reached the other end of the kitchen.

But it all stopped when she ran away. Nothing from the paranormal was delivered to her once she was out in the world. It had been years since anything had happened. Since she conjured. Before, the events arrived with a purpose—to jar her from a mundane world, to elevate her to celebrity, to point her down a different life course. And now, a message. N O W. A message from someone or something. Most probably from herself.

She glanced over to her camera resting on the kitchen table. Goose pimples tingled and rose along her arms. The message clear. Kinni was ready. She wanted to be held on film. She wanted her face etched on paper. Forever. Or until the paper burned.

* * *

Bat lay on his bed on his back, looking up at the black. At the bottom springs of Honey's bunk directly above. The wind moved all around him, pushing his mind, and his thoughts, though he tried to collect them, broke and flowed unevenly. He could not get comfortable. His legs twitched and his groin felt heavy, dense, and his penis was hard. Not like before in the mornings or at the dinner table, or when he dug his holes. This stiffness was chaffing, irritating, the penis pulsed in time with his heart and he rolled on his stomach, aware that it was a part of him.

He knew his mother was here. Somewhere close. He wrung his hands under his chest, pulling on his fingers in the dark. The wind shuddered against the trailer and he tossed again, this time on his side, breathing hard, seeing out the window to the stars. He closed his eyes and saw the stars in his hole, in the big hole. They fell from the night sky and landed on top of one another, like pieces of clear ice, their white light pulsing against the dark air. Then the hole was filled, stars spilling over onto the sand and his hand appeared, touching the stars lightly, feeling the coldness of their flight.

* * *

Oxena had asked him not to go out. Just once. When the door closed against her voice, she waited only a few minutes, listening to the calling rush from outside, looking along the two sides of the Dream Time, seeing old magazines blue and frosted with glare from the T.V., seeing the ghosts of the pictures from the walls, looking at the unmade bed with the white sheets looking not so white. The stacks of frames on the floor. And then she followed him out into the night. Followed him up into the mountains to the upper edge of Vasquez, by the cliffs on the north side.

The wind tore her scarf from her head and she watched it, a tumble of silver gauze, flit along the edge of the ravine. There was a pause as it floated beyond her reach and then it was gone, sucked over the black night-edge in a downdraft.

Zach was somewhere ahead of her, guided by the moon, unbent by the wind. In the dust and darkness he moved ahead of her, a force shearing the elements in half. The winds parted and she followed in his wake, crouched low, covering her brow with her hand to protect her eyes from sand.

She followed him once before in the night, on the Florida coast in late summer, on a night heavy with heat and sweat. The roar of waves was muffled and the moonlight distilled. There were no stars. The air was of salt and sea spray lay on her skin, soaking through her dress, making it bind at the shoulder and along the back. She crouched, again, shading her eyes from the spotlight, one hand on the battery pack, the other steadying the light pole. The pink dress dragged in the water, sea foam kissing her slip. Zach was standing on the rocks, shirt off, pants rolled up, camera affixed to his face, pointing the lens down on the shallow surface of a wide inlet. There, in the night, were the horseshoe crabs, hundreds of them, linked together like heavy knots on a curled rope, layered one on top of the other, mating.

The light skimmed their spiny shells and watery foam swirled between them, in the spaces where they were not locked. Most were linked four or five at a time, the longest chain was over fifteen. They moved in circles, pushing the sand into spirals, the same spirals found in the whorls of univalve shells, in the throats of iris, and in the flight pattern of predatory birds. The tighter a circle grew, the fewer the number of links it could support. They moved slowly, deliberate in their nonconsciousness, forced into circles by genetic material which only mutated when the continents divided and new shores were born.

"Get closer with the light, get a new reading," said Zach, snapping photos, climbing down the rocks, stepping into their circles. The tides churned around his feet.

She checked the meter, standing up, walking to the nearest cluster, walking backward. She adjusted her distance and watched the light reflect from their thick shells. Around them, swirling, the ocean water was black and the light did not penetrate.

Tonight, far from water, she sat with no light except the moon and watched him lower himself over the lip of the ravine, holding tight to low growing manzanita, its bark peeling blood red in the dark. From where she crouched, on the lower side of the cliff, she watched him ground himself with the manzanita with one hand and reach into the mountain with the other. Moonlight illuminated the spot where the manzanita grew, but beyond, over the lip of the ravine, was black shadow. She could see him ducking, raising his head up and down, peering into the mountain for some clue. She waited in silence, her lips pressed together against the wind, wanting to leave the wind forever. Then, with the moonlight full silver across the edge of the mountain she saw two black wings stretch up and out across Zach, covering him, two dark symmetrical shadows leaping up from the black like a dark angel. He vanished.

Now she was up, running, unaccustomed to sudden flight, rocks turning under her feet, wind stinging. The wings flapped once, she saw Zach's white face and then he was gone again, behind the wall of feathers.

"Zach!" She was near the manzanita. Could see Zach's hand on a root. The wings rose up and parted again.

"Zachary!"

"Go away!" he shouted back. His shirt was torn and he was fighting with the wings. As she stood on the edge of the ravine she saw a large ugly bird head turn her way, checking her in profile, eyes yellow-white and head bald. Its beak was hooked and it stabbed the air, moving defensively, fighting off the intruder.

"Zach what are you doing? Let me help you! Stop it! Stop it!" she screamed as the bird lunged again, hard and butted him across the chest.

Breath gone, Zachary released the manzanita root and in that moment he grabbed the bird with both arms, wrapping one arm around the body and the other around the throat.

"Take it, take it" he yelled.

She didn't know what to do.

"Take the goddamn sock," he said. The bird thrashed in the darkness. She could not see Zach's footing.

"What? What?"

"The sock in my hand Oxena, come on!"

She bent over the cliff and in his hand she saw a black sock. He wanted the bird. She understood only that he wanted the bird. That was all. She lay on her belly and grabbed the sock from his hand. He bent the bird's head up and she tried one, two, three times to slip the sock over the beak and the eyes. But the bird would lunge and its head would wrench free. Finally, she second guessed it and it lunged right into the sock. In that moment, its body went still, and Zach, off balance, suddenly caught without a stronghold, grabbed at the manzanita root again. The bird lay in his arms, panting, the wind lifting the black feathers.

"Good job," he said.

She said nothing. Her knees ached and she had lost a shoe.

"Help me take it home."

She stood and stared down at him, wiped her nose and looked out over the void of the ravine.

"What are we going to do with it Zach?"

The bird moved again, ruffling its feathers with a muted hush, and he held it still.

"We're going to save it."

"From what?"

He said nothing.

She turned her gaze back to Zach and the condor. She recognized it now. The black wings were not the extension of shadow, they were real. All nine feet of wing.

"It's a female," he said, looking up at her. "Please help me with her," and he held her up, awkwardly, not letting go of the manzanita.

Oxena knelt down, rubbing her knees with the palms of her hands. "Are there any eggs?"

"No."

She opened her arms wide and felt the weight of the bird against her arms, the smoothness of the feathers, the coolness of its body.

* * *

Wind did not exist where Zeus lived. Zero particles were tossed into existence, created from nothing and moved by invisible forces. Once created, however, they did not decay into quarks or positrons or electrons. They held in place and though they spun within Diana between layers of polarized steel, they were not bound by the forces Parker and Puez studied. Zero particles were immune to the four forces, Electromagnetism, the Strong Nuclear force, the Weak Nuclear force, and Gravity.

There was, in fact, a fifth force. The godless force of Creation. The force which could pry into each of the others and link them together or build upon one or the other. We perceive existence in four dimensions: three of space and one of time. Creation exists outside these four, and accounts for particles which appear for 10^{-21} seconds from nothing and turn back into nothing. These are virtual particles which make a link from nothing to something. Particles forced into these negative milliseconds by Creation, to touch us in four dimensions, to make a connection between that which can be tested and that which cannot.

Creation is like the wind. It is invisible, but it has force. If you took wind away, the landscape would appear the same. But over time, without it, there would be no rainfall, no erosion, no change, no growth. The same is true of the force of Creation. Every particle in the universe exists with a froth of virtual particles enveloping it, invisible, arising from a vacuum only to disappear. But without this aura, without this foam of virtual particles popping in and out of existence, there would be no change, no growth, or birth of dust or thought. The force of Creation, this fifth force cannot be measured, tested, secured on faith, or ignored. It can only be glimpsed through conduits.

Parker Limpid knows nothing about the force of Creation. He does know that, on paper, particles will arrive from nowhere and disappear in theoretical, incalculable moments. He also knows that if he were to scrape up all these wayward particles and discard them, the earth and the galaxies would appear to be unchanged. He does not see their necessity. They are a mathematical problem that Zeus was supposed to help him solve. And Zeus is growing increasingly uncooperative.

Zero particles are building in Diana, living in our four dimensional world far beyond their normal time range. Zeus has succeeded in cutting off their passages from dark matter. A particle is also wave. As wave it can reach one destination point by traversing two paths simultaneously. These Zero particles of Zeus's crisscross bonds and overwhelm each other and have recently begun, for the first time, to acquire mass.

HYPOTHESES

Hattie dreams. She is even aware she is dreaming. I am dreaming...this is a dream...this is not real, she finds repeating over and over in her mind. She is not telling herself this, the message comes from someplace beyond herself. She does not know why. Something is wrong. She must hide. The heat is terrible, like a terrible pressure. It fills her lungs.

Hattie wakes. Sits straight up in bed, eyes wide, the sound of the wind somehow grounding her. Her heart is beating hard and she is very thirsty though she waits to get out of bed. Waits until thirst overcomes fear. When she does go to the sink, she turns on every light on the way: her nightstand, the hall light, and the light above the sink. The glass of water shakes in her hand. The presence telling her it was a dream is gone.

She turns on the small transistor radio by the sink and looks at the clock above the stove. It's two a.m. Her face feels heavy, her eyes pressed open against sleep. The static is harsh and she rolls the dial listening to the crackling swell and ebb of vacant stations until she finds voices: a radio talk show. There's a man speaking and Hattie fine tunes against the wind and sits down at the kitchen table, the glass of water nearly empty.

"...yeah. Broken down into groups of five or six. And out of my group I'm the only one still alive."

The transistor sits balanced upright in the center of the table, a faint green light pointing to the station. Hattie takes a sip of water and sighs, leans back in the chair. The room does not seem threatening though she is glad the hall light is on and is comforted by the yellow light spilling from her room. Glad there is a trail.

"So what you're saying is that these people were killed?"

"I'm not sayin' anything. What I'm saying is that they're not around."

"But how did you stay in touch with them. I mean why would you stay in touch with them?"

"Why would I stay in touch? I couldn't help it. I mean we were all practically local folks. I knew two of the other guys in my group just to look at and the one woman played bridge with my wife. I mean when something like that happens in your city and you were there, you don't just go home and forget about it."

Hattie traces a long scratch on the Formica table with her finger.

"How did these people die?"

"Well, out of the six of us questioned, three died in accidents—"

"When?"

"Whadya' mean when?"

"How long after?"

"Just two years."

"Two years."

"Yeah. One guy was hit by a car as he crossed the street, even though he jumped back on the curb. I mean man, he tried to get out of the way and he was mowed down. Just mowed down. Another guy had his neck broken while he was taking a shower. For no apparent reason. And the third one, a dock worker, was crushed. And two more died of cancer a year later. That woman and another guy. A welder."

"Didn't people talk? Locally about what was going on? Didn't the newspapers pick it up?"

"Hey. We tried. I tried. Before my wife and I moved, I tried to write a story and it went nowhere, man. That woman, whose name I won't say, who died of cancer, tried to get a story in the paper. But no one would touch it. I found out about this later, from a friend of mine who used to work, and I mean used to work, 'cause he got fired, on the paper who said she tried to place a paid ad warning everyone who was across from the grassy knoll, but they wouldn't run it."

Grassy knoll. Grassy knoll. Her finger keeps tracing.

"And then there was me. I was the sixth and I thought, 'they ain't gettin' me,' so we moved fast and I mean fast—no warning, no two week notice, no nothing and we went to where I am now and I'm not sayin' a word about where we're livin' either so don't ask me. But there were lots of others. Lots. Just about everyone who saw those shots and that smoke are history now. History."

"So you're saying anyone who knew there was a second gunman was killed?"

"I'm sayin' there ain't anyone around whose goin' to back me up. Not now."

"And it's all a conspiracy?"

"That Warren Commission—nobody from that Commission never questioned me man and—"

"So what's your theory after all this? That Kennedy was killed by the—"

"Kennedy was killed by the feds. And by the feds I mean all those guys who get in bed together, the Mafia, the CIA, business, all of them. I mean, Jesus, I saw it. I saw it. I saw with my own eyes and no one believes me. And he was the end. They knew if he was killed that would be the end. I mean those guys were there rounding us up into little groups before that sedan even got to the hospital. They knew what they had to do. But they're not doin' it to me."

"So it's your conclusion that Kennedy was killed by the second gunman..."

"He was killed by Americans you asshole. Can't you hear a word I'm sayin' to you. He was killed by people just stickin' their heads in their asses and—"

She rolls the dial with her thumb and static pricks through the twang of a country music station. KSWG, the station with swing. The wind bangs against the trailer, knocking down along the full length of metal. She stares at the scratch. She was eleven years old when Kennedy died. She had been watching Mighty Mouse when Walter Cronkite came on the air. She remembers feeling angry that she couldn't see the rest of the show, upset by all the grown-ups talking on the screen, and frightened by the way Henry sat in front of the T.V.

* * *

The baby sleeps and wakes, sleeps and wakes and Melody lays with him in dream, on her side, in bed with him close, naked. She stares into his face, perfect in the poor light. She listens to the whisper sounds of breathing and sighing and his small weight moving on the mattress. He sleeps as if caught in a watery current, his arms and legs rise in slow underwater movements, and she cannot stop touching him, lying with her head on a pillow looking down at his black hair.

119

Throughout the night the wind wraps and pulls hard, she can feel the trailer wave. The infant, used to rippling movement, sleeps, and stirs only to root, moving closer to her breast and then to nurse. When he finishes with the left side, she breaks the suction with her finger and then shifts slightly, rolling further on her stomach and offers him the right breast. He is not as hungry as that first feeding in the mine and he dozes between swallows, his jaw moving only every now and then, his eyes sliding back behind his eyelids in bliss. His skin is not from the earth it is so fine and soft and she kisses his forehead, feels his quick breath on her wet nipple, and touches the curve of his shoulder.

She does not allow herself to think of Henry, outside with the wind.

At four thirty she is startled to find herself waking up. He wants to nurse and is arching his back, his face twisted up in tiny wrinkles and a small cry forces out from his lungs. She hurriedly gives him her breast, but he is panicked and drops the nipple, thrashing. Now she is anxious and tries again, her heart racing, panicking for a moment thinking he might not ever take it. But he does, and his tiny body relaxes and her breast lets down milk. Her sigh is deep and long when she finally relaxes as well. It isn't until he has finished nursing and they both lay near sleep again that she realizes the wind has stopped.

* * *

They put the bird in the shower stall. Oxena has opened the glass door and now she helps Zachary into the house, taking care not to let the bird's wings unfold. He stands in the shower, leaning over the bird, his hands holding the bird's body hard. When the bird is released, she stands straight, hops once and remains still. The sock is still in place over the condor's head and neck. It's an old, black, gold toe sock of Zach's and it's stretched nearly full length. Zach steps out of the stall and pulls on the chain for the light above the sink, turning it off.

"What do we do now?" says Oxena and the bird tries to jump again, its head weaving from side to side. It knocks against the stall two or three times before it is still again. In the hazy light Oxena notices the dark chocolate smear of blood on the stall floor and she

120

glances at Zach to see if he's seen it. But the blood is from her knee, not the bird, and she steps back further from the shower. She and Zach stand for a time, separate but united in a kind of meditation, focused on the condor and the need for silence. She does not know the reason behind the condor's presence. She does not understand how she feels standing next to Zach in the darkness, but she is aware of a grappling with an unknown she had long ago forgotten existed.

After a while the bird visibly relaxes and its posture slumps into repose. It squats down, stepping lightly from side to side, gingerly sitting, standing upright, stepping side to side, making another attempt. Finally, she sits as if nesting, her legs tucked underneath her body, her head balanced back against her neck. The profile is typical of a vulture, but the outlines of its face are lost under the sock.

Oxena crosses the small space and sits down in the living room across from the blue white static of the T.V. Soon she hears Zach carefully closing the glass shower door, pressing on the clasp to avoid the metallic click. He throws a thin, blue cotton bed spread over the glass door. He moves into the kitchen, moving quietly, gently opening the cupboards above the sink. He passes her, a dark thin shadow against the flutter of the T.V. screen, and hands her a small glass of Scotch without ice. Cracking the ice tray would have made too much noise.

He sits across from her in his overstuffed chair.

"Should I turn the T.V. off?" she whispers.

He shakes his head.

White noise she thinks. It will hide their voices.

They sit and sip Scotch for a long time and the banter of the wind courses under the snow of the T.V. Her scotch is hot in her throat, a stream of fire from lips to sternum. Her chest seems to open up and her breath is warm. She does not drink Scotch, usually, but her knee has begun to throb and her hands hurt.

They hear nothing from the shower stall. No flailing. No objection to captivity and she is unsure of motives.

"So what do we do now?" she says, feeling the last dribble of Scotch wash the back of her throat.

"Hmm?" His head nods up and she sees he holds his chin in his hands and stares past her.

"I said, what are we doing?"

There is a long pause and she feels the rush of the unknown, of being swept away by a force greater than she.

"We may have the last wild California condor," he said and leaned back and picked up his Scotch. "The last one. We have to save it. Save her."

She looks at her hands folded in her lap. There are little scratches across the palms from their struggle on the cliffs. And then there is the quick slip of hope, ungrounded and fleeting, rushing around her, filling her heart, giving her power and then, just as suddenly, it is gone. And she is left alone, betrayed once again by dreams.

* * *

Kinni sleeps as if dead. In repose, her face is upturned, no pillow, her jaw slack, perpendicular to her neck, arms parallel by her sides. She has not slept since mid-morning, and then only slept a couple of hours before being awakened. She did not return to sleep until after midnight. She is exhausted, limp, dreamless. Now she is unconscious during a time when she is usually awake. Her world has reversed itself. Light, the beacon of day, has always bathed her while she slept and she has grown accustomed to drifting away with the red void of daylight against her eyelids. Of seeing blood and life and shutting her mind against their force. Tonight, though, exhausted, she fell into sleep from a dark cliff, sailing over the top, plunging down into darkness. There was no force to shut her mind against. Blackness surrounded her and she succumbed.

* * *

Lani, too, is asleep, naked in the hot night, the T.V. still on but with pictures and cryptic messages both gone. She waited until just after one in the morning to catch a second message, waited without appearing to wait. These things usually don't happen again especially if you're watching for them. And nothing more happened. There was a only a late-night news rehash and a cropped version of *Butterflies are Free.* She sleeps on her stomach with her head turned toward the wall, red hair fanning across the pillow behind her. Freckles across her pale back appear dark in the night, like tiny stars, in negative of the sky above. Moonlight slips across the floor, competing with the white static snow of the T.V. But the white of the T.V. cannot move and the moon spins. The walls of her room are bare. There are no pictures, no photographs. No evidence of her camera. And though she stirs in her sleep and shifts her position slightly, she, too remains dreamless.

* * *

Monday morning Raceway is vacant. Even the wind has left and dust is still. No one is out walking. Melody will call in sick. Kinni, for the first time in years, is asleep in these early hours. Bat is not going to be allowed outdoors right away. Lani stirs but does not wake. Hattie, too, sleeps. Oxena will not drag out her chaise lounge this morning and Zach will not wander around the Dream Time with his polish and shammy. Only Henry and Barday circulate in the sand, each independent of the other, each moving away from death and returning to Raceway, each coming forward from different directions. One from the east and one from the west.

Henry has blood on his work pants and dirt under his fingernails and he uses the shovel as a walking stick. He has buried the woman in the mountains and has moved through the night with the wind tearing around him while he remained isolated from himself. With each left step he throws the steel tip of the shovel into sand and there is the sound of soft grating. Barday has blood everywhere. The wind brought a night of battle and defeat deep in the woods in Virginia. The forest rang with gunfire and the cries of young men and old men, women and babies, all wounded and dying. Even the dead screamed in the wind. Echoes linger and he tries to make Tip walk faster in the sand, kicking him with the heels of his brown boots, needing to retreat from the scarlet wetness of the forest. But the horse remains slow and steady and does not sense the same danger as Barday.

Henry buried her on the steep side of a mountain, in a tunnel facing east, sunrise, guessing she was Hopi. First he dug the tunnel, then he went to the mine shaft. She was small, not heavy to lift, and he did not look at her face or think about her over his shoulder when he made his way across the path in the wind and the night. The wind kept her smell from overwhelming him, though the tang of blood still stained the back of his throat. He thought once about her blood in his mouth in the moment when wind slid off her back and whirled around into his face, but he closed his mind. When he reached the tunnel, he lowered her onto two thick elderberry branches, like a stretcher, and pushed her deep into the mountain and began throwing shovelfuls of dirt back into the tunnel. He knew she should face the east, that her arms must lay folded across her chest, to place a single smooth stone over each eye, and to pray. The hillside was steep and he had trouble with his balance in the sway of the wind. When her feet disappeared, he stopped and began rolling large rocks into the hole, a safeguard against roving coyotes. Then more dirt. And then a prickly pear dug from a few yards away, placed in the center of the fresh earth. Then handfuls of sand and small stones. The stones took on a pink hue before Henry felt the wind die and sunrise began silently and without birdcalls. His hands were callused and his eyes and face felt dried out and numbed by wind.

He had never prayed. Not even for Arlene. But now he prayed for her in her way—as a courtesy, offering respect, summoning an aura of exhausted awe at her mortality. He shook slightly as he made his way off the face of the mountain and he chose his steps carefully. He did not look back. He wanted to be able to forget which mountain kept her. In the darkness and turmoil of the wind it was easy to forget the slope and the spot of prickly pear and the rose of sunrise was not going to make him turn around.

He walks in the sand, head down, aware of the direction for Raceway, moved by an internal compass. He hears the sound of his shovel in the sand suddenly matched by a second sound of plunging and sees Barday mounted on Tip coming towards him not more than a hundred yards away. Henry quickly looks back at the ground. But the outline of the Union hat was clear against the reddening sky and stays clear in Henry's mind. Horse and rider are silhouette ghosts, useful fodder for the force which wants to overtake him. But this morning there is no pain. No flash of agony. No sucking in of air, and Henry looks up again, in spite of himself, as if to test. But Barday has disappeared, gone around in back of the trailers and is out of sight.

Henry stops and leans on his shovel, squinting into the sun. And then he hears a baby cry softly from the desert and he hurries, thinking it is the infant. Remembering the infant and Melody. But it is an echo from somewhere else and Barday hears the same cry.

When Henry enters the trailer, there is only the soft drip of water from the spigot in the kitchen sink. The pan of water is still on the kitchen table. So are the scissors. He takes off his shoes and walks down the hall to the bedroom, careful not to make noise. He stands in the doorway and watches Melody sleeping, still on her side, facing him. A sheet covers her and from her shoulders it falls over the baby. Only the infant's hair shows above the white—a soft, depthless mound of black. He can hear them both breathing, Melody's metered slow and laborious, exhausted with sleep, and the infant's in quick startled breaths. Henry sits across from them in a blue canvas butterfly chair, tilts his head back, lights a cigarette and then puts it out again in an old cup of coffee on her dresser. As his eyes close he feels salt water pressing heavy in the outer corners of his eyes and he blinks. The tears are released. He does not know where they come from—if they are from being with the wind or from being with thoughts—and he falls asleep with heavy tears slipping from under his eyelids like warm mercury.

* * *

Barday has spent the night on Tip, riding out as far into the desert with no direction, only purpose. His purpose was to win in combat, but like a flag shredded into long thin streamers from battle, his purpose became confused and fragmented, bandied about by the wind, and pieces were tossed and snapped by forces in his mind too powerful to overcome. The desert faded, the rocks and the sand vanished and only the wind and stars remained, shining over the forest in Virginia a day before Antigua.

What followed was not victory. Defeat was strong and sudden, the poise and heart of the South stabbing the tremulous righteousness of the North. And this poise and heart would carry forward in time. So would tremulous righteousness. Barday enters his battles with the handicap of foresight, of coming to them from the future. Like a time traveler, he knows the outcome of the war. So even though tonight he

125

was deep in the forest of Virginia, he entered that forest with echoes from his own past far in the future, of buses and lavatories, drinking fountains, separate and volatile and children escorted to school by men with guns. It is because of this foresight, he always loses his battles.

He cannot remember tonight's battle clearly. He does not see Henry walking towards him with a shovel in one hand and his other limp by his side. He only catches glimpses of the battle, tight, close snapshots of blood and human gore, fathers killing sons, brothers killing sisters, babies left standing over parents, blood across their cheeks, hysterical and alone. Men's chests ripped open, blue and red uniforms smattered with bone and blood, hands and legs lost, eyes open and dead. The battle ended when the wind stopped. The shards of his purpose came back together in the calmness of morning and he found himself returned to the desert floor, with Tip heading home.

Barday cannot go into another battle. He is drained and he coughs, hard and long as he reins Tip in along the back of the trailers. He begins to weep, bending forward, at first covering his eyes and feeling his tears running into his hands and then he lifts his head up to the sun, shuts his eyes and holds his breath. He must not cry. He knows he has returned. He must lie down. Tip stands by the back door of the trailer, stiff after his long walk in the wind, and the leather saddle creaks as Barday dismounts. The earth moves under him and Barday steadies himself with a hand on the pommel. His joints of his knees ache. He uncinches the saddle and it slips off heavy in his arms. Tip's back is wet with sweat and the horse turns and looks at him, the great hollows above his eyes deep with morning shadow. The horse's face is covered with small thin scars, a labyrinth of battle wounds. It is as Barday reaches up to pull off the bridle that a cry comes across the desert, like an infant's wail, and he stands unmoving waiting for the echo to pass. The wooded forest is far away, too far away to carry echoes and he begins to cry again.

* * *

Parker Limpid has not slept for much of the night. But this fact does not have any implications for him. Where he lives there is no night or day, only the imperceptible spinning of the earth. Instead he dozes in periods of one to two hours, intent on solving the Problem, aware of the 2:00 am shift arriving and of Dr. Puez's return a little later at 7:00. She will not stay down under for more than ten hours. "I need to surface," she's told him before and this statement has led him to question her dedication.

Just before Dr. Puez returned, Parker Limpid sat rubbing his eyes. There was a discrepancy in data and he was working with different models, trying to make an appropriate adjustment to account for the data. But nothing within the realm of what he wanted to believe would account for the figures in front of him. The discrepancy existed and he was left with only theoretical models. Nothing in three dimensions worked. And Parker hated multidimensional models. Mass was building in Diana, but there was nothing to account for the mass. No particles retrieved. Had they trapped a sliver of dark matter? A block of heavy nothing? The discrepancy was that the mass appeared to vacillate, decreasing slightly, increasing more, decreasing again, and then increasing each time so that the total mass was slightly more than what it originally began with. And it appeared these increases and decreases followed a four hour cycle. Perhaps particles were leaving and those left were then attracting like particles. But according to Zeus, there were no particles in Diana. The final piece of unexplained data was the fact that Zeus had apparently sealed off Diana, refusing to report back to Parker, not answering specific questions and physically charging the detector to deflect all possible incoming particles.

Zeus was malfunctioning. It was clear. The reality must be that there was no mass building, the four hour cycle was the period of time it took for the error to loop, and Zeus's silence around Diana was the final indication.

"So, what's the prognosis?" asks Puez as she sits down.

"Zeus's a sick puppy." Parker rubs his face. "That 'mass,'" he says, index fingers up and curved in quotes, "in Diana is still building and he's still saying there's nothing there."

Puez swivels in her chair and doodles with her pen on a yellow legal pad. She is making circles within circles, not connected like a spiral, but separate, concentric circles, like a bulls eye. This is the pattern she always follows when Parker Limpid begins an explanation.

"Now we're stuck because I don't know where to look. I'm assuming it's a program problem given the four hour lapse time. I guess all we can hope is that this is an isolated incident."

She sighs, puts down the pen and says, "Isolated over a seventy-two hour period? So you're calling it a malfunction?"

"Well, yeah. There's nothing else to explain the data. I mean the data is gibberish."

"What Zeus is saying is that something is appearing out of nothing and that something has mass, but no energy or form."

"Yeah. And he's being a pain in the ass about it."

Puez smiles. "You mean he's being tightlipped?"

"He's being a pain in the ass."

"Should we shut down?"

Parker Limpid looks at her and again questions her ability to reach effective conclusions. "If we shut down, we won't be able to run any diagnostics first, and second, it would set us back weeks, possibly months, and we have to answer to dozens of funders and at least that many senators."

She pops a Kingston Trio cassette into the tape recorder and sets the volume low. "So I guess we're not shutting down."

He turns back to his computer. "No." He feels a question from her. "What?" he sighs knowing whatever she going to say is going to irritate him. Then he knows..."Oh, you think these might be real. That there's—Oh Christ," he unpeels the paper wrap from a Snickers bar and takes a bite, staring into his computer.

"So I guess you don't think there's any danger."

He continues to stare at the screen. "It's a problem, Puez. A mathematical problem. The numbers aren't going boil up from the ground and explode."

There is a silence and Puez begins to stand. "I think I'm going to do a round," she says and a moment later, as she lifts her legal pad, the sound of a cry is heard, loud, bright. A single wail with the trail of an echo. Though the sound is not loud, it is foreign and it seems to shake the steel walls—it is close, above them, below them, around them and Parker feels a flash near his heart. A chemical flood of adrenaline.

"What the hell was that?" Parker has not moved from his chair.

"Shh."

They can hear the slap of heels and squeak of rubber tennis shoes on linoleum as people in the room behind them scurry trying to read information.

"Is this a fuckin' joke or what?" Parker yells, tilting backwards in his chair. "Someone's gonna get fired." Now he is rising, standing, not looking at Puez. The glass double doors open and Dr. Francis says quietly, "We don't know what it was." The door shuts again.

Puez is sitting back down, her mouth slack and all thought lost as she searches for a second sound, another chance for analysis. But there is only the busy silence of a sound not heard. She and Parker will spend the morning hearing the wail again and again, faint, hollow, a haunting they themselves create.

VARIABLES

I woke up late that Monday, past nine, really late for me. I woke and kept waking. It was cooler than it had been for a long time. The wind from the night before scoured out the valley and the crisp dry breath of morning air was a heavy sedative. I could barely move. I finally shoved a pillow behind my back, leaned over and picked up the Almanac off the nightstand. If I started now, I could get a lot read without having to really think. This twilight state was good for all kinds of chores. Early morning's the best time to do the dishes—you don't even notice you're scrubbing.

I was finishing up the Disasters section, and had rolled through Major Earthquakes, Some Recent Earthquakes, Major U.S. Tornadoes Since 1925, Hurricanes, Typhoons, Blizzards, and Others Storms, Floods and Tidal Waves, Explosions, Fires, Major Railroad Wrecks, and Notable Aircraft Disasters Since 1935 the evening before. Now I was faced with Principal U.S. Mine Disasters. I rubbed my eyes and took a sip of lukewarm water from the blue glass on the floor by my bed.   There was an interesting note preceding the entry which declared: Before 1968, only disasters with losses of 60 or more lives are listed. After 1968, all disasters in which 5 or more people were killed are listed. Only fatalities to mining company employees are included. All are Bituminous-coal mine unless otherwise noted.

My eyes, accustomed to the preciseness of columns swept across and down the page:

date	location	deaths
1867 Apr. 3	Winterpock, VA	69
1869 Sept. 6	Plymouth, PA	110
1883 Feb. 16	Braidwood, IL	69
1884 Mar. 13	Pocahontas, VA	112
1891 Jan. 27	Mount Pleasant, PA	109

1892 Jan. 7 Krebs, OK	100
1895 Mar. 20 Red Canyon, WY	60
1900 Jan. 1 Scofield, UT	200
1902 May 19 Coal Creek, TN	184
1902 July 10 Johnstown, PA	112
1903 June 30 Hanna, WY	169
1904 Jan. 25 Cheswick, PA	179
1905 Feb. 20 Virginia City, AL	112
1907 Jan. 29 Stuart, W. VA.	84
1907 Dec. 6 Monongah, W. VA	361
1907 Dec. 19 Jacobs Creek, PA	239
1908 Nov. 28 Marianna, PA	154
1909 Jan. 12 Switchback, W. VA	67
1909 Nov. 13 Cherry, IL	59
1910 Jan. 31 Primero, CO	75
1910 May 5 Palos, AL	90
1910 Nov. 8 Delagua, CO	79
1911 Apr. 7 Throop, PA	72
1911 Apr. 8 Littleton, AL	128
1911 Dec. 9 Briceville, TN	84
1912 Mar. 20 McCurtain, OK	73
1912 Mar. 26 Jed, W. VA	83
1913 Apr. 23 Finleyville, PA	96
1913 Oct. 22 Dawson, NM	263
1914 Apr. 28 Eccles, W.VA	181
1915 Mar 2 Layland, W. VA	112
1917 Apr. 17 Hastings, CO	121
1917 June 8 Butte, MT	163
1917 Aug. 4 Clay, KY	62
1919 June 5 Wilkes-Barre, PA	92
1922 Nov. 6 Spangler, PA	77
1922 Nov. 22 Dolomite, AL	90
1923 Feb. 8 Dawson, NM	120
1923 Aug. 14 Kemmerer, WY	99
1924 Mar. 8 Castle Gate, UT	171
1924 Apr. 28 Benwood, W. VA	119
1926 Jan. 13 Wilburton, OK	91

1926 Nov. 3 Ishpernig, MI	51
1927 Apr. 30 Everettville, W. VA	97
1928 May 19 Mather, PA	195
1929 Dec. 17 McAlester, OK	61
1930 Nov. 5 Millifield, OH	79
1940 Jan. 10 Bartley, W. VA	91
1940 Mar. 16 St. Clairsville, OH	72
1940 July 15 Portage, PA	63
1943 Feb. 27 Washoe, MT	74
1944 July 5 Belmont, OH	66
1947 Mar. 25 Centralia, IL	111
1951 Dec. 21 West Frankfort, IL	119
1968 Mar. 6 Calmuet, LA	21
1968 Nov. 20 Farmington, W. VA	78
1970 Dec. 30 Hyden, KY	26
1972 May 2 Kellogg, ID	91
1976 Mar. 9, 11 Oven Fork, KY	26
1977 Mar. 1 Tower City, PA	9
1981 Apr. 15 Redstone, CO	15
1981 Dec. 7 Topmost, KY	8
1981 Dec. 8 No. Chattanooga, TN	27

The world's worst mine disaster killed 1,549 workers in Honkeiko Colliery in Manchuria, April 25, 1942.

April 25th is my birthday.

The next section was Historic Assassinations Since 1865, but I'd had enough. My eyes were closing back into slits and I needed to wake up. The book lay spread open, spine up on the bed. I rolled over, swung my legs down and remained bent in half enough to retrieve the sheet of pink marbled paper and my good gold pen from the lap tray on the floor. I stood and wandered down the hall to the kitchen, feeling the oversized T-shirt fall loose and wrinkled against the back of my thighs. The transistor radio still sat in the middle of the Formica table and I stared at it for a moment before opening the refrigerator. No juice. Just some ice water. Perfect. I sat down, glad that the glass didn't sweat immediately, and wrote:

My Henry,

Life is counted by increments of time, by small incidences layered one on top of the other like a stack of papers. Don't try to upset the stack. Time can't be shuffled around. I love you. I love little Henrietta, and I love having breath and thought. But these loves of mine will be lost soon and you must commit them to memory. When you read this, I will not be in your life, except as a presence. Time is fixed, straight and long, disappearing over the horizon line on either side of you like two infinite steel poles—one stretching behind you, the other in front.

I need to know that you will walk forward to that horizon line.
Arlene

This would do. It wasn't bad. It would give him something to mull over and take his mind off of the pain in his legs. That pain. I sighed. I had to get him to the doctor's today.

I glanced at the clock. A quarter to ten. He'd be at the Shell station. I leaned over to the counter, lifted the telephone and dialed. But he wasn't there. And Betty, the owner was not pleased. "Tell him he'd better get his ass in here or call me the next time when he decides not to show. I'm sitting here doing everything myself and I can't do it all. Ralph Pearson called in sick yesterday and I bet he doesn't show today. Jerk. I mean I can't do it all, and it really pisses me off. Now if your Henry's sick, really sick that's one thing, but if this is just him laying bed with a hangover, now that's another and I won't tolerate it. I can't and I won't. I can't do everything myself."

Betty Jarless (pronounced jar-LESS) was about sixty, shorter than my 1952 Hotpoint refrigerator and probably triple its weight. She wasn't round though. She was as square as that fridge, with a little square haircut over a square face, wearing square glasses and little square post earrings. A cube of flesh. She was strong but not fast and couldn't take the heat and dust at all. She was her best just after a rainstorm, which meant she was her best about five days out of the year. "Doing it all," meant pumping gas every half an hour for a lost visitor and opening the broken Coke machine for the local kids every time they slipped in money. Not a high pressure job. Of course, who am I to talk? And Ralph Pearson was an addict who was always sick, never in and looked like a long, thin, thrashed green bean. But he was eager to please and tried to look straight. He could have been twenty-five or sixty-five. There was no way to tell by his face. I avoided the Shell station.

I folded the letter from Arlene in half and stuck it my T-shirt pocket, rubbing the crease with my fingers to give the appearance of time. I should really try to find him. He'd either be at home in a stupor, slumped on his bed, back to the door, barely breathing with the room reeking of gin, or he'd be at the Volcano. I looked at the clock again. Of course, the potato fryers warm up at Denny's at 11:00, so he could be out in Palmdale dipping into the blue cheese.

I got up and went to the cupboards, dragged out a loaf of bread and smeared peanut butter on a slice. When I was a kid, Henry would buy Wonder bread and that thick chocolate milk with the viscosity of watered glue and we'd sit and eat margarine and sugar sandwiches and gulp down the chocolate milk straight from the carton. I remember my hands always were too rough for the bread. I'd just touch it and the surface would bruise.

I could hear Celeste outside yelling at Bat to stay close to home and I peeked out my side window above the sink. I saw him sitting in the sand. But he wasn't digging. He was staring straight ahead, sniffing the light air, very focused on something in the distance. Something either out on the horizon or in his mind. He knelt, something I'd never seen him do before, and his back was very straight, hips above his knees, his arms crossed in front of him, fists against his chest. It all gave the eerie appearance of prayer. He remained still, caught in some electrical or chemical trance the entire time I stood at the window and finally I turned away.

Sometimes I wished I smoked. This was one of those times. I could hear the letter rustle every time I moved my arm.

* * *

Hattie knocked on Henry's trailer. No answer. Odd, too, that the front door behind the screen was closed. Maybe because of the wind last night. She knocked again and then turned the knob. The kitchen was exactly as it was the morning before, with old fried egg floating in the iron skillet in the sink and a mug of something with flies on the rim.

135

"Henry," she called and went to his room.

She never liked his room. Even as a child. She didn't like to watch him sleep and in her mind "his room" meant where he slept. There was too much to know and too little she understood when she watched his face in repose. Unconsciousness left him even more vulnerable and his moaning at night used to keep her awake. As a teenager she really despised the times they'd have to share a room. She resisted the need to protect him—if she allowed herself to be swallowed into his painful sleep, to allow herself to be pulled into his deep black reverie of remorse and isolation, she somehow sensed she would never be able to move away from him. That's why she began calling him Henry, to loosen that obligation of custody and care. To remain free.

His room was empty. There was the acrid, burnt smell of evaporating gin and old cigarette butts. The window above his bed was open and a light film of dust covered the pressboard bureau and turned the surface dull. Everything was coated in haze from the wind. Even his bed billowed desert dust when she fluffed the pillow.

There was a small picture of her when she was seven on the bureau. Hattie picked it up and wiped dust off the glass. She always liked this picture. Her hair is unkempt, sticking straight out, wild. She is smiling, equally wildly, and has all four front teeth missing. That was the summer she had to eat artichokes and corn on the cob by turning her head to the side. She is holding a green garden hose and standing in a small plastic baby pool, wearing nothing but her underwear. She still has a little girl's body, flat chested with a slightly protruding tummy and water is splashing over the edge of the pool. It's the only picture she's ever seen of herself as a child and she is always impressed by the little girl. Hattie looked hard, trying to capture that feeling she used to have as a child—that glorious sense of self importance, of having something no one else had. Of having something secret and special.

She pulled the letter out from her back pocket, folded it twice more and stuffed one end up inside the little frame, leaving just a flicker of pink flaring out from between the cardboard backing and the picture. She set the frame back down on the bureau and walked out of the room.

Hattie left the trailer without shutting the door and the screen slammed against the jam twice before remaining open just a few inches above the top step. She saw Honey out on her swing set, looking up into the sky. She looked up too.

"See that bird again?"

"Naw," Honey said, not taking her eyes off some depthless spot in the sky. She was riding the pendulum again.

"Have you seen Henry around?"

"Nope. Haven't seen anybody. Just... hey, do you have Cheerios?"

"Not now."

"Well, the next time you get some, can I get the prize out? Last week I got these," she said and rolled her hand around the chain so Hattie could see two rub-on tattoos above her knuckles. "I'm going to school pretty soon," she announced, "but Bat's not." And with that, she launched herself into the air and landed close to Hattie, folded up on the desert floor, and then struggled up. "That stinged my legs," she said, stomping her feet. "That bird's gone too," she said, quite seriously, looking Hattie right in the eye. "And so's Bat. Mom's mad at him and he's in trouble again."

It was true, Bat was gone again. When Hattie got home, there were just two long prints in the sand where his legs had rested. For the first time ever, there were no new holes to sidestep. Hattie climbed the stairs into her trailer and sighed. Henry was gone, Bat was missing again, even Oxena and Zach were absent from the morning scene. There was no pasty smell of wax and polish wafting through her kitchen window, no odd little tip of the lemonade glass as she'd walked back down the line of trailers. But the weather was perfect.

* * *

The morning hours were cool. Oxena sat stiff in her chair, her legs asleep. She felt dirty. The T.V. was turned off. Zach's chair was empty and she moved to find him, a crick in her neck making her wince. She had to turn her whole back and hold her head carefully, to see him flat out on the floor next to the shower stall with a pillow under his head. Setting her legs down slowly, she rubbed each calf until the tingling stopped and then she went quietly to the refrigerator, stepping next to him on the floor, not caring to look down, not daring to look in the shower stall. She opened the refrigerator carefully, first breaking the suction with her finger and then swinging the door open slowly. She crouched down and looked around for the thawed chicken breast from the night before. It lay uncovered on a plastic plate.

When she turned, Zach was squatting next to the stall, peeking in behind the cotton bedspread through the glass. He glanced at her and saw the plate of chicken and smiled and nodded slightly. It had been years since she'd seen that nod. It was quick, led from the chin, and made her feel woven into his life, full, as if they were truly one. The nod was more than appreciation, more than respect. It was conspiratorial. She never sensed she gave him anything as complete and over the years had forgotten how he could, with such a simple act, at once dissolve her into him and yet make her more aware of how beautifully separate they were.

Zach opened the door and the condor jumped, her head stiff and straight ahead, straining for sound. In dual moves Oxena slipped the chicken to the shower floor and Zach pulled the sock from the condor's head. Her wattle was collapsed and cold, the red fleshy hood deflated, but her black eyes were bright. She darted her head from side to side, catching them both in her vision from different angles. She did not try to fly. Oxena could see her breathe through the large holes in her beak, and her toes, unused to walking on flat slippery surfaces, remained curled, her black talons clicking on white fiberglass.

Zach closed the glass door and she walked straight to the piece of meat. Oxena watched as she closed one foot around the chicken breast, her hind talon neatly piercing through ribs. Without another glance to them, her head dropped and the black feathers on the nape of her neck opened in even lines and her beak shredded off a piece of chicken the size of a finger. Within minutes only the white of bones and tough cartilage remained.

Again in dual movements, Oxena reached in and grabbed the breast bone, and Zach slipped the sock back over her head. This time she held quite still and seemed content to have her eyes shrouded. They closed the door and replaced the bedspread. As the spread slipped across glass Oxena saw her huddle in one corner of the stall, squatting back on her thighs, her magnificent wings ruffling along her back. There was something in her poise, in the way she carried herself, the careful placement of her lower body against the floor that made Oxena realize she was full, ripe, laden with an egg.

* * *

Lani's camera swings like a pistol around her neck. Absorbing heat, even on a cool day and when it touches her chest, it burns the skin above her tank top. Celeste's calls for Bat had woken her from a black sleep that morning. She had peeked out her window and seen Celeste on the top step, hands on hips, pointing to Honey to look around the trailer park. Celeste was getting ready for work. Just a month ago she'd gotten a part-time job working for the Sand Canyon School System as an assistant and now she stood on one leg, trying to finish pulling up her panty hose with her hands. Bat would go with her and stay two houses down at a sitter's, five hours a day, five days a week. And now he was making her late. Lani opened her door to call out:

"Celeste...Celeste! I bet I know where he went."

"He was just here a second ago. Up by Hattie's. I'm going to be late again."

"Just go," said Lani and she waved her arm. "I'll get him. I'll keep an eye on him for you today," and she stepped out on her front steps.

"You sure?"

"Yeah."

"Really?"

"Yeah."

"What if you can't find him?" She was hustling Honey into the car.

"If I can't, I'll call you."

Celeste disappeared back inside her trailer and came out slipping on her shoes as she ran down the steps. She tossed her purse into her Dart and walked across the sand to Lani.

139

"Here's the number." She held out a slip of paper. "If you don't find him in an hour, call me. Call me when you do find him. He's a handful. You watch him."

So now Lani is walking toward Bat's hole in the middle of the basin, certain to find him there, digging in the midmorning sun. She is barefoot and in her cutoffs, the weight of the camera pressing its need to be used. She'll take pictures of him she decides. She will shoot Bat working in his hole, separate from the world, focused on an accomplishment, methodically turning over earth just as our ancestors did, moving human kind from antiquity to agriculture, from peace to war. His actions, however, are without purpose yet fluid, and she wants to record them.

When she finds him, she is surprised to see him not digging. She comes up over the horseshoe rocks to the lip of the hole, which is now a good nine feet in circumference. He squats in the center of the pit, four feet down, his back curved to her again, breaching once more. His head is dropped and he is scraping at something with his hands. The spoon lays to the left of him, catching sunlight and sends it to her eyes in a blaze. She steps to the right to avoid the glare. She hears him sigh and sees him shift his weight.

"Bat," she calls down. "Bat, what are you doing?"

He stands immediately and looks straight ahead and then turns his face to her, tilting up to find her eyes. She feels goose pimples rise on her arms. He smiles at her and claps his hands. Sand clings to his fingers and then he quickly bends down, slaps the ground with his open palms and stands back up, searching for her eyes again. Lani looks down into the crater, between his feet. Nothing is clear. But something pulls on her, some force which makes her feel the rush of the unknown and she sits down, dangles her legs over the side and slides into the hole.

"What have you done Bat?" she says softly and feels the earth with her feet. He has dug very deep, passed sand and dirt and now he has hit clay, a kind of red spongy clay which feels warm and soft under her feet, almost like flesh. In a few hours it will dry, cracking and peeling like burnt skin. She sees their bare footprints clearly in the earth and she bends down, squatting like him and in a moment they both hover above the clay, their hands in the earth, digging.

"What are you looking for?" she asks, feeling his breath on her arms.

"Stars." He says the word simply, clearly, and with definite purpose.

She stops digging and sits back on her heels. Her hands are red with clay and she rubs her fingertips on her cutoffs. Red earth rolls off her skin in long fat rolls and her fingernails are stained.

She stays crouching, squatting back way on her heels, her back against the rock and dirt wall of the pit. She lifts the camera and the weight releases from the back of her neck. She centers him in the viewfinder, adjusts the lens, bringing him into focus. His face is determined, his jaw tight, his eyes following the movements of his hands. Her finger is on the shutter release, she can see the red blur of clay next to her face. The back of his head and the top of his forearms are in sun, the rest of him in shadow and she sees how sunlight dips across his shoulders, its absence leaving dark pockets in the hollows above his collarbones. He tenses and bends down even closer to the ground, she hears him breathing hard and his face is lost to her. Then he looks up, quickly, right at the camera and his arm straightens and through the viewfinder she sees there is something in his hand, balanced in his palm.

"Star," he says again. Clearly. "Our star."

She feels the weight of the camera back against her neck. She takes the star from Bat, stands, and rubs red clay from its crevasses. The more she rubs, the more she trusts the rush. She brings the star into sunlight and she sees it is bone. Bone turned to rock. A piece of bone three inches long and half an inch wide. A piece of something—a note of song.

She hands the bone back to Bat. He has filled both hands with stiff clay and they are cupped together as if drinking water. She presses the bone hard into his hands. It sticks in the clay. Crouching back down, she makes him find her eyes again and when she sees the golden flecks she takes the camera from her neck and lays it on the clay bed next to them. Lani will not take any more pictures this morning.

* * *

There is not just one horizon line, but many, each pressed against the other in strips of tinted time, rock and dirt colored by geologic forces, the face of eons reflected in brown, mauve, red, gray, white. The strata of lost horizons is all Bat sees, a multi-colored wedge of earth rushing up to meet the sky. But the sound is the same.

I here. I here. I here. I here.

In front of Bat are the slow curves and colors of time, rolling one on top of another, locked in earth. Some layers are of fine sand, paler than others, some rocky and dark. He smiles as they come in and out of focus, alternating with the curves of her face. He still feels the star in his left hand. He sits very still, his penis is stiff and she is holding it very hard. His legs feel tight and he hears himself moan and he leans back, lying down and rests his head against the soft clay. Now there are no horizons at all, past or present, only blue sky and for a moment he shuts his eyes. The pressure mounts and the sound is louder.

I here. I here. I here. I here.

Her hair tickles his face and he feels her nipples brush against his lips. They are soft and smell like clay. He latches on to nurse, his mouth filling with skin and then he feels all of her body, all of her weight pressing down and then his penis is hugged very hard, tight, stretched up and down and he feels himself gasp around her breast and he opens his eyes. The nipple slips from his mouth. He sees her face rocking in his vision and she places his hand on his penis. He squeezes hard, as hard as when he lifted the star from the clay, and a connection is made. It is at the moment when he looks from the sky to her face, and from her face to her eyes, that he feels the pressure release and his back leaves the ground, trying to pass through her to the sky and she rises with him. She feels light against him and coming down, her breasts flatten against his chest and his legs tremble. He feels her shake slightly, her hips and arms, and her breath matches each shudder.

When the blue sky returns, he feels the star still in his grasp. He is aware too, as she lays against him, heavy and quiet that now there are two sounds. Two pairs of sounds. He moves under her, at first gently and then struggling. He sees her face again. Her face is in pain and her eyes are full. He knows somehow she is worried. He pulls himself up and back into shadow, sitting against the curve of the pit, knees up, head down. He feels her touch him on the shoulder and he flinches. She wipes his hand with a napkin. He feels tears come from his eyes. And they are his tears and he knows why he is crying. He is scared. Bewildered. Confused. Because for the first time he realizes the sound, the I here, I here, I here, I here he has always heard did not come from her—does not comes from anyone outside himself. The thud of soft comfort resounding with the curving horizon lines is the echo of his own heart.

He understands he is separate.

* * *

Melody sat in the plaid chair in the front room, alone. The infant was asleep on her bed, and her breasts felt cold and heavy, her arms light and empty from having only the cool weight of air. She wanted to smoke, but it had been too long and now she hated the smell. She really just liked the idea of having paper between her fingers, the familiar bend in her arm, and the sound of her own breath as she exhaled, the taste of tobacco lingering along the roof of her mouth.

Henry was pouring her coffee from the percolator.

"Black?" he said.

She nodded and he passed a chipped china cup, white with a faded yellow and pink rose pattern. He sat down to her left, his back to the window and the closed drapes, a mug of coffee between his legs.

"So what do we name him?" she asked.

"What?"

"What do we call him?"

"He's Native American. Indian."

"You sure?"

"She was Indian. I know she was Indian. She probably came from over past Pearblossom."

"There's no reservation there," Melody began and then lowered her voice, "but I guess people can live anywhere."

"There's a few Hopi families living out there. Not a tribe or anything like that. I think there's a Pueblo family too. Or maybe they're Navajo."

Melody did not want to talk about her any more—the woman under the mountain. She meant the end of everything. If she were found, the infant would be taken. Her existence was not to be uncovered. She was a threat, real, lurking, stronger now than Death and, for the moment, far more pressing.

"His name is Clay."

Henry looked up at her and saw her staring at him.

"Clay what?"

"Clay Colliery." She paused. "Sort of an aunt I had."

The silence was long and clear and Melody finally let a sigh escape her lips and felt the heat of coffee in her mouth give way to cool air on the inhale.

Henry finally brought the mug to his mouth and took a long drink of coffee. "Well," he said and he smiled a stiff smile, his face unaccustomed to the wash of something warm and beyond himself. "Sounds good to me."

Melody sat back in her chair. A purpose had wedged itself in her life and she could hardly stand the lightness of the room, the clarity of thought. For a moment she was alone with hope and then she was crying again, hot tears sliding down her face and Henry was kneeling beside her holding her in a funny position, trying to lift her long hair back from her face but succeeding only in awkwardly patting the side of her head.

A little later, after the baby woke, Henry brought the Valiant around to the front door. No one was out and the sand was empty. Not even Zach and Oxena were in sight. He left the passenger door open and skipped up the steps two at a time to open the door for Melody. She carried a large paper bag from Vons in her arms. The bag was full and lumpy and when Melody sat down in the car she lowered the bag carefully on her lap. Henry got behind the wheel and in a moment they were out onto Rte. 14, dust lifting behind them. Neither of them saw Hattie peeking from her window, pulling her front door open, or her face when she saw Melody look around and then reach into the bag, pull out an infant, and place it to her breast. As the car drove passed Hattie's open door, it slammed shut.

* * *

Kinni moved, shivered on the bed, woke and was left sightless by the shards of light shining in sheared lengths through the slats of her venetian blinds. Light and dark in a regimented pattern that made her grope to the tie and snap the binds completely shut. She was a creature of the dark and she was not prepared to be revealed between light and dark, unwhole and in pieces. She heard Tip whinny outside and when she walked to the kitchen to get a glass of orange juice she saw him standing outside with his bridle still on, chewing the weeds which lined her concrete patio out in back. Her trailer and Barday's faced the desert and Tip's corral of barbed wire and old railroad ties was just beyond the concrete slab.

She took small sips of juice, staring at Tip, trying to decide why it was he would be eating the weeds, his dull yellow back still wet and dark from a long ride, easing his weight from side to side as he grazed. Tip looked up for a moment and saw her through the glass. He shied slightly, stepping on himself, and his head dipped and then he stepped on his reins and he was down on his knees, one front leg out, the reins caught under the bent leg. He lunged once and blood appeared on the concrete as he gashed his leg.

Kinni rode ponies in Japan. Little tiny ponies, much like Shetlands except they were small boned and sleek instead of thick and chunky. She always rode them when they went to the country to her uncle's house on the edge of that stream. The uncles had three ponies, all golden with cream manes and tails. She had no favorites. She liked the way they smelled after they ate hay and mash and often she sat in their feeding bin, pushed and prodded as their big heads moved against her in their quest for food.

Tip was up. Both knees were bleeding. She set the empty glass of juice down on the counter. But it was when she heard him scream, a kind of long howling whinny and he stepped back from the concrete slab and his eyes rolled, that she moved toward the sliding glass door. Her bathrobe was on the back of the kitchen chair. He howled once more, head up, nostrils flared and the reins danced dangerously under his feet again. He was alone.

When she stepped outside, she was unaccustomed to the feeling of air against her face. She felt light, distended, somehow floating above the scene which all seemed too bright, too clear, too unwebbed. She had to squint very hard to protect her eyes. She saw her arm reach out and catch the reins. She laid a hand on his neck he pulled against her once and she jerked down hard on the bit. He froze, still tense and quivering, panting from his ordeal and then, as she stroked his neck and face, he began to relax and his head dropped closer to the ground. Her fingers rolled unevenly over the tiny white scars on his face. She led him over to the barbed gate, aware of the sky and the sand, feeling almost lost by space suddenly revealed, and lifted the wooden latch and walked in with him. He lowered his head obediently and she slipped off the bridle, spit falling in frothy white flecks from the bit. Her bare feet, unaccustomed to the heat and rocks were tender and she stepped from side to side as she watched him move to the bath tub and drink large gulps of water. She draped the bridle over the fence. When she closed the gate again, Tip came over and nibbled at the twine hinges. She turned back to the trailer, focused on the sliding screen door as a destination point and crossed the concrete patio, her eyes dropping only once to see the blood on the blue-white concrete slab.

She just stepped inside when she heard the moan. At first she thought it was Tip again and turned on the top step to look back toward the corral. He was standing attentively by the porcelain bathtub, looking off to her left, flicking flies off his hind legs with swishes of his tail. His ears tilted forward. He shifted his gaze to her and then back to his focus point again. She turned her head to the left, took a step down, and followed his stare.

There was an old pile of bricks right outside Barday's back door. Nothing had ever been done with them. They were used brick and chunks of mortar still clung to them. It was the red of the mortar that struck her first, the blood like spilled burgundy, soaked up by porous baked clay. Barday faced her, chest down, eyes closed, blood across his forehead, the Union hat knocked a few feet away in the sand. She climbed back down the stairs and walked over to where he lay, focused on the rubble, on the angles of the brick, of where there was blood, of how today, now, there was no dust or smoke rising from the rubble and no cries coming from underneath. Barday lay sprawled on his stomach, his right arm underneath him, his left foot twisted half buried in the brick. He was beginning to move, coming out of a drugged dream and moaned again, softly, his free hand next to his face shaking. He tried to blink, but blood dried across his eyelids. He coughed, raising his head slightly and blood came from his lips.

When Kinni reached him she said nothing

"Who's that?" he called out and she saw where he had bitten through his lip.

She reached down and removed the bricks from around his foot. He moved his leg and the cavalry boot dragged across the pile of brick.

"I think I fell. I fell in a well," he said, disoriented, lost, his voice quivering. Kinni put a hand on his back and pushed hard to help him sit. The touch of his back, of feeling bones under her palm was repugnant. Of feeling someone alive. The hand and arm which was under him was cut and bleeding and spread dark stains under the blue coat.

She bent down further, put her knee against the brick, placed his good arm around her neck, and pushed up with her other leg. When they stood, the weight she carried seemed familiar, not difficult, but she could feel his breath against her face, against the skin on her face and she turned away.

"I cannot see in front of me, not a stone or rock or–" he mumbled as they climbed around the pile of bricks and up the two steps to his trailer. The back door was slightly ajar and she kicked it open wide with her foot. It smelled musty and alive, like wet canvas. She got him to the sofa, old, dark, ripped with coarse cotton bulging from along the back and had him sit, slowly, his head tilted to one side and up, resting against the batting, his neck exposed. She saw one arm fall on the arm of the sofa.

"The baby cries alone in the wood, and if I could see and make do where I stood, I'd find that baby–"

Kinni moved in a trance to the sink, shifting dishes aside, ignoring flies and greasy water, found an old tea towel and ran the cold water. In the desert you always have to wait for cold water–here water lays hot in the pipes. She held the tea towel under the spigot for just a moment, wrung out the towel and crossed the small room to the sofa. She did not see the piles of canned goods stacked along the kitchen floor four feet deep or the dirt and mold etched in the linoleum floor or the pieces of carpet worn away and the rough brown of exposed plywood underneath. She could barely see Barday and she had to consciously focus her attention on him, on him lying back against the cushions, on the gash on his head, on his need for her right at this time, or she would lose him completely and walk away from the sofa.

She sensed all this without reflection. And when she looked down on her white bathrobe and saw his blood streaked across her sleeve, she knew enough to look away, quickly, and not allow herself a second chance at thought.

LIGHT AND SPACE

Hattie on closed spaces

My heart is a closed space. Tight, dark, pinched. Usually I ignore its cramping, the sharp ache of contracted muscle, pretend I am as wide as the sea, and people say, "Oh, Hattie Peach—such a nice person." All knowing, all forgiving. But then something happens: I watch friends leaning on each other, or see a hurried mother's sudden smile, or spy a young couple's soft anticipating touches, or watch an elderly pair sit silently in the sun—all acts bred from familiarity—and I feel the cramping and I'm disgusted with myself. I need that familiarity, and I don't have it. All I ever succeed in doing is catching Henry's hurt looks, glances and turns of the head which tighten my heart even more.

Even the times I thought I was in love, my heart remained brittle and I ended up sending them off, and watched them join the Air Force, go to college, disappear on a Harley. My first love was named Alan Parks and he was sweet and kind, but slow and watched too much basketball. When he found out I was still a virgin at twenty-three, he left me ripe and sweaty in bed and stood out under the stars, looking up at the night sky, overwhelmed by what he called his "responsibility" to me. We ended up making love two nights later and six months after that my interest dissolved. It evaporated when I realized what I was pretending was love was really a farce and I could not love. Too many closed spaces. The safest love is from afar.

That is why my door slammed when I saw Henry and Melody leave with the paper bag. I could feel ventricles constricting. I saw Henry moving gently, helping her down the steps, a hand on her elbow, watched her lift the baby from the bag and press the infant's head to her chest, saw the expression in Henry's face as he watched them, and as the car rolled by my door, saw only my own face reflected off the glass of the passenger window. It was a small, squished face, and one that I don't want to see again for a long time.

I sat for a long time on the sofa, looking nowhere, waiting. I've lived my whole life refusing to name the elements of my world. Because nothing is named, nothing is familiar and the intimacy I crave remains elusive. But there was something familiar about that face reflecting back—there was a link to the past I could draw on and I realized I had sat in the same state the morning after Henry threw the trunk away. When all her things disappeared. When I had slept out against the round rocks, on the stiff river grass and cried. I was betrayed that day. And I was betrayed again this morning, by both of them. Just like before. First Henry and Arlene and now Henry and Melody.

Melody was just supposed to nurse children, unseen, giving them nourishment and security, not harbor a child for herself. She was supposed to remain wide open, endless in her capacity for giving love all in rough counterpoint to me. I saw us as a kind of informal team, with her making up for all my closed spaces. Just being with her, watching her arms move with wrestling children, hearing her laugh and seeing little fingertips against her skin was enough for me. Though handicapped, I could still live through her and she carried a limitless capacity for taking on the needs of others, whether she knew it or not. That in itself drew me to her. That she could extend herself so much and not even be aware of what she was fulfilling. But it was over. All of it and I was being left behind, to fend for myself.

I knew by the way she held the baby the infant was hers. No one else's. This child would demand all of her and she would embrace her role without ever recognizing the huge gaping hole she leaves behind. Even Henry, by his face, is being left behind on some level. He is trying to be with them, become one with the two of them and he is being shut out, off, hungry, incrementally circumvented as only fathers can be.

And Henry has betrayed me. This is probably the worst. After all these years of not wanting his pain, of learning how to measure and occupy distance, he remains not just unaware of my efforts, but is caught in the illuminating web of new life. He has stepped from death to life without a glance back at me, leaving me with the marble paper and thoughts unsaid and unwritten. I don't know how he managed it, this transition, so quickly. But I envy him and hate him—envy because

I still need to fill that marble paper and hate because he's left me behind as well. It's as if he's forgotten how often he licked his wounds and that he's always done it in front of me.

Now you see how hard and how quickly my heart can tighten. I used to feel the same anguish trapped inside that trunk, with her smell breathing around me and sometimes I'd kick the sides, hard, as if still in the womb, angry with her, furious and blind, knowing that soon I would have to leave her crimson satin sanctuary and venture out into the world. Once, I held her black little box of watercolors against my chest, the lid open and as I cried I could feel the cool smoothness of the oval colors as they lay hard and symmetrical, and, ultimately invisible.

Melody on open spaces

There has always been too much space around me, even when I lived with the nuns. I could be alone in my tiny little room, lying on my cot, but thinking about everything around me and of how it could all disappear. Because of all the space out there. Space isn't empty. It's filled with cars and airplanes, murderers and rapists, cells that won't stop dividing, rude people, fascists, liars, floods, fires, earthquakes, tornadoes, nuclear power plants, bad wiring, and even simple things like glass or lightning. Just think of it. Out of that vast huge and endless sky, filled with nothing but space, can come a sword of electricity bent and jagged, aiming just for you.

That's why I try to fill up space with people. Little people who don't hurt me and who depend on me to keep the things in that space at bay. I noticed a long time ago that I almost never have bad daydreams when I'm with kids. I never feel the impact of my own death when I'm nursing. Those thoughts which leap from the outside never penetrate my brain and I relax and am content. The mothers always comment on how calm I am with the children. That I don't worry and that it's good I let them play the way I do, without holding them back. But I have to stay alert, I can't afford to be caught daydreaming when I'm with them.

When I woke that first morning with Clay right there and Henry sitting in the chair I could feel all that space pressing, bearing down and I was paralyzed, frozen, even before I looked down on his little sweaty head and pouting lips. He was so vulnerable, so small and fragile, so near death at any moment and yet he was life and I would give him life. Life had suddenly turned to glass and could be shattered at any moment, not by daydreams, but real tragedy. He could just stop breathing. His liver could stop functioning. He could choke on his own spittle. I could drop him. He could get an infection.

Giving him a name made me realize that there was something lurking out there in all that space more threatening than what I could imagine. It was real, immediate and was going to happen no matter what I did. One day, either tomorrow, or next week or ten years from now, someone was going to come and try and take him away from me.

So I have to act. I have to be sure no one will ever succeed in separating us. I have to be certain in my own mind he's my son. No matter who shows up: the state, the social service people, lost family. It doesn't matter. He's mine.

Henry and I have said very little to each other. We both seem to know what must be done, because Henry's a big part of this. When we got in the car and pulled out onto Rte. 14 heading east to Palmdale and the airport, I knew we were all connected like pieces in a puzzle. I watched Henry driving the car, holding his cigarette out the window, smoke screaming behind us as the needle hit sixty on the speedometer. I looked out the window and saw Vasquez looming up in back of Raceway, bathed in sun, all those rocks lying sideways. And I saw purple mountains behind them, way in the distance, and all that blue blue sky.

Clay needed to nurse then and the road curved behind a mountain. By the time he was sucking, we came out from around the curve and were looking out over a different panorama. This time, foothills and yucca rolled on and on and seemed to flow forever to a rolling horizon line. The views were nearly the same in all directions: mountains, scrub oak, yucca, and rock. I realized how simple it was to scan all that space and I sat back, saw Henry looking at me, and I smiled.

Lani on the properties of shadows

Shadows are tricky. If you do it right, if you take your goddamn time, shadows can make a black and white shot really dramatic. That's why I like black and white. Even if the take isn't exactly what you wanted, if it's in black and white even your stupid mistake appears intentional. I guess people take black and white for face value–they don't question it. But color's a tricky thing. With color, shadows can absolutely ruin a shot. Somehow intent is a lot clearer with color and if you fuck it up with bad shadows, everybody knows. But if you do it right, shadows can bring out depth and texture. You can make someone pay attention to hidden dark places and different shades of color–make them aware of the dark space while taking in the light. The effect can be fucking awesome.

But black and white is safer. The risk is small. Basically, no chance of failure. And if you do fail, no one needs to know. They just nod and say, "Ooh, that's kind-of stark." And I like starkness anyway. That's why I live out here.

When I saw Bat with his head on his knees and I thought I heard him crying, everything was in color. The yellow light on my arms, the brown and gray of rock and sand, the streaks of white between the brown, the red earth below and the blue sky above. Even the air around us had a quality of color, making everything bright, sharp, allowing shadows to accent the scene around us. And there was Bat sitting in shadow, his color outlining him against the lines of earth, all pitched into darker hues because of the lack of light. I wanted to do that shot. In color. Nothing could go wrong. But I didn't take it. All I had in my camera was black and white film. And I didn't want him in black and white. For the first time I wanted real risk, I guess.

But I felt bad in a way. My heart was heavy and lumpy and I wanted to cry too because I know he knew, somehow, what we did. Not that we fucked, because we didn't. That wasn't fucking. But we were very close and I know he made some tie between me and coming, a connection between me and him and I think maybe that's the first connection he's made. Ever. In his whole life. I mean, it was pretty intense. I mean I still don't know what I even feel about it. Christ, he's eight years younger than me. A kid.

I guess in a way it wasn't really even sex. I mean with sex, there's got to be some kind of appeal. I do it because I like the way the guy's butt hangs, or the way his voice sounds, or how his arms look, and, let's admit it, it feels fucking good even if I don't come. And the guy does it with me because I wear my high heels in the desert and both my legs and hair are long and I'm willing to do it—I think that in itself is appealing. It's like desert-fantasy or something: woman shows up from the shadows of desert rock to fuck unsuspecting man's brains out, and she disappears. No ties, no commitment, no phone calls.   Christ, I'm every man's fantasy and that's not saying a hell of a lot.

But with Bat, he wasn't after me, he was after himself. Coming was probably just a physical thing—I mean if you rub it enough, it's going to happen—but it was a physical thing with himself, not me. It made him aware of himself and because he found a piece of himself, he was able to find me. As for me, I know I'm not attracted to skinny fifteen year-old boys.

That's why I can't really understand why I liked all the color and saw the shadows so perfectly. Usually I'm afraid of risk. Especially now of all times, when I think I'm at the beginning of love. I don't know anyone who's been present at the origins of love. People fall in love with each other and they watch it unfold, I guess, but to be there as love is being created...to see something evolve from two completely empty slates? Bat wasn't even there enough to know his own name— he's a guy walking around with no past. No present. No future. No something that could be named. Nothing connected. And then I connected with him. And I think that started it off, really. I think love was the first seed in his consciousness.

And hell, my slate is about as empty, let's face it. But the only reason I know that is because of how hard I was crying sitting next to him in that red clay-hole.

I just put my arms around him and held him while he cried, hoping he'd realize sooner or later that the same person was still sitting here with him. And that the person holding him was me. That was really important.

When he finally lifted his face, he found me right away and I could see little red veins in the white of each golden eye. I tried hard to stop crying, afraid it might scare him. He blinked and heavy tears melted from each eyelid and slid down his face. He opened his eyes again.

"Bat," he said.

"Lani," I said and bit my lip.

"Star," he said. He dropped an arm, opened one tight fist and handed me the bone.

The sun was very bright and lit the hole completely. I wiped my eyes, but the feel of the star in my hand made them fill again. I had to shade my eyes with my hands as I leaned forward to kiss him on the cheek. When I stood, I realized it must have been noon, because all the shadows had slipped away.

Kinni on the properties of light

I do not understand light. I know that light is different in Japan. The passage of light equals the passage of time and I have no need to record the turning of time. Light is a particle and a wave. Days are either filled with tiny separate, instantaneous events or with situations which flow easily from one to the other like water. I know only that reflection occurs only in lighted space.

I wipe Barday's eyes with a damp cloth, dipping the towel into a bowl of warm water and bringing it to his face over and over again. The repetition is good, keeps me from watching him. He mumbles something and tries to move my arm away, but I am stronger than he and his hand is light and hot against my cool skin. I continue to wipe his eyes and he leans back, relaxes, and lets the water run off his temples crimson and warm.

The back of the sofa is growing wet with blood and water and I must bend him forward to remove his coat. I can barely stand to touch his skin and as I pull off his white shirt, I see how very old he is. Papery thin skin, pores collapsing into sagging lines and wrinkles, chest hair brittle and gray, veins filled with tiny knots just under the skin lacing his arms. There is a tattoo on his shoulder, an American flag, waving on a simple flagpole. The colors of the tattoo are vibrant only because of the pallor of his skin. I take off his boots, one by one, and then push him down on his side.

He is naked now, lying under a sheet I pulled off his bed. He is asleep. I empty the water in the sink, watching red mixing with old food, and then return to kneel beside him. I tip his head up so it falls back and I can wash his forehead and find the gash.

But it is still quite dark and I cannot see. I reach up and turn on the light. The switch works, but the bulb is burned out. I stand and pull back the curtains, old heavy green carpet drapes backed with canvas and light floods the room. I am caught in a maelstrom, forced back to my knees and must focus on the towel, wiping, bring my hand to his face again. Repeating the pattern.

And then he moans. The sound of pain. But time does not stop, and I am searching for the gash, looking through blood and matted hair for the cut and find it, dirty, jagged, a three inch tear just above the hair line on the right side. I do not understand how I am able to watch him with his eyes closed, or wash blood from his head or see the pulse in his thin neck beat. Each beat I see is a particle of time.

The wound is clean, as clean as I can get it with dish soap and water. I have laid toilet paper over it and wrapped a piece of sheeting around his head. This is the best I can do. Though I feel the need to leave, I do not. I sit, careful to remain in the shadow of the room, but look out across the trailer park. No one can see me, but I have a vantage point. I sit and watch from my spot on the floor. The day, I see, is beautiful. The sky is cloudless and deep blue. The sun is bright but does not glare. I hear him sigh behind me on the sofa and stir slightly. He says something softly, but I do not turn my face to hear.

I do not turn, because from where I sit, in shadow, I can see directly across into another's kitchen and hall. And standing in the hall is a huge bird, black as night, and though no light penetrates its feathers, it is lit from behind by a second window I cannot see. It stands illuminated in the hall like some apparition. And then I see it is eating. Eating flesh, strips of meat, feeding slowly, not rushed by fear, but in time measured by hunger.

It is when I feel the heat of the sun on my chin and I see Oxena appear at the window. She turns directly to me and I sit back suddenly, feeling my face slip into shadow. The blinds of the kitchen shut quickly and I put a hand over my face. Properties of light, of heat and warmth, are seductive and I need my veil.

NOTES OF SONG

Parker Limpid tries to slam the glass door behind him, but it is equipped with hydraulic hinges and closes with an irritatingly slow metallic whisper.

"Can't find it?" says Puez, setting down her coffee mug.

"No. Francis and Guillepse are running more diagnostics, but we're coming up to the four hour loop again and I know he's going to tell us Diana's filling with mass." He flops into his chair and it swivels him into position in front of his computer.

"Maybe we can freeze the data there, inside the detector."

"What we need is something what we don't have the technology for yet. A terminal display of the particles in a visual format, laid out where we can see what he's reporting." Parker scans his screen, touches a couple of keys and the monitor flickers.

"But according to you, we'd be facing a black screen."

"Maybe. He thinks it's there. He thinks he's got something in there. Zeus must be making up the projections themselves. And if he's doing that at least we could see what the hell he thinks he's got."

"So you still see it as a math problem. You think Zeus's making up the figures."

"Hell yes."

She pauses for a moment. "What if we are at the beginning?"

"Of?"

She is nodding slightly and notices her heart is beating harder and between each breath, coming quickly, lightly, is the thrill of secrets.

"Time," she manages to breathe.

There is a moment between them that is pure, full of hope, and then he ruins it with the tone of his voice.

"Jesus, Puez."

She will not be put off. "We've been able to take it all back, back nearly to the beginning, take it back 10^{-35} seconds after the big bang to some sort of symmetry breaking event and then everything gets muddy. It's not until 10^{-11} seconds afterward, when bosons were created, that we can pick up the thread again."

He is watching her, not saying anything.

"But between those two points is the desert. That stretch of time when nothing is supposed to have happened. Nothing. But something happened to give us all four forces. Something happened or we wouldn't be here."

"So what happened?"

"I don't know. But maybe Zeus here has managed to glimpse some sort of primordial particle. The mother of all particles. We could be looking at the face of time, Parker."

He sighs. "This is too ethereal for me. He's malfunctioning. It's obvious."

Puez sits back, arms folded. "And he's just making this all up from nothing."

"Well I don't know if he's doing it from nothing. There's a reason for the malfunction."

"But not a physical reason."

For a moment Parker sits very still. "I don't know." He pauses. "It's been postulated that photons can communicate with each other over light years, without ever traveling anywhere near each other. If this is true, maybe there really is something in there, a kind of antiproton and you may be right. They exist on paper." He shrugs. "But I doubt it. It would be momentous. You and I would have Nobels up to our necks."

"Like whale songs. The photons you mean."

"I don't know. What about whales?" Parker knows very little about living things.

"Their calls can carry over thousands and thousands of miles. Without all the garbage in the ocean, a whale could sing to another whale in a sea on the other side of the world."

Parker grins. "Am I right here? Are you trying to equate whale songs with photons?"

Puez glances at him. "Don't you think that's fascinating?"

"What?"

"That a right whale off the coast of Chile could communicate with a sister off the coast of Alaska."

"What was your dissertation on?"

Puez takes another sip of coffee. He is probing for some reason. He never asks personal questions. But she feels the question is safe. None-the-less, she begins with an apology. "You know I'm a physicist at heart, not by training."

"I know, so what was your dissertation on?"

She shrugs, "It's embarrassing."

"So."

Puez sighs. It was years ago. She was the only woman in her class. She was sexless and that was the best way. "The genetics of race horses."

Parker laughs. "Race horses?"

"Yes, and no jokes."   She is suddenly aware of their age difference. He looks like a kid. A skinny teenager. Pale, tired, hair wild with talk of horses and the race track. She can tell she has his interest. "It was actually a very good paper. I published it several times. Not much has been done with race horses, then or now." She settles back, comfortable with her coffee. Glad not to hear the echo-cry. "I thought it would be interesting to trace the dynamics of how people took something as man-made and fabricated as the structure of a race and the need to win, that competitive challenge—whatever you want to call it—and somehow implant these urges into an animal. Horses don't race in the wild. They run in herds. They don't compete with time, we gave them that need. How, though. That's what I wanted to know."

"So you're an animal freak." Parker smiles and taps his desk with the eraser end of a pencil. "Well, did you solve the mystery and win a Nobel?"

"No.   I mean who knows? My quest became very narrowly defined very quickly, and I ended up studying the bloodlines of the first twelve thoroughbreds. From Spain." She glances up at her terminal.

"Thoroughbreds. What were you a jockey in a former life? Hey, do you have a bookie topside?"

"When I was a girl, way before your time by the way, I read about a horse named Eclipse who ran the Preakness, fell on the home stretch, picked himself up and not only finished, but won. When he was taken to the winners circle, he dropped dead."

"Heart attack?" Parker swivels to face his terminal.

Puez nods. "He'd also broken a leg. But the most amazing thing was when they opened him up, they discovered he had only one lung."

Parker stops tapping and swivels back to face her.

"Yeah. Somehow, we bred into that poor horse the need to kill himself." Puez glances at the screen above her head again and set down her coffee cup. "What the hell?"

She looks at Parker and then back at her screen and she can feel the odd quiver of uncertainty and a sliver of fear move like breath down her back. She clears her throat.

"Zeus's shutting down." She adjusts her glasses.

"What?" Parker Limpid does not hear her clearly or believe what he hears.

Puez half rises from her chair and glances across the instrument panel. "I think he's shutting down, Parker." She does not understand what is going on and for an instant she thinks she hears the cry again in her own ear.

Dr. Francis opens the glass door again. "All detectors are closing out," he says and Parker does not like the opaque blond-red of Dr. Francis' beard. "And the cathode gun is shutting down."

So they sit and watch, quietly, without having the ability to check what they see or a chance to analyze the event, as small lights, one by one, are extinguished from a broad black glass display panel above their heads. More of the crew step in to Parker and Puez's office, standing, necks stretched, cause and purpose not just escaping the observers but their absence providing no hypotheses either.

"They're not all closing out," says Puez, smiling, though she does not know why the smile has appeared, "Diana's is still functioning."

Parker whistles low and even, just one note.

FORCES

Hattie sat on her stool at the volcano. Bert was not talking. He was watching an old Star Trek re-run on Channel 13. The picture was fuzzy and rolled and he leaned back against the bar and exhaled smoke, his head tilted up, the side of his face to her.

Bert had a breakfast special, a cup of coffee, a piece of toast and an egg for 69 cents. Hattie always got two pieces of toast, no extra charge. She laid the egg, which he cooked over hard, on top of one slice of toast and saved the other to smear with grape jelly from the bowl of teaspoon sized plastic jelly packages on the counter. That piece of toast was to have with her coffee. When she was little, back in Chicago, Henry would make her toast with boysenberry jam and a cup of hot chocolate. It was wonderful. Grape jelly and coffee could never come close, but would have to do. Henry would tell her stories, history stories while she ate, legs dangling from the kitchen chair. They both pretended not to remember the woman lying in bed in the next room.

Of the stories he told, her favorites were of the Trojan horse, of slaves bound for America, the underground railroad, the families hidden in Germany, famous escapes, the fame of Houdini, the wave of immigrants from Ireland and Eastern Europe, the internment camps in California—stories of people who were forced into hiding from the point of strategy or survival. There were many, many of these stories to tell. He always told them as if he had really been there. That's how he taught his classes in school. The one about the Trojan horse she liked the best.

"So," he'd say, the toast popping up, "I hated the way the inside of that horse smelled. Too many men, we were all Greeks you know, and not enough air. The road was so bumpy. I hit my head on the roof, it was curved, every time we'd hit a hole in the ground. We knew," he would be setting out the jam by now, "we would either die or be victorious against the Trojans."

There was hot chocolate to sip. "What kind of wood was it?"

"It smelled piney. I think it was hemlock and sap was all over the walls on the inside. Sticky stuff," and to prove the memory correct, he'd make a face at a dribble of jam on his fingers and press his index finger and thumb together.

"How far did you have to go?"

"Miles and miles and it was dark. We couldn't light fires because we'd burn up the horse."

"And you won? They got tricked?"

"We slaughtered them," he'd say and smile. "Troy was ours. It really worked. We got up inside where they lived and they closed their big old gates behind us and then we busted out."

"But why?"

"Why?"

"Why did you have to sneak around like that?"

"Because it was the only way we could win. Why else?"

This Monday, there were no stories, only Captain Kirk talking about eternity being sacred. It was noon and hardly anyone had been in all morning. But it seemed Bert was about to get a rush. A moment later, a man and a woman stepped in, outsiders, tanned and lean and serious. They both carried clipboards with papers curling at the ends and both wore large wide brimmed straw hats.

"Excuse me," said the man, blond, in his mid-thirties. "We've been tracking a California condor for the last several weeks and we've lost it." He focused on Hattie. "You know the kind of bird I'm talking about? It's a big bird, gigantic wingspan. You couldn't miss it if you saw it. A little black girl over at that trailer park told me she saw a big bird yesterday."

"I haven't seen a thing. Sun's bad for me," said Bert, quite chipper, and then he added, "Can I get you folks anything? Sandwich? Something cold to drink? Beer?"

The man shifted his gaze from Hattie to the menu taped to the cash register, but the woman was watching her.

"I saw it yesterday too," said Hattie. She sat up a little on her stool. "I saw it about two o'clock, I guess. It circled right above the trailers and then took off."

"Hey Cheryl, what do you want?" the man tapped her on the arm. "Pastrami or turkey, that's what the guy's got."

She glanced back at her partner. "Pastrami." Then to Hattie. "We had it tagged with a radio emit like this one," she said, holding up what looked like a tiny transistor radio with a stubby antenna. "Oh, I'm sorry, I'm Cheryl Henderson and this is Matt Durrel. We're with UCLA and the Condor Project."

She was in her early forties or so, perfect build, strong looking legs and a thick wedding band. Her straight hair was graying and neatly pulled back in a ponytail. With her khaki shorts, leather work belt and white polo shirt, she looked fresh from the pages of National Geographic. Hattie felt caught up in the search and a little put off by her own eagerness to be helpful. There was a sense of importance and purpose and they invited her, Hattie Peach, to join them.

Cheryl continued. "We found this emitter by its nest early this morning."

Hattie looked down at the smaller version Cheryl held in her hand.

"It tore off?"

"No," said Matt, collecting change from Bert, "We think someone cut it off."

"See, this was a female we were tracking. But most important, it's the last one in the wild. We also," Cheryl paused and looked at Matt, "we also found what looks like fresh digging on the opposite side of the mountain from where the nest was. We don't have shovels, but if something's buried it up there...I mean if someone killed it... and there's a whopping fine, and, well, we just need to know what's going on. We just need a little help," Cheryl said.

Hattie cleared her throat. "What do you mean?"

Matt, grabbing two greasy sandwiches and hugging them in their paper plate cocoons said, "We need someone who's got a shovel."

* * *

Hattie watches them dig. She feels odd, detached from the group, but pleased to be with them. Shadows are gone, it is noon and the side of the mountain where they have taken her is on the edge of Vasquez, where they rocks ebb back into the dirt again. She is vaguely aware of being excited, aware of a tremulous thrill of being with other people, different people who are on a very tangible search. She is watching Matt dig straight down, the shovel slipping easily into the light with stones moving a little too freely. They all notice how strange the earth is, too unpacked, too uniform. Cheryl and Matt ask her questions about her past, how long she's lived here, chit-chat. They cast their eyes to the sky every now and then, still searching for the huge silhouette. Hattie watches only the shovel.

The tip hits a rock and the handle twists in Matt's hands, and he and Cheryl lean down to move rocks out of the way. Cheryl waves Matt aside and kneels against the mountain herself. Together she and Hattie move several large stones out of the way, and Matt continues digging, but there is nothing underneath. Hattie can tell the ground has grown suddenly hard and unyielding and after five more minutes, Matt glances to Cheryl, sweat pouring down his face.

"Let's give it up."

The two scientists stand in the heat appraising the situation, and the tremor of excitement leaves Hattie. She feels suddenly out of place. Out-classed.

"No, wait a minute," says Cheryl and takes the shovel from him. "This is just too weird. Something's got to be here," she says and squats down, sticks the edge of the shovel into the side of Matt's hole, into the mountain, and gives it a hard push sideways with her foot. A large mound of crumbling earth loosens easily into the cupped blade and she staggers slightly with the weight. Hattie watches her dump the dirt off to the side, re-insert the shovel and then drop the handle.

In slow motion, Cheryl sinks to the ground, holding her throat, making odd squeaking noises from her mouth and Hattie steps up and forward, looking down, looking long enough to hear Matt say, "Holy Jesus Christ. Cheryl. Oh my God," and then peering sideways into hole to see a human foot, blue-gray and waxish sticking out from fallen earth.

Hattie sees just enough to feel sick. She steps back. Everything is bright. Too bright and she squints. She picks up the shovel. Fear moves her now. Real fear, primal, coming from her middle and flaring at her hands, beating in her temples, circles upon circles, a supernatural fear that the force has finally reached up through the ground and sucked Henry straight into Vasquez.

She can hear Matt yelling at her to stop, but she has no control and in another moment she is digging, moving earth, turning dirt over, revealing another foot.

"Put that fucking thing down."

He is shouting at her and Cheryl has moved way down the side of the mountain. Hattie sees her turn and run toward Raceway. She fills the shovel again and again, fast, because Matt is trying to take it away from her, but in another second her quest is over. It is not Henry. There is a floral print sticking up now through the dirt like the tuft of a red, pink and white flag.

She feels the force of Matt's grip and the shovel is pulled from her hands. He tosses it aside. She steps back and steps back again, tripping slightly over loose sand, rocks, the shovel. She looks down and for the first time notices the rusty brown smear on the wood. Up by the socket. She knows it is blood.

"What the hell was that all about?" Matt shouts at her. He is standing with one hand on her shoulder trying to pull her even further away. "What the hell are you doing?"

"I thought it was my father," she says, aware of her hair in her face and how hard her hands are shaking.

"What?"

How could she explain that somehow between this morning and this moment Henry could have been buried, sucked under by riptides.

"Leave me alone," she whispers.

"What?"

"I have to think," she says and looks down to Raceway. "Somebody has to—has to call the police," she says.

She watches him back away from her and suddenly realizes he is afraid of her. There is something very funny about this, about the way he is looking at her, and she laughs, a high, nervous laugh which ends equally suddenly when she feels vomit fill her mouth.

* * *

It was a woman. An Indian woman who died and was buried. Definitely buried they said, though no one noticed she was facing east and when they exhumed her body they didn't bother to cross her arms over her chest and they took off the beads from around her throat and put them in a manila envelope. She was lying on two branches of wood inside the grave. There were four police cars, two ambulances, a coroner's car and a fire truck all parked at the base of the mountain. Everything was mowed down Hattie noticed, yucca, cactus, flowers.

They roped the side of the mountain off with fluorescent orange tape, looping it over yucca to keep people well removed. Even Hattie and the group from UCLA didn't see the body. Just a hand that fell from the stretcher and was quickly stuffed back under the sheeting. There were photo sessions, kids yelling from down the hill, a dog was kicked back beyond the orange ribbon.

Hattie was up on the mountain until nearly three in the afternoon. They spoke with her the longest because of what Matt told them about her. About grabbing the shovel and digging and the comment concerning Henry. Plus she was local. Maybe she knew this woman. Maybe she knew who might have killed her.

But no, no, said the coroner, walking over, a man in his mid-twenties, very young, with a fine complexion and thick black hair, no, I don't think she was killed, sir. I think she died of a hemorrhage. Shut-up is what the sergeant says back to him and the sergeant looks at Hattie as if she were pressed under glass. I know I'm right, is what the coroner says. She hemorrhaged to death. He glances at Hattie and smiles. She gave birth and the placenta peeled badly or she burst something afterwards. She died at childbirth. Or right after. Or maybe she attempted an abortion or something, but if that's the case, she was pretty far along. It does happen you know. Great, says the sergeant, you just blew it asshole.

Hattie cannot feel the sun or smell sage. She is standing alone now on the side of the mountain. She can feel the weight of the shovel in her hands, though it is lying spade down just a few feet away. She is afraid to look at it for fear that her eyes will betray the brown smear on the handle. The sky is still very blue, growing purplish with late afternoon and shadows are beginning to lengthen slightly. She is caught between what she has just seen and what she is seeing right now. Now she is seeing the brown paper bag and Henry's face.

* * *

Lani and Bat walk back from the hole across the desert, toward Raceway, in single file, Bat in front, Lani two steps behind. She plays an old game of setting her foot in his tracks, something she used to play with her mother when she was little. As they near Raceway, they shift positions and she takes the lead and then his hand. But she doesn't know where to take him. She can see Tip standing in his corner looking thin and dusty and as they come closer she sees Kinni, all dressed in black coming from her trailer, across the backyard. Black pants, black sleeveless shirt, black veil. Kinni senses them and turns. Kinni holds very still and Lani speeds up, pulling on Bat, feeling him move along with her.

Kinni turns the veil to them completely as Lani and Bat come around the corral. The breeze is dry and warm and moves across the veil rippling its surface as if the black lace were water. From the depths comes a voice.

"Now is the time," she says, and then, shyly, "If you want to take my picture."

Lani stops and drops Bat's hand. Her camera hangs from her neck again, though now she does not feel its weight. Black and white, she is thinking and decides it will be fine. Kinni's face will dodge light and fill with shadows and the film will see both. Cut off from her, Bat is slowly moving away, adrift and she takes a few steps and lunges for his hand.

"He has to stay with me," she says, "I'm watching him for Celeste." She pauses. "Where do you want to do it? It's up to you."

"Somewhere where there is light and dark," Kinni says slowly. "Somewhere where we can be alone."

"Alone," repeats Lani and thinks of Bat's hole, but they can't return there. Not now. Not so soon at least. Bat is tugging at her hand, pulling her around toward Raceway, pulling hard to make her feet move.

"What?" she says, "What?" He stops and looks at her directly, then drops her hand and, in an awkward movement of arms and wrists, he flings the bone-star up into the air, over the trailers. He looks at her again and smiles.

"Alone," he says, and a moment later, "Heavy sound."

"That would be a good place," says Kinni. "A place where sound is heavy."

* * *

It is one o'clock, they are on the west side of the canyon, up beyond the desert floor and Bat has disappeared into the mineshaft. Lani pauses outside for a moment to see if Kinni will really step inside. She has been slow to follow them and Lani does not know if this is due to hesitation or the fact that time is not a relevant means of measurement. But Kinni does follow Bat inside the shaft, deep enough to move from sun to shade in the twilight of the opening. Bat crouches down, careful not to scrape his head on the crystals above. He sits against part of the wall where there is too much sand to support the crystal growth, and folds his arms across his knees, clasping his wrists down by his ankles. He looks out the opening, eyes blank, unseeing, blind again.

Kinni bends over as well and sit in the center of the mine floor.

"It is smooth here," she says and kneels, sitting up straight. "Are you ready?" she asks, her voice wavering slightly—the quicksilver of the unknown running between her words.

"No, no not yet," says Lani, fumbling with the case, "Yes, yes, now, wait, no. Let me get a light reading on this," she says and holds out her meter.

Kinni lifts her arms and begins to unwind the lace from around her neck. Kneeling as well, Lani raises the camera and centers Kinni in the viewfinder, bending her head down to see the image coming through the lens. The ends of the lace hang long and loose, like obsidian hair over each shoulder.

"I am," Kinni says and her voice is a heavy whisper.

"Go ahead," says Lani and does not look up from the viewfinder.

Through the glass window she sees Kinni bend her head low, and for a moment they mirror each other, kneeling, heads bent, chin to chest and then the veil and cap are lifted off to lie in her lap against her folded legs. She raises her head and though she is still in shadow, her face glows white and all features are presented in clear curving lines. A high, smooth forehead, deep dark set eyes below broad swaths of lids, flawless, poreless cheek bones stretched high above the shallow inward curve of soft cheek dusted with shadow, a tiny flat nose, symmetrical above two slightly pared lips, dark lips outlined by the whiteness of her face. Her jaw is small, an even curve from ear to ear, a clean, round slice of white above the darker hue of her neck and her hair is dark and thick, cut very short, around her ears. Black hair streaked with white, surrounding a face which is unlined, unmarred by time, by wind, by change. Her face has been trapped, caught underneath lace and unconsciousness, and the image is that of a young woman. A child. Lani fingers the trigger, presses and releases many times.

Lani backs out of the mine carefully, easing from the twilight of the shaft, coaxing Kinni to follow. She positions herself outside, the sun burning her left shoulder, and looks again through the viewfinder, standing this time, waiting. Waiting for a long time.

"I'm here," she calls. "I'm still here. Whenever you're ready."

Slowly she sees Kinni's face, slipping from shadow into light, from the mine into day-space and then she sees her whole body moving with small graces from the shadows. Kinni's clothing is gone and Lani depresses the shutter release, rewinds, depresses again, rewinds, again and again as Kinni begins to turn slowly in front of the gaping black hole. Her body is as slender as a young girl's, her breasts very small and flat and the black of her pubis is a closed "v". Her collarbones are perfectly straight, horizontal to the ground and her body is closed, restrained. As she turns, her buttocks move tightly and her hips are small, like a boy's. She does nothing else but turn around once in the hot sun, a small dark pool of shadow lapping her feet.

Lani does not stop once to look up, she is rewinding, pressing, rewinding, moving up a little, back down.

Then she hears Kinni's voice: "I want you to tell the people that I am from Nagasaki." Her lips move like perfect pieces of ripe melon. "I want you to tell them I was there in 1945."

From the mine opening there is a howling, like a coyote, full, haunting. Bat comes into the viewfinder, staggering, his hands—Lani raises her head and shades her eyes—covered in dark red blood.

* * *

Melody steps out of the car. It is two o'clock. She carries Clay with her up the steps to the Homestead, hoping now that someone will see her. But no one is around. Henry is right behind her with a large baby bag, and he makes three more trips out to the car and back to bring in grocery bags full of disposable diapers, cotton swabs, alcohol, baby wipes, cotton diapers, suction nozzle, little fingernail clippers, three glass bottles with nipples, four tiny stretch suits, a couple of flannel receiving blankets, and a baby bucket.

On the fourth trip in he looks different.

"What?" she says. Clay moves in her arms. He is fresh, with clean diapers, baby powder, and wrapped tight, as newborns like to be wrapped, in a white and blue checkered receiving blanket. "What?"

"Look out there," he says, standing behind her and she can feel his arm move as he raises it to point at a spot above the trailers, below the sky and against the mountains. There are blue and red flashing lights, a dot of bright red and the outline of several cars all parked along the hillside in the distance, caught in perspective between the power lines of the trailer park.

Melody holds very still, like a bird testing the wind before flight.

"I have to go," she says. "I have to go. I have to leave."

"He's ours," says Henry and they both stand close to each other and he feels the space between them buckle slightly, wavering with a thread of nervous intimacy. For a long time intimacy has been fed only with memories, with depth but no substance. This moment, there is someone standing beside him, tangible, touchable and there is a kind of quivering pressure he can feel.

"I can't go through with it right now. I don't want them asking questions right now." She looks down at Clay. He is asleep, his lips moving with small pouts and sighs. "We have to go away. Now. Right now Henry or I'll break down. I can't handle it. I'm telling you. Let's go to your place. They're going to be here asking questions you know it. They'll be asking everyone.

Henry looks at her. "So we go to my place. What if he cries?"

She feels her heart begin to beat up inside her chest, hard against her ribs. They do have a story, but she is not ready to make it real. It is still just a story, weak and untold. What is more real is the daydream she is having of someone in uniform coming up to her and pulling Clay from her arms.

* * *

The condor ate half a chicken. It was to be Oxena and Zach's dinner and now it was bone. The bird seemed at ease with them both, looking up expectantly when the bedspread was pulled back and the glass door released.

Oxena had seen the blur of a woman's face at the window, across the way, at Barday's. Just for a moment. Just long enough to know the condor was being watched and long enough to make her hold very still after she had snapped the blinds shut. They had let the condor out of the shower, watched her walk in the hall, her body lean and tall, her head standing three and a half feet at least from the floor. Several times she spread her wings, not to fly, but simply to relax and smooth her feathers and it was then the blinds snapped shut. She jumped at the sound and Zach looked up sharply from his crouch in the hall. He was cleaning up the bones.

They still were not speaking to each other.

The bird walked into the living room, looking at the snow of the TV, which Zach had turned to no station to drown out sounds of the trailer park. Her head bobbed from side to side, up and down, as the white light caught her eye. And then she began moving around the room, walking slowly, looking at everything from all sides, head tilting, the dull patter of her feathers ruffling the only sound besides static. Oxena sat down in her chair again and watched her make her rounds.

Several hours later Oxena woke with a start. Someone was knocking at the door. She didn't remember even falling asleep again and was surprised to be awake. She had no concept of time or how long she had been sleeping or where the bird was in the room. Zach moved fast down the hall and there was another knock again, louder, more insistent. She heard the wings beat in the shower stall and then Zach stood by her, squeezing her shoulder, stepping to the door. He looked at her once and again he gave her that nod and she realized she was gripping the sides of the chair. She released her hold as the door opened.

"Yes?" Zach said.

Oxena could see two men standing outside on the step.

"Mr. Turnbill?"

"Yes?" repeated Zach.

"There has been an incident up in the mountains and we'd like to speak with you a moment."

"Oh? Yes. Do. Come in please, though," he paused, "I'm not feeling well today. Either is my wife. Flu or something."

"Well, we'll be quick about this, I'm sure," said the first man and stepped inside. A second one followed. Oxena waved weakly from her chair and smiled a wan smile. "Sorry ma'am," he said.

She coughed.

They asked about transients in the area. If one of the residents was a Native American. If they had seen any cherry pickers leave a woman behind. Did they know an Indian woman who may have come to the Volcano on a regular basis? How about in the last couple of days? Did they know that there was a body discovered up in the mountains early this afternoon? No? Well, she was dead and had not been dead too long. Had they noticed anyone out at night? Lights which seemed odd?

Zach reminded them the rocks held ghosts and the two men looked at each other.

Maybe a car which hung around but didn't belong? The woman wasn't killed, they didn't think. She died of natural causes. But someone buried her.

No. Nothing. Oxena shook her head too. We really don't do too much outside, you know, especially now, in the summer.

The two men nodded and turned to leave. The first man held out a business card just in case she and Zach remembered something. Oh, said the second man, "Did you notice a black condor anywhere around? There are some folks from UCLA, who are studying it and they think someone killed it. There might be some kind of connection between the two."

What two? Oxena can't see the two men well. Zach has the front door open again and peach light is blinding her. They are silhouetted against the doorway.

"Maybe the Indians buried her and killed the bird for feathers or something," says Zach.

The men shrug their shoulders and the first one said, "Now that would be ironic. That bunch from UCLA is going to riot if that's what turns out happened."

A half an hour after they leave, Zach lets the bird out of the shower. She stands quietly, looks at them both with small, round bright black eyes, and sits in the hall. Oxena feels how comfortable the bird is with time. The condor is a dinosaur, a living feathered slip of time from when the desert was flooded with salt water and vines and trees dipped into the surface from what are now mountaintops. The condor is simply waiting, waiting for them to make a move.

"We have to leave, Zach." It is the first time they have spoken to each other since last night.

He says nothing and looks at the bird.

"We have to leave and give her a place to nest." Oxena watching him.

Walking to the kitchen counter, Zach opens the cupboard and gets out the wax and shammy.

* * *

Inside Diana, particles are joining, bonding. There is a force pressing them to revert to nothing, to move through wormholes smaller than 10^{-23} mm back into nothing. As if as a last resort, they begin to bond, one to another, their masses building until millions of them form something they were never meant to form. They were not even to exist simultaneously, never to share space together. Forced into this unnatural state, they begin to imitate.

Hydrogen is one of the most common elements in the universe. It is life. It is in matter and antimatter, space and dark space. The particles are chameleon-like in their need to pass as hydrogen. Imitation is their only hope of escape. Zeus will not screen hydrogen. What Zeus has trapped deep inside Diana is a sliver of creation. Of that space-time which brings forth creation. The particles are only supposed to occupy our space for instantaneous moments, flashes of less than 10^{-21} seconds and then recede to the other space from where they came. They are to give the impression of coming from nothing and exploding into nothing. But this is only impression. Not fact. They exist in dimensions outside the three we see and the fourth we call time. Now they have been trapped and it is dangerous.

Time was not always linear. It was not always separate from the three dimensions, extending in straight lines. When the universe was not a universe, when space was tightly compressed, the qualities and differences between space and time did not exist, and time was in effect, a fourth dimension. This fourth dimensional space was curved around like light without a source, folding back on itself, illuminating many things at once, and the universe had no beginning. Time had not unraveled itself into linear form and would only do so as the universe began expanding. The particles in Diana come from such a place, a place where time is not linear, yet where time still exists as space. Like angels in cumbersome skins, they are not accustomed to having mass and order and they move up, wary of new parameters, determining, like water, the point of least resistance.

The pulse of coreless hydrogen meets the electrical field and Zeus allows them to pass. They move fast now, within a second they pass through Basilosauras, a speck of energy reverting to nothing. They begin to scatter again, bonds loosen, they shed their mass and they are still moving up, seeking their wormhole, looking for that hollow thread linking two worlds. They break though the top fin of Basilosauras and then red clay, and though the difference between air and earth means nothing to them, it is at this point that they begin to revert. They dissolve quickly, in trilliseconds, the energy released making a pale glow. Then. in a moment, they shoot up to the sky. A wormhole has appeared and will only exist for a millionth of a second. They stream to its entrance, the density of the wormhole an overwhelming force.

The particles are separate now, without mass, and shedding energy, shooting toward a target where they will disappear. From earth to sky and then gone.

Below Basilosauras, Puez and Parker watch Zeus panic. His treasure is gone. His duty has been stripped and rebuked and he scans all three detectors in a desperate effort to find his zero particles.

It is 7:00 p.m. and Puez has been here too long. She wipes her eyes and tries to concentrate on the screen in front of her. "What does he think he's doing," she said.

"He doesn't think Puez,'" says Parker. "He just does."

"Oh, like involuntary muscle movements or something'?"

Parker says, "Yeah. Right." He sighs and watches blips on his screen and types in code. Waits a moment. Sighs and says, "Well, we're fucked."

"It's not that bad," she says. "I think we need to keep still and figure out what happened. I still say we should shut down. Give him a cooling off period and reboot the entire system."

Parker doesn't argue.

"The worst thing that can happen is that he'd malfunction again. He'd do it all over and we'd be right where we are now."

"Right. A couple of months from now. We wouldn't be here Puez, we'd be way behind."

"We're behind now." She pauses. "Look, he could have really trapped something, you know. Something we don't know about. Let's just say, now don't scowl, let's just say there were particles, unknown, that he found."

"He is supposed to report abnormalities."

"Yes, but let's say these particles don't have the properties of particles as we know them. Maybe they're tachyons."

"Oh, right. And they're moving faster than light and zipping backwards in time and if I could only tap into them, I could quit and become a psychic and know all about the future."

"Or some kind of particle force?"

"Have you been reading that crap in the bathroom that Guillespe's been pinning up?"

"Let's see. Can he give the dimensions of the mass..." Puez taps the keyboard. "Now let's just do a simple calculation. Nothing fancy Parker, we just want to keep this simple. Always striving to be simple."

Parker watches her and is suddenly exhausted. His face feels heavy. He has been living underground his whole life, it seems. And the last three days, he has existed at this desk. All he has left in the refrigerator is a can of soda, a yogurt, and an éclair from yesterday morning.

She swivels to him and looks in his face. "Now see. I'm trying not to get excited, but look here. The mass divides too neatly into separate but equal variables. Just think, what would space and time look like at the subatomic level?"

"I'm lost."

"What would it look like, think."

"Like shaving cream."

"Yeah. It would be all foamy like sea foam bubbles and bridges. What if some kind of virtual particles were created in this sea foam?"

Parker leans forward. "And then Zeus broke down the bubbles and made the space too smooth or small for them to disappear again? Can you image," he leans even closer to her, a smile really moving fast across his face, "Can you image if Zeus did trap virtual particles and was able to hold them? Even for a second? That would be historical."

"Well, according to this," Puez slaps the screen, "He held them for forty-eight hours.

Parker sighs and sits back in his chair. "'We're fucked," he said again "Totally, completely fucked."

"Why?"

"That didn't happen Puez." He looks at his terminal. "You know about the horizon problem right?"

"What's that got to do with this?" She does not want this explained to her.

"It's the same kind of problem. If the horizon distance, the total distance light could travel since the beginning of the universe, exceeds, and it does, wildly, the radius of the entire universe then the fundamental laws which we all and I do mean we all cling to are invalid. Big bang didn't happen. Inflationary models don't work. Back to the drawing boards."

Puez shrugs her shoulders. "So."

"The same thing is true for Zeus. I mean quarks, antiquarks, virtual particles, all that crap is really just a platter of mathematical ghosts. We can't prove they're out there. And if they don't exist, the whole mechanism for understanding how the universe works comes to a grinding halt." He rubs his eyes again. "I think we're going to be stuck here making up a whopper to explain some data and there's no way to prove any of it." He cocks his head and says, "T'ain't there if I don't see it."

"Well something happened here. I felt it. We're at the beginning of something."

"Yeah? What?"

CORE ELEMENTS

I did not see Lani and Bat and Kinni come out of the mountains. I was released from the neon tape, allowed to leave the mountain, and walked slowly, trying to find the vestiges of the trail. I had no reason to hurry. The air was sunburnt-cool and my skin sensitive to even the light pressure of the breeze, as if I'd spent too much time in the ocean and now salt had dried in tiny crusty swirls over tender skin.

I was not thinking of anything except the next letter I wanted to write. To Henry. From her. But I wasn't able to make the words straighten out into sentences. In my mind, the words and Henry and she ran over each other and all I could hear was a deep roar. I needed to send him off into the unknown. And what I wanted, I realized, was revenge. To hurt him. Badly. With the cold calibration of ice. To wound him myself through her and let him suffer. Suffer in a way so that, for once, just once in my life, I would know the exact reason for that suffering and wouldn't have to summon the energy to try and understand his world. I would know because I would be the core, the source of that pain. Not her.

When I walked down my line of trailers I saw Barday Tullis standing on his porch, unsteady on his feet, a blood stained piece of cloth tied around his head. He looked so different, ghost-like, that I was uncertain for a moment that it was him.

"Barday?"

He turned and looked at me, not aware of time or where he was. He seemed confused and touched his head with one hand while leaning against the door jamb with the other. He wore a light blue flannel shirt, unbuttoned, long sleeves rolled up to the elbows and a pair of very old, very paint-splattered Levi's. I had never seen him in regular clothes. And he was barefoot. There was something sad about his feet, having them naked, yellow toenails exposed. Something more disturbing than the blood on the cloth.

He finally saw me coming up the steps and he said: "Tip's dead." In a moment he made a grimace, his lips pulled down and his eyes brimmed. He caught his breath a little and wiped a hand over his face. The hand shook. So did the collar of the flannel shirt.

"Oh Barday," I said, my arms heavy by my side. "I'm so sorry."

He removed his hand from his face and though his brow was still deeply furrowed, he controlled the corners of his mouth. "Come here, come with me, so I can show you his last bed." Not even attempting a rhyme.

We came through the trailer, I put an arm around him and felt how light he was, thin, like a bird with hollow bones, and we moved slowly through the dark trailer to the back door.

I could see Tip, or at least a portion of him through the open door. What I did not see right away was Lani and Bat kneeling next to him. Or Kinni, with her back turned to me with the horse's head in her lap.

"See, see, there he'd be," said Barday and let go of my hand and moved from the support of my arm. He walked through the sand and stood above Tip.

As I came up to the horse, I saw Kinni's hair. It was black, like the veil, and I hadn't noticed she was bareheaded. And then slowly she turned to me, tilting her head up and around until her face met mine. Completely.

"Hi Kinni," I said, feeling a lightness in my chest from relief at the smoothness of her skin and the hammering awe of the perfection of her face—an escape from the unknown into the known. So this was Kinni. With a face of marble and eyes of black light.

"The horse is dead," she said.

"I think it just died," said Lani. "I mean shit, it's not even cold yet."

I turned and looked at her. She had her camera. Of course. And Bat. I stared at him. His hands were red, with smeared blood. Lani saw me looking at them. She reached over with a towel and tried to rub more off.

"Something was in that old mineshaft," she said to me, almost whispering. "Something dead. An organ or some shitty thing. He found it."

Not dead, I wanted to explain, just finished with. As if you grew a heart for just nine months and then pushed it out your mouth. That woman on the mountain would always be there. Like the myth of treasure, part real, part fable. A private myth. And that baby in the paper bag would grow up in the long shadows of her myth, with a legend of its own.

Barday slowly crouched down next to Kinni and she moved over slightly so he could cradle the head. Tip's eyes were closed and flies tried to land on his lids, but Kinni kept them away with delicate passes of her hands. Like an incantation. Barday petted the forelock and smoothed it down, between the ears, patting the flaxen hair.

The men from the mountain would come from around the corner of the trailer in a few minutes and enter our circle with suspicion. A dead horse, a old man with a bloodied head, a disturbed teenaged boy, a young woman with no bra and a camera, a Japanese woman all in black, and me again—the one who thought she was digging up her father on the hill. They had every right to be suspicious. There were too many lives crowded around the edge of the horse.

When they explained why they were there and told Lani and Kinni of the woman in the mountains, Lani only looked at me once. And she took Bat's hand as he looked up into the sky. Kinni's expression never changed. She told them she was from Nagasaki, that she was there in 1945 and kept patting Tip's sunken neck with her hand. Barday didn't say anything either and when they finally left, he leaned forward and pressed his cheek against the flat bone between the horse's eyes. I watched him rub his hand along Tip's nose over and over again, not weeping, but with his eyes tightly closed and all memory gone, concentrating only on the immediate moment, on the tactile qualities of hard bone, short stiff hair, soft nose. His hands looked strong because his fingers were thick and curled, but I saw how frail he was as they shook, his hands hovering and caressing the tiny scars across the horse's face. Like a parent looking for signs of broken bones, touching gently, touching again, afraid to touch.

"I know where to bury him," said Lani.

I looked at her. She was still holding Bat's hand.

"In the star," said Bat and followed her gaze to my eyes, and I felt a note plucked.

My stomach turned. She was right. He wasn't blind. He saw me. He knew who I was. I felt suddenly self-conscious under his pure gaze.

"Yeah. Out in the rock pile, out there," she said and pointed beyond the corral. "There's a big hole out there, pretty deep. I'm sure it'll hold him."

"How do we get him out there?"

"Load him in my truck."

"Who? Us?" I wasn't feeling strong.

"Since when are you so crabby?"

I stared at her.

"In the star hole," said Bat, his glance never wavering. His golden eyes were luminescent in the pale air.

"At least I think it's big enough." Lani turned to the desert.

"I will go and see," Kinni said and rose, gracefully, purposefully from her place in the sand. She gently touched Barday's shoulder as she reached over to pick up the veil. It was the first time I'd seen it not masking her. It was benign, much smaller than I remembered, deflated. "I will be back soon," she said and he reached up and for a moment held her hand against his chest.

When she left it was with the straight poise of a water bird. Back rigid, head up, veil tucked under her left arm.

"You know she found him there," said Lani looking over at a pile of old bricks just outside the back door. "And she brought him inside."

"She tended to me as I did sleep, she came to my aid and my heart did keep," said Barday slowly and we became very quiet.

A little while later, I saw Henry, my father, coming from his trailer, walking straight out after Kinni, as if sent by messenger. I didn't like the way he walked, hurried, with expectation. I looked down at Tip and Barday and then out to Henry's back as he trekked across the basin.

* * *

Melody ended up with Clay at the rocky edge of the horseshoe, disappearing. It was Henry's idea. They both knew the rocks were there, knew it would be a good place to hide and they lay in the opposite direction of Vasquez. And it was far out from the trailer park, nowhere near a road. She could hide there until nightfall, until the cars went away, and everyone would think she was working at K-Mart.

But she and Henry didn't know about Bat's star-hole. As Melody came up to the crest of white boulders her eyes kept dropping down, trying to find ground. When at last she saw the bottom of the hole, she shivered, not understanding why it was there, but somehow comforted it existed. The earth seemed to have pulled apart and widened just for her. She squatted, swung both legs down and, cradling Clay carefully, slid into the pit. She walked around in a circle for a minute or two and then found a soft spot to sit, where the wall curved to meet her back. She pulled down the receiving blanket to look at his face. He watched her eyes and face, his mouth a tiny sealed "o" and she lifted him to her face and rubbed her cheek against his. They were safe. Suddenly he gave a lusty cry and her breasts tingled deep in her chest.

He nursed twice more before she heard the sound. It was beyond late afternoon, closer to evening she supposed. Six or seven probably. The sky was clear and pale purple, washed by fading sun. She had dozed on and off and now her leg was asleep. She hadn't brought a diaper and he needed to be changed. But she didn't dare move. Henry would come and get her when the men left. That's what he said. When all was safe.

The sound was of footsteps, soft sounds of sand and walking. But it wasn't Henry. Henry's sound would be heavy, tired. This was quick and light, then hesitating, then fast again, searching. Searching.

She wanted the walls to bury them. The flash in her mind was of crumbling earth, of stratified earth coming apart, falling together into heavy powder, released from the walls of the hole like water from a dam. First there was the rush, the sound of earth moving and all the horizon lines mixing into nothing, then the impact of dirt on her body and she would curve herself around Clay, like the mothers of Pompeii, protecting him against Fate.

The footsteps came closer and a finch pecking at the ground above, flew away. But the sand and earth around her and the infant were not about to give. She wanted to run. To take Clay and leap up like a gazelle and tear across the desert floor. But she couldn't move. So she sat in the sinking shadows, trying to flatten herself against the wall of lines and dirt, her mind blank, all hope gone in the wish she had stayed home. Her eyes, straining to see what would appear on the fine line separating sand and sky, were unblinking. She did not breathe.

The long thin shadow spilled down into the hole before someone's head appeared against the blue sky. Someone with white skin and flattened eyes and nose. Someone who looked down at her and said, "And this is your child."

It was Kinni.

Melody saw her face, saw perfection and the beauty of timelessness.

"Yes," she said.

"What is his name?"

"Clay. Clay Colliery."

"And how did you come by him." Kinni was standing above her, dressed in black, the lace veil beating under her arm in a stiff breeze.

The question caused a reaction and Melody tried to remember her stories about him. Which had they chosen: the aunt dying in childbirth; the teenaged cousin; a sister's mistake? But she couldn't remember the details and the stories fled from her. So she could not answer and stood not looking at Kinni, not looking anywhere, except straight ahead.

Kinni stared out across the desert, behind her, toward the sunset.

Melody swallowed, coming out from the shadows.

"He is just and only your baby then."

"Yes."

"That is good. And now I make a trade. My lace for Clay. Just for a moment. To hold him." The veil of black lace and the cap landed by Melody's feet, in the center of the pit.

She was so beautiful, standing there above Melody, against the purple sky, her short hair moving with wind, her brown arms curved awkwardly out in front of her, ready to hold the infant. Melody stood and lifted him up and his arms waved as Kinni took him. In the next moment, Kinni turned from the lip of the crater and disappeared.

Melody froze for an instant. Then she was up, moving, out of the pit only to see Kinni pressing her face against his and the two of them facing the sliver of sun balanced on the horizon line.

Kinni's voice was soft, "He is a beautiful baby." Melody saw Kinni lay her face gently against his head and breathe in the smell of his hair. "You are very happy now," she said, to both of them, separately.

Melody looked east.

Stars began to shimmer in the eastern sky, out past the horseshoe and across the desert floor. Hearing her name called, Melody turned to see Henry walking from the west. He was walking fast, nearly running and waving and she knew all the cars had all gone—at least for tonight. Kinni knew the truth. Someone else knew the infant was hers.

Henry came up to her and she felt his arms hold her, just for a moment, and his hug was hard and bony. He looked at Kinni holding Clay and Melody said, "This is Kinni."

"I know that," he said.

"I am from Nagasaki," she said and smiled. "I was there in 1945."

1945.

"I see," he said and did not even remember the possibility of pain. That force was gone, either slipping away with the sun or fading with moonlight, but the force which wanted to pull him into the earth had evaporated like mist.

"Here," Kinni said. "He wants his mother," and as the sun disappeared and the sky widened with stars she passed Clay back to Melody.

It was on the walk back to Raceway, as lights from the trailer park lit one by one and they walked steadily as if heading toward a new found oasis, that they hear the sound. A cry. Plaintive and jubilant, a cry of escape. The sound came from behind them, from the eastern sky, black with space and lit with stars, and it coiled around them and then disappeared like a delicate fragrance.

Kinni, then Melody and Henry turned and first they saw nothing but stars and sky and then in the not so far distance, they saw a glow. A soft surge of light which seemed to come from the hole, glowing for a second and then shooting up into the night sky like a pulse of sound or a bubble. From earth to sky. Then it was gone. The reverse of a falling star.

* * *

Melody is the first to appear from the dark, holding the baby, the glow of the oil lamp making her features yellow-white against the dark. A moment later, the second form materializes and there is Henry, and then Kinni. She is the hardest to see and her black clothes and pale cream complexion give the illusion that her face is somehow floating above ground. Like a ghost following Melody.

A small group has formed around Tip and Barday. Besides Hattie, Lani, and Bat, Celeste and Honey are standing with the oil lantern, and Oxena and Zachary Turnbill have arrived each with a flashlight. Several other neighbors, whom no one really knows, have come around asking questions and have left. Someone across the way is playing acid rock very loudly, but no one notices.

Lani has pulled the truck up close to Tip's head. The tail gate is missing. It is an old Ford half ton pickup, rust patches showing through the dull gold finish. The side mirror is missing from the driver's side. There is a large dent along the front, the back bumper is missing, and the inside door handle doesn't work—to open the truck from the inside she has to reach out the window.

Zach has brought rope, some slick nylon webbed rope and he and Oxena tie the rope around the horse's head. Then Henry takes the rest of the rope and hobbles the legs, binding them together and climbs up in the truck bed.

"I think we're going to need a ramp or something," says Hattie. "To get him up in there."

"I've got an old piece of plywood under my trailer," says Celeste. She and Honey return, dragging a warped five by three slice of plywood along through the sand.

"There," says Hattie, as she and Celeste rest the wood against the edge of the truck bed. Zach, Celeste, and Lani climb into the truck bed, joining Henry, and then Lani helps Bat up, and wraps his hands around the rope as well. Hattie, Kinni, and Oxena then climb in and pick up the rope tied to the head. Barday and Melody stand off to the side, watching and Honey sits in the dark with her elbows on her knees as if waiting for a campfire.

"Everybody ready?" says Henry.

"Everybody pull," says Hattie.

Tip moves and Hattie shivers with the weight against her hands. They count to three and pull again. Her hands burn with rope. They pull again and Tip stretches up the ramp. They pull again, pausing to catch their breaths, to keep what they've gained and to pull again. When the body is on the edge of the truck bed, one hip drops and they have to stop. By now, Celeste and Lani and Oxena have climbed down and are pulling from the ground, on either sides of the doors and the others are up on the cab. Then Henry lets go of his hold on the rope, jumps off the truck, and comes around to push the rump.

Tip is in, neck and head arched backwards against the wheel wells, tongue out, lips folded back, teeth exposed.

Lani drives. Bat sits between her and Barday. Everyone else rides in back with the horse. Three shovels rattle against metal. No one says anything. The night is long and black, lit only by stars and a sliced moon turning Tip a cool, buffed silver.

The horse lands in the pit with the sound of earth. As if they had rolled bags of dirt out of the truck. There is no air escaping, no hard grunt-thud of a fall trying to be broken. Just the heavy slipping of something large. They all stand around the edge of the hole and look down. But there is nothing to see. The horse is already buried by shadows and all that can be clearly seen are his hooves, still bound together, resting against the south wall of what is now a grave.

Melody sits in the truck and nurses. Honey falls asleep in Celeste's arms. And Celeste, sitting on the edge of the hole watches Lani with Bat. Sees the way Bat's eyes followed the body into the ground. Sees Lani standing next to him and catches, for just a moment, the glitter of stainless steel, the curve of his spoon at the bottom of the hole, against a far wall, the last place where moonlight penetrates, the space itself curved like the crescent moon.

Hattie, Henry, Zach, Oxena, Kinni, Lani, and even Barday take turns shoveling. There has been no rain in a long time and Bat's earth is soft and light, not compact. What has taken him months to dig, they fill in an hour. The moonlight slides over the grave, silent, unconscious, picking up tiny shadows of rock and crumbled earth. When they are done, when the new earth is feathered with the old and the top smoothed, Barday brings two rocks and lays them in the center of the round grave. Then the seven stand and begin walking in circles moving out from the center to the periphery of the grave, tamping down earth. Celeste has scooted off to the side, still holding Honey's head in her lap, looking into Honey's face, thinking of eyes: Honey's closed, Tip's closed, and Bat's moving.

"When I go, when I die to his right I will lie," Barday announced, suddenly, loudly, standing in the center of the circle, between the two rocks. Some watch as Henry puts an arm around Barday. Hattie looks away.

People begin to leave: one by one, some in pairs until only Kinni and Barday remain and then she, too, rises and walks away in the night, leaving him behind with a blanket of stars.

* * *

I arrived back on my doorstep, so weary every time I blinked my eyes all I saw was dirt and sand. And fractions of Henry. His profile in the night air, his arm around Melody's red shoulders, his avoidance of my eyes. I was filthy and I wanted a shower. A hot, steamy shower to wash off the dust and blood and everything from the day. Lani dropped me off right outside my door and as I climbed the steps, my foot knocked against a good sized stone. I heard it roll unevenly and stooped to pick it up. It was long and slender and glittered when I turned on the kitchen light. I washed it off. There was still work to be done with the earth apparently.

The dirt was brownish but washed off scarlet red in the water. The more I rubbed, the less red the water became and within a minute or so the water under the kitchen tap ran clear. I dried the stone with wadded up paper napkins and looked at it under the light. It was a bone. A fossil.

When you grow up in the west, you know what fossils look like—from the swirls of snails millions of years old to fish bones etched in solid sand. But this was fossilized bone. Bone turned to stone. It was as long as my little finger and about as wide. Stone had filled the marrow and over time crystals grew like weeds, filling up the core, taking over the bone mantel. Conditions had to be perfect.

I set the bone on the counter and took the sheets of marble paper left on the table and laid them in the sink. It took me awhile to find some matches, they were with the charcoal over in the corner between the fridge and the garbage. The flames were yellow, bright yellow and I was surprised they weren't solid pink.

In a minute or two all that remained of the marble was a pile of thin black ash and the dull smell of burnt paper. I ran water over the ashes, watching them tear and melt, swirl in the sink and jam the strainer.

The shower was hot and I felt muscles in my back and legs loosen as water poured over me, pulling my hair straight, sliding off me in sheets. I ached all over, especially in my chest. I turned to the source of water and though my nipples hurt with force of the spray, the heat took away some of the cramping under my ribs.

I stepped out, wrapped my hair in a towel and dried off with a second one. I shut my eyes as a kind of test and instead of seeing a pile of dirt I saw the red water in the sink. I shook my hair out, watching the curls bounce back, released from the weight of water, lighter again. They wrapped wetly around my face and I looked in the mirror. I did not recognize the face that looked back. She really didn't have much to do with me. I brushed my teeth. Picking up the stone from the back of the toilet, I left the bathroom, walked into the bedroom, and looked at the clock. It was midnight.

The Almanac sat beside me on the bed, closed. I scooted back against the pillows and opened the book to the dog-eared page marking where I'd left off: Celestial Events of 1981. The stone made a neat bookmark, the pages bowing open slightly around the wedge of bone when I closed the jacket. I would not open it again.

* * *

Henry sat and watched Melody making tacos. He held Clay gently, gingerly. The Homestead smelled of olive oil and refried beans, cheddar cheese, and onions. There was a jar of salsa opened on the counter. And a sliced tomato. Melody moved slowly, as if recuperating, and leaned heavily against the counter. It was late, after midnight and the yellow of the kitchen made her hair a flat sheen of gold. He liked watching her.

189

Clay moved in his arms, small stirrings, but strong and Henry had to shift his arms slightly. The last time he held a newborn, it was Hattie. She was pink and white and he didn't know how to love more. When she turned her tiny little face to him for the first time and her dark blue eyes held his gaze, he felt a surge of something primeval. If anything threatened her, he would stop it. Or die trying. The surge wasn't the acceptance of his own death but the release of power with knowing he would die with a purpose. She was a perfect person. Complete.

And now there was Clay. Someone else to know. Another life. And he had that surge again, just holding him, looking into his face—a sudden acceptance of an impulse either instinctive or highly cultivated—that he would protect Clay. And he knew he and Melody would see Clay move through the flitting stages of childhood. Henry knew it passed quickly, an infant became an adult in less than a flash, and the only true measurement of gauging his own age was in terms of Hattie, but holding Clay it seemed impossible that time would accelerate. Clay would always remain an infant in Henry's arms. Melody would always be just as she is now, turning and smiling a tired smile.

She came over to him and said, "Let me try to nurse him before we eat," and she sat down next to them on the sofa and lifted her shirt. Henry lifted Clay to his face and kissed his cheek.

"Look at him," said Melody after he'd latched on. "I swear he's gotten bigger already."

Henry stroked her hair for a moment and she leaned back and closed her eyes. The way the shadows filled her face, the light left her looking old and he saw clearly what she might look like years from now. When Clay was gone.

He took his hand away and got up and walked to the bathroom. He stayed by the sink, running water for several minutes trying to take the heat and sting from his eyes with splashes of cold water. Arlene never grew old, either in life or in his mind. Clay, fresh, tender in all ways, would now live as a measure of time. He dried his face on a thin yellow towel and pushed his sleeves down on his shirt. He sighed. Time would never reverse itself. He felt the light stiff weight of the pink marble paper in his shirt pocket. She was right. It stretched on past the horizon line. Hattie would never again be the little girl in that photo, and Arlene would never laugh or stroke his hair or look at him hungry and warm. Time was long and thin and he needed to follow its forward direction. The fact that Arlene somehow avoided its linear form and circled back to retrieve him was no longer a puzzle he needed to believe. He knew she could not have written the letters.

When he came out of the bathroom, Clay was strapped in the baby bucket, sated and sleepy. His lids were thin and lightly veined, closed against the light and his little clenched fists were on either side of him, parallel to each other in sleep.

* * *

Oxena and Zach loved the night air. It was cool and light, and stars hung arid and pale in the thin sky. The walk back from the grave was silent and they moved side by side, like gears, barely touching, but turning an entire mechanism. When they came close to Raceway they stopped and he reached over and took her hand. It felt awkward to her, having his hand closing over hers, but she relaxed and when he dropped her hand it wasn't because she failed to respond. It was because they were moving again.

The condor was asleep in the shower stall, head folded back against her wings. She did not hear them enter the trailer.

Oxena knew she was dirty and her hair was stiff. She felt old.

"I need to take a bath or something," she whispered. Zach nodded.

They stood in front of the kitchen sink and stripped. Oxena brought out towels and washcloths. Zach found a bar of soap in the cupboard and a shampoo sampler.

They washed each other's hair. First Oxena bent over the sink and she felt Zach test the water with his hands, then run it through her hair and lather her head with a cold spot of shampoo. He rubbed his fingers over the base of her skull, her crown, along the temples and the hairline. Then he took the hand spray and with gurgling sounds of soapy water, rinsed her hair clean. The water was shut off and a towel draped over her hair. She raised her head and stood still for a moment to get her balance. She gave herself a quick towel drying and then slipped the towel over her shoulders. "Your turn."

So she did the same for him. She saw how creased the back of his neck was and how numerous the moles and freckles across his shoulder blades had become. It was easy to wash his hair, just the fringe along the sides and back, but she soaped the bald area and rubbed her fingers into his scalp just the same because she knew it felt good. When she leaned over to rinse, her breasts sagged against his back and his skin felt warm.

She turned the water off. He stood up and she handed him a towel. His eyes were still tightly shut and she moved him, while he was still off balance slightly, in a circle to face away from her. Then she turned the water back on and soaped up a washcloth.

"It time for a bath," she said and rubbed the washcloth down his spine. She moved down his body with smooth practicality, and with a gentleness that surprised herself. He shivered once and she wrapped the towel around his waist. Then he reached for the bar of soap.

She was surprised how gentle he was when he washed her. Though he was kind, he had never been sensitive or gentle in bed and sex was not an opportunity for quiet exploration. But tonight he moved slowly, deliberately, being careful of her breasts, the inside of her thighs, the inner pink of her labia. He even used caution with her feet, testing the pressure to avoid tickling her. As if he were trying to be her in her skin. She watched his face. Though he did not look at her, he was seeing her. He laid a heavy towel across her shoulders when he was through.

"There you go," he said.

They dried off and spread the damp towels on the floor to absorb all the water. They walked to the back of the Dream Time, to their bedroom, and she put on a cotton sleeveless night gown. He took out a pair of light blue pajamas with a faint paisley print.

He sat heavily on the edge of the bed. "So when do you want to do this?"

"Tomorrow." She was combing her hair, standing in front of the little square mirror above the vanity.

"Tomorrow," he repeated.

"We don't have to wait around for anything right? You've done the polishing. I'll call the post office in the morning and the utilities. I say tomorrow."

"I'm glad," he said in such an odd voice that she turned around. He was lying flat on his back, looking directly at her. His hair was still wet. "I'm glad we're going to do this."

She knew what he was thinking. And then she realized that sometime during the last day she felt him again. Inside her. Feeling those liquid bonds which move and tear with the current, and yet keep joining and rejoining over time. And as she sat on the edge of the bed and leaned over to kiss him, their history relaxed into the past and their future trembled, emptied of expectations.

"Tomorrow," she said and covered herself with the sheet. It fell lumpy over legs and stomach. She felt Zach move next to her. They lay side by side, on their backs, staring at the black ceiling, each trying to remember which constellation was pressed in the sky above them.

* * *

Lani parked the truck, shut off the lights and watched Celeste and Bat and Honey go inside. Honey was groggy and Celeste had to carry her up the steps. Bat stood quietly behind, watching, head tilted up to the front door, one hand on the railing. The moon was bright and bathed his face in shallow light.

She sighed and reached around to open the door. Celeste did not say anything to her, but she didn't have to—Lani saw it all in her face. A line had been crossed and no one knew what to do or how to talk. Bat, too, had crossed lines, from nothing into something, from a place of no time or substance to a place of dimension and color. Celeste watched them, Lani knew, saw them hold hands, saw Bat turn to look at her. Bat could see and his vision allowed him to name things. Star. Heavy sound. And, over the grave, "Good good horse." Language, an element which had always existed in a whirling solution, never having any organization or meaning had suddenly precipitated into thought. He always knew the word "horse." Now he understood what it meant.

Lani watched Celeste's face when he took his mother's hand getting into the truck and suddenly pulled it to his chest. "Mommy,"

193

and without drama or emotion he looked straight into her face. Celeste held his gaze for just a moment and she gasped slightly, lips parted—not questioning any act, or him or Lani, but aware that events were moving, pushing Bat into consciousness.

Lani had looked down at the ground. Celeste would not say anything to her the rest of the night except, "Good-bye," as she climbed out of the truck bed. But she knew. She knew her son could see.

Lani took a bath, feeling the water swirl around her, watching her nipples peak above the waterline. She was lucky to have a bath. Some guy helped her install it, an old porcelain claw foot with a stopper that leaked. She could hear water tinkling down the drain every time she moved.

When she found the bloody mess in the mine, her first thought was that an animal had been killed. Whatever it was it looked like a big piece of liver, or a heart. An organ. Large and dark. The back of the mine stank. But when the two men came around, she understood what it was. She chose to say nothing.

She climbed into bed, this time in flannel pajamas, and buried herself under covers. She was chilled. And she shivered, teeth chattering, trying to forget Barday's face, the heavy weight of the horse, the image of its tongue, the sound of shovels.

* * *

Bat listens to sounds. Of his mother grunting with Honey's weight, of the light full snap of sheets being aired and spread. Of the shower running, of her hand on the door jamb, nails tapping slightly as she leans forward to wave him inside. His clothes, as they fall, muffled to the floor, and the grate of the shower door as he steps inside. There is a familiar smell that is missing and he pulls the word from the chaos, slowly: "Soap," and then there is a bar in his hands and the shower door closes again. He washes himself and can see his mother like a multifaceted shadow moving in segments behind the milk glass door. His hair feels heavy and grows long with the weight of water.

When he stands he hears the towel buffeting around his ears as his mother dries his hair and the sound of elastic against his skin and

194

feels the waist of his pajamas snap against his own. His arms feel good inside the top, and he concentrates on the feel of cloth, the smell of his mother, the order of the day and the event of the shower and says, "Soft. Tired," meaning the pajamas are soft and he is tired.

He can hear his mother's heart now, clearly, and he knows it's not his own and he puts his arms around her awkwardly. New responses. She asks him, "Are you sleepy now?" and he hears the word "sleep" and from the whirling comes the vision of his bed, his pillow, and the feeling of lying down, limbs quiet and heavy, darkness.

"Yes," he says a long time later, after she has closed the door. He listens to sounds around him, inside him. Of Lani, high against the blue sky, her breath against his neck, of the release of his own breath as he throws the star, the sticky sound his hands made in the wetness of the mine, the varying sift-calls of the crater as it slowly filled with sand.

He holds a vague image of a tomorrow, and his pillow remains undented by thrashing. He knows tonight the sun will follow him tomorrow. He is calm, laying still, looking up and seeing, for the first time, patterns.

* * *

Kinni sits on her bed, unmoving. She is the only one who will not bathe. She needs to feel the dirt on her, to gather its heavy smell and not relinquish it. Today she became a part of others. Today the ground swallowed the veil. Today air touched her face and sun filled her eyes, both unfiltered and in pure form. Change came to her.

She turns on the light by the bed, stands, moves to the window on the end wall, and pulls the curtains open. Something she's never done before. The light shines in front of her making her reflection on the night black glass perfect in shape and color—like a pale mirror. She steps forward, closer to the window and some of the light fails to reach her face. Her features become hollow, as if time had rushed in swirled in a cloud around her face, leaving its impression of age. She looks old. Of times to come.

She smiles, her mouth small and pink.

195

She takes off her clothes and leaves them in a pile on the floor. The smell of sage and sand clings to her arms and her back and there is dirt between her toes. She reaches up and feels a line of grit creased in her neck. She looks at her legs and arms as she sits on the bed, lays back and holds her hands above her face, following the lines in the palms of her hands. Her hands are a labyrinth of lines, too many, and their crisscrosses stand out, stained with earth.

She reaches over and turns off the light, feeling the air around her, cool, cold almost and she begins to shake. She is flat against the bed, arms by her sides. First her thighs tremble and then it rushes to the back of her knees and then her ankles quiver. She likes the shuddering cold and she holds her breath, reaching down between her legs with her hands. She feels the bristle of her public hair and turns her head. Her eyes are wide open, staring into the dark, looking for the stain in the ceiling, but the resemblance is gone. She shuts her eyes and imagines her body. Pictures herself in the night, on the bed, naked. One hand feels her breasts, carefully, lightly, stroking, and her nipples suddenly grow hard. She sees them full and round, riding soft and flat on her ribcage and she can see the shadows of her ribs as her breath deepens, her chest widening as her legs spread open. Her fingertips are light against the skin of her breasts and her other hand rubs fast, quick, but not fast enough. It is not until she imagines her own face, eyes sealed shut, tears leaving moonlit streaks down each temple, mouth open slightly and then shut, lips trembling, that she is released. Released into something beyond control. And instead of chaos, there are patterns, primal and ageless, and she moves with the core force, flowing in waves with the course of instinct.

She falls asleep under blankets with one hand on her abdomen and the other around her waist, embracing herself. She, alone, survived in the backyard. She, alone, survived the burning rains. Now she survives herself.

* * *

Puez takes a sip of Coke. She has just woken from a nap in the lounge and swings her legs down to the floor as Parker walks in with, "It's after midnight."

"No shit," she says.

"I don't think I've ever heard you swear."

"Sorry. It's my upbringing."

"So what's the occasion?"

"It's gone."

"What?"

She shakes her head and coughs. "It, Parker, It. It's gone, and we're never going to get it back."

He sighs. "It couldn't be an It, it's not a thing. I'm telling you, 'It' is just a blooper of numbers stuck in some microchip somewhere and when I find out who did it, I'm going to kill them." He sits down next to her on the sofa.

Puez puts a hand up to her eyes and feels the thickness of the skin on her face. She feels fanned out in too many directions, opaque, not whole, and the conversation seems surreal.

"Nothing's that easy Parker and I don't want it to be. Don't you see, Zeus woke up. Don't you see it? He woke up and found something that doesn't fit here. Whatever it was, it didn't belong here and it left. Maybe it was part of a superstring and it came from some ten dimensional space or some crap like that. But we missed it, Parker. And we have no data. And I'm sick of having no hope. I need some kind of hope Parker. That's what this is all about right? Isn't that what this whole frigging five mile long tube is about? Finding the origins of the universe, breaking things down to get at some core? I think we had it and it slipped away."

Between them there is sea foam, invisible, undulating, and moving on the subatomic level. A wormhole appears wriggling in the froth. A single virtual particle appears from nowhere like a piece of cork and vanishes back into nothing. The wormhole snaps shut and spreads into a bubble. The entire process takes no time. No one can imagine time in such small increments. It is easier to think of particles of time like sand, but they are not.

"Look," Parker says, sighing, "If it's there, it will always be there. And one way or another, we'll get it."

"Maybe we're not supposed to."

"That sounds prophetic. Since when did you find God?"

"I'm not talking about God." She looks at the walls. "I'm talking about the universe. Those photons," she waves a hand, "yacking to each other across light years. Without ever touching. All that space— It's just filled with noise. I want to listen in."

Parker watches her. She is exhausted. The problems of tomorrow are still not real to either of them—how Zeus will have to be rebooted, will the systems work, what will he do with the detectors, and Parker is irritated with himself that he cannot stay focused on the impending issues at hand. But the day began with a cry and ended with the escape of something which does not exist. Parker is caught in a wave of thought which engages his senses. He is aware of the smell of the lounge, controlled, cool, medicinal. He is aware of light and how patterns of faint shadow fall, cast by the long fluorescent tubing above their heads, pooling under tables, chairs, along the bottom of the whiteboards along the wall, at his feet. He feels the slight give under his left thigh where Puez's weight settles in the sofa cushion. With all this he feels, suddenly, human, beyond himself, and is somehow connected to everything in the room.

"I want to hear too," is all he says and they sit together on the sofa, not touching, but feeling, for the first time, the presence of each other.

EMPIRICAL THOUGHT

Hattie on movement

I've never liked fast moves. Picking up, moving here, relocating. From the Waldheim to Vasquez. I don't like people who talk loud or make fast movements either. If you move too fast, everything becomes blurred and you might as well be blind. And blindness scares me. It really does. So I moved slowly that night under the stars, over Tip's grave.

My steps were slow, methodical. I began walking those concentric circles over the grave with great care, plodding. The more I walked, the heavier I became, and the tighter I made my steps, the safer Tip would be. And then I realized that under my feet was a dead horse beginning to decay and up in that mine was a placenta rotting and somewhere that poor woman was being hacked apart in autopsy. I felt Henry brush against me in his circle and then Lani with Bat, and finally Kinni. No one seemed to notice that I traveled slow. Or if they did, they said nothing.

I lifted my left leg and stomped, feeling earth shudder under my step. I could imagine the ground surrendering and all of us falling into the hole, being covered up with sand. I had a desperate need to save everyone from this fate and was swept away with the urge to pack the earth down, making it so hard that it would become rock, so it couldn't ever surrender. Ever. I took another step, and another, using my weight, raising little puffs of dirt with my heels as I went along. I went faster, passing Lani and Bat, Henry, Kinni, then Lani again, not seeing them, but feeling their presence. I could feel my arms working too, up and down, back and forth, two pumps adding force. Then I was dancing on the perimeter, along the edge where the two seams of earth met and I stopped to catch my breath. My shirt clung along the straight line of my spine and the denim jeans were binding behind my knees. I was shaking, tremors radiating from the center of my body to my fingers, down my legs to my heels. It was a whisper of the same force which sought out Henry and I looked around, watched for others, tried to ground myself between the grave and the earth.

One by one the others I'd passed joined me on the seam of dirt and then would return to the center. I could feel them around me, pressing down dirt. But the circle didn't turn to stone. It lay pale and wan, a sphere of crumbled, smooth earth. There was no starting point and no end. I didn't want to lift my foot and go forward again. The shaking got worse and I felt sick. I dropped my hands to my knees to catch my breath. I did not want to go on. Movement seemed pointless. Escape was impossible. The earth would swallow us all and there was no action to take. All movement was really static, a cruel hoax.

I looked up from my bent stance, my hands sweaty and still on my knees and watched the others move in their circles, as if shuffling in some pagan dance. Passing shadows, they'd emerge from darkness, monochrome and then come close to the lantern blossoming in to full color and then recede again into gray. Some moved faster than others and I'd see them come into the light more often. To be seen on the periphery you had to move twice as fast as those deep in the center, just starting out, because you had farther to travel.

I stood straight. A breeze lifted the shirt from my back and the shaking left me with a sudden chill. I took a breath. The stars were very bright, speaking to each other in soft light, their echoes mingling with moon breath. Slowly, I felt everything breathing: the earth, the sky, the sage and the wind, moving with the effort of the people on the grave.

So I started out again, made a conscious decision to walk that curved line between earth and grave and I walked it with light, quick steps, avoiding that pull down. And it was as I imagined it—around me everything became blurred, unfocused. But when I completed my circle and stepped back onto the undisturbed earth, I felt a kind of melancholy victory, as if I'd found out something I'd always known. Like when I found the bone on my step. And burned the pink marbled paper.

* * *

I had the same feeling when I saw Oxena and Zach pulling out of Raceway early the next morning. It was six o'clock, the sun was up and I heard the guttural waves of a revved motor.

I stood sleepy, wiping my eyes on the stoop. Their '57 Chevy was bright navy blue, the metallic glitter in the paint gleaming in direct sunlight. The chrome was thick and heavy, like bands of solid mercury, reflecting everything back in fat, wide angles. Attached to the back of the Chevy was the Dream Time.

"What are you guys doing?" I scratched my arm and yawned.

Zach looked up from his crouch behind the Chevy's rear bumper.

"You're leaving?" I said suddenly, staring at the car and the trailer all peach and white, sparkling in shades of newborn pink from the sunrise. The car and the trailer were strung together like two bright round beads.

"I have to wire the lights," said Zach.

"She seems fine," said Oxena, opening the front door. She saw me and seemed startled, glancing quickly down. The porch steps had been dragged way off to the side and stood useless in the sand. Three shallow steps up, leading to nowhere. The electric line was capped and tied to the pole, strapped with black electrical tape.

"You're leaving," I said again, and dropped to the next step. "I don't believe it."

Oxena stood in the doorway looking at Zach's back. "We're leaving," she said.

Leaving. I saw the tan flash of the shammy as Zach wiped the tail lights on the Chevy. Oxena jumped down, hatless, slammed the door shut and walked to the passenger side of the car. She leaned against the open door, one foot on the car floor, one still on the road.

"Good-bye Hattie. Good luck," she called and waved.

Their flight suddenly became real. "You're going right now? Now?"

"What do you think?" said Zach, coming around to the driver's side.

He was right. Now was better than later.

"Where're you off to?"

They looked at each other over the top of the car and settled on the bench seat. Zach's hands rested on the steering wheel. "Someplace we can let a bird go," said Zach and turned the key.

"Don't look like that Hattie. It's just time to go." She got in and rolled down the window. The wheels of the car began to turn and the Chevy crawled forward, pausing for an instant, picking up the weight of the Dream Time. Sand fell softly from the wheels as the Dream Time moved forward.

I saw Oxena's face as they drove by. Her passenger side window was rolled down and she waved a white handkerchief with one hand, pressing her fingertips to her mouth with the other. I couldn't tell if she wanted to cry or laugh.

"Drive fast—drive real fast," I called out, feeling the same sense of relief yesterday when I found Kinni's face. A lightness. A hope. She looked startled at first and they were almost passed me now and for an instant I was afraid she didn't understand. Then they were beyond me and all I saw was the back of the trailer. But then she waved harder, up and down, the white handkerchief bobbing up and down like a buoy out her open window.

* * *

Two weeks after the Dreamtime pulled away, the story of Clay was born. A myth, and just like freshly died fabric fades in the beginning, the tale eventually took on its own hue, and remained fast. I even heard the folks at Caldonia's talking about Melody, her aunt, the tragic coma, the unknown father. For those of us from the mineshaft, we said nothing. I never lowered my eyes or looked away, I just always simply smiled and nodded when the story circled around and I was present. It was a conspiracy of which we were all silently proud. Lani considered herself an aunt, the real aunt. Kinni would hold the baby and walk him up and down the rows of trailers singing lilting children's songs, all in Japanese. Clay's favorite, she told me several times was the one about the bamboo princess who returns to the moon. Bat would sit for hours and touch the baby, gently, either in short sweet strokes of his hand, or with a single index finger and delicate pressure on the tip of Clay's nose, eyes, mouth, ears.

202

And Henry. Henry, who should have trusted me, his own daughter, kept the secret as well. We never discussed what must have happened in the mineshaft, and yet I'm sure he knew I knew about the ghosts at Vasquez. He moved in with Melody and Clay four days ago. He just brought over some clothes and left his own place to banter with the wind. His idea is to turn to turn the Traveler into a kind of library. Packed with history books, waiting on four wheels, but, this time, moving nowhere.

He called me over to the Homestead last night looking the same: thin, brown, papery somehow, as if a strong wind would shred him like crinkled crepe paper. He wanted to know: "Do you want any of her things?"

"Like what?" I said, trying not to look at Melody on the sofa with Clay.

"Well. I have a pair of earrings," he said, digging in his pocket. "And a frying pan, a little glass vase. Oh, and this."   He held out a shallow black rectangular box.

I stared at him. I remembered the vase. It was milky pink with little yellow flowers on it. I never knew it was hers. The closed box was the watercolors. Her watercolors, closed for thirty years. Those same hard ovals I laid with in the trunk.

"And I have these," he said and pulled out three marble pink letters from his breast pocket. Three.

"Oh, but Henry, those are yours," said Melody and moved uncomfortably on the sofa.

"Well, not really," he said. "Well, one of them is mine. I'll keep it. But the other two are really yours. Right?"

I saw his hand shake slightly as he held them out to me. Not from any force but from age.

I took them and felt how smooth they lay in my hand.

"I didn't know about that other letter," I said, watching his face.

"I know you didn't," he said. "You didn't write it. Melody's right. It's mine."

It must have really been from her.

"Do you want to see it?"

"Yeah. Sure." I thought it cruel he should be offering me her when Melody was sitting right there. It seemed wrong, as if they were speaking of their adultery right in front of her.

"It's to me only. You understand that?"

"Yeah."

"O.K.," he said and passed me the third letter. I saw the yellowed fold and was careful to open the sheet of paper carefully. I felt my heart swell and pound in my throat and then the pressure fade from the base of my neck. The faded marbled paper bore a small child, a portrait, light, ethereal, the colors all orange and pink, outlined with Indian ink. A portrait of a little baby all swirls and sweeps of brush. By her. It could have been of any round white infant, anywhere.

I heard Clay cry loudly and the sucking sounds of his mouth on Melody's breast. I saw Henry sit down next to them on the sofa and put an arm up along her shoulders. Melody smiled at me and her blond hair fell softly. Clay had grown this last month and he was fat and healthy, brown and had lost most of his black downy-thick hair. He nursed with sighs. I saw the three of them sitting on the sofa as I held the empty paper. I felt awkward and suddenly light. The cramping in my chest seemed gone. I moved to sit down next to Henry.

"I'll take the vase," I said. "And the watercolors."

I slipped the portrait back into the front pocket of his shirt, leaned over and kissed Clay on his forehead.

Melody on measurement

Death is all around us. All the time. Just like I thought it was. But it's not circling around like an evil god waiting for the moment when my guard is down, waiting to make reality out of a daydream. The ghosts, the floating nuns, the emptiness of space cannot be measured. But death can. I saw it in the mineshaft. In her dry eyes. That measurement was final. I saw it when Tip fell into the hole, the moonlight on his teeth, his tongue out. I see it in Barday's eyes, moving like shadows across his iris. He knows death as well. And I see it in Kinni. In the way she stands, straight, tall, feigning strength I don't think she has yet.

And I see it in Henry. I can measure Henry in increments of death. His mother and father, a younger brother, those in the war, the woman in the mine, and Arlene's. Hers, perhaps, is the easiest to measure. Time has passed and yet the strings still pull him, long strings stretching backwards that can be loosened, but never cut. And I can measure them—there has been a price.

I always thought, that in the end, death won. It's stronger than anything else. Final. There is no other force as complete. That night, out in the truck watching everyone trampling Tip's grave, I felt the dark pressure of all that dirt piling up, sealing me in. I lost my breath for an instant and felt my heart beat hard, without oxygen, floundering in my chest. But the stillness between beats was not a cover for death. When I felt Clay push against me, I looked down into his face and saw pale moonlight reflecting in his eyes and was able to breathe again.

I can't measure that. I can't measure life. As I see Henry more I cannot measure that either. Love? Affection? A bonding? It's impossible to say and even if I could, there is no way to measure a warm sleepy arm around your stomach, a child sucking your nipple, the sounds of breathing all around you.

Death is relevant to time. It's always linked inextricably to time. He died too soon/she was just a child/he lived a good life/why did she have to die now?...these are all said in the context of time. It wasn't his time.... But this other thing has little to do with time. Time can be a piece of it all, but not a measurement. Love is not bound to time. Thought is not measured in seconds. That same arm will feel warm ten years from now. Though suckling will stop, there will be early morning talks, a finger on my cheek, my glimpse of a fumbling first kiss, the scent of shaving cream on just his chin. None of which can be measured.

I talked to Hattie once about this, but she's too concrete. Time is linear, straight. For her, there's a past, present, and a future. Even that Almanac she used to read is set up that way. Everything is counted, dated, stamped with time. Death is measured in hundreds of different ways. But not life. I've never seen tallies and scrolls for all the moments in life. Death is final. Life is infinite.

Lani on angles

When you take a picture, you don't just take a picture. You take many shots, shifting position, moving slightly, making adjustments, using different angles.

I developed the shots of Kinni in the mineshaft myself. I can make my own darkroom by taping black vinyl over the windows in the bathroom and I've got a small stock of chemicals. I didn't want anyone else messing with those shots.

Kinni emerged from the clear bath suddenly, a human form like a huge drop, then lines appeared and shape, and she was standing, her back to the camera, two half moons under each butt curve, her head half turned to reveal just the shimmer of cheek and the tip of her nose. She was all curves and smooth skin, indentations of pale shadow behind the knees and in the hollow of her elbows, like a baby. There was no sag in her skin, no evidence of time. She was taut, full. The light was perfect and she stood like a pale statue, legs together, feet slightly pointing out, hands at her sides.

It was a great shot.

Not all the others turned out as good, though I liked them all. There was another, a close up of her face in the mine and of the six I took in there, it was the best, though they all came out a little underexposed.

In this one, her eyes are half closed, lids heavy as if she'd just wakened from a dream. Along the back of her head and on either side of her face are clumps and lines of crystals. Her bangs are tossed to one side, uneven little black and gray wires lying in light twists across her forehead. Her hands are up by her face, just by chance, cupping her chin like a giant clam, her fingers resting by her earlobes. Her lips are slightly parted, sexy in a way, and I can imagine her breathing. All shadows are forced by the smoothness of her face to pool up behind her and the outlines of her hair grow fuzzy and dissolve in the black-space of the mine.

It was Bat who made me get out the magnifying glass, grab the negative and blow the picture up.

I showed him the original, the 8 x 10, and he looked at it, crouching in the sun, not moving at all, just blinking his huge golden eyes in front of the picture. Then he hands it back to me and says, "many angles." So I sit down next to him and ask, "What do you mean?"

"Many angles," he repeats, brushing a finger along the sides of her face. The sun glared off the glossy print. "Many Kinni's. Hundreds. Thousands of Kinnies. We see many Kinnies here."

I took him back into the bathroom and shut the door. I cropped the negative and blew up the picture, keeping only the lower left-hand corner of the original—her chin to her ear, across the cheek to one half of her nose and down to the chin again. Just a quarter-block of face. But what materialized out of the clear bath was a picture of many pictures.

In the original, the crystals gave the shot some texture. Something rough against something smooth. Here they were real, separate, unique. A blanket of broken, gray glass. In each, in every gray flat facet, was a perfect face, all of them reflecting a different face from the one I'd photographed. From different angles, that is. Kinni was captured in whole on hundreds of tiny pieces of gray glass, her face perfect in each.

I keep the blow up in a drawer. It's too artsy fartsy for my taste, but I actually hung the original. It's the one picture I've had framed, matted and the whole bit. I like looking up at her, knowing that it's not a picture of just one face. And whenever Bat comes over he likes to hold it in his hands, lifting the frame right up to his own face until his eyelashes brush against glass. Sometimes I think he sees his own face reflecting back in all those gray crystals.

He's coming out of gray, you see. Slowly. And he's doing it on his own. Everyone's noticed. It's a kind of weird miracle. Everyday there's more color, he sees more shades. It's like a slow leak and colors are spilling out on a dry basin, trickling at first and then moving faster and faster as the fissure slowly widens.

We haven't touched again or anything like that since. To tell you the truth, I was really out of my mind for the next couple of days, wondering what the hell was the matter with me. But that short time on the clay slab left a lingering bond of intimacy that grew stronger as weeks passed. We only needed to crawl around inside each other's skin once I guess. Once was enough. And now we talk. As much as he can. And we share things, I know we share little moments that are usually reserved for lovers or very close friends. Glances, touches, the feeling of relaxing into each other without the stress of the unknown. It's like that one moment on the desert was the plunge of a stone and we are floating and bobbing along on the ripples—except the ripples aren't fanning out and fading, they keep growing stronger.

The other day I took a picture of him. Just a quick head shot, full color. He was eating cotton candy, pink cotton candy outside at the county fair. The breeze had just lifted one end of a long strand and sent it flying across his face, like a twist of pink gauze. That's when I snapped the shutter. He's laughing, his head thrown back, eyes nearly shut, lashes curled. One hand holds the paper stick up by his face, the other grabs the end of the strip of cotton candy. His shirt is bright yellow and navy blue, striped, with big red plastic buttons. Red is also in his hair, the coppery highlights and in the background you can see the merri-go-round with all the colors spinning together.

I didn't bother with different angles. It was a one-time shot and it came out just fine. I'm thinking about hanging that one too, framed and shit. Celeste is getting ready to move into Palmdale, across the street from a school for disabled kids. I get to volunteer at the school and help out twice a week. I want to give all those kids cameras. Every one of them, little Polaroids so they can take their own pictures. In the meantime I am going to get this picture framed. It would be nice to see him eating his cotton candy. To wake up and see that face every day.

Kinni on energy

I am weak. I have been weakened and I feel this weakness in my chest, my hands, my legs. This weakness comes from lack of action, of being caught in a long reaction in which energy was released and never recouped. I never thought or wanted to stop the reaction—I assumed it would continue until death. That I would simply slow down until I could no longer move.

Energy is a constant force and can be harnessed with the smallest movements, like my head on Barday's shoulder, my arms taking Clay, the toss of the veil into the hole. And energy can build momentum, acquire speed and direction of its own.

This is why I am weak. I am not prepared to reverse the reaction. But yet I understand my weakness in the rush of change around me. I must move slowly, cautiously, test my strength against this force before each undertaking. But my caution doesn't come from fear—it comes from the need to assess, to gather resources, to proceed.

I care for Barday now. I am not accustomed to caring for anyone. There are tentacles of feeling, warm threads woven with worry and hope, pity and concern which gather him close to me. This is part of why I move slowly. Most of the day he sits on the top step of his trailer or in the beach chair Hattie gave him. He sits and watches the desert. I will sit with him and read the newspaper to myself. When I am finished, he will tell me about a battle, moving his hands slowly, wiping his eyes, still looking out across the desert, never seeing me.

Before I go to work I fix his dinner. I prepare only Japanese meals. Often he does not know what he is eating, but he is polite and always thanks me. His teeth are bad and rice and bean curd are what we eat most often.

I am careful to touch him often. My touch soothes him and is a reminder of the real world and that it can be gentle. When I touch him, I am reminded of a past not of my own, but a part of me. In Japan, there was a time when progress was assessed and rejected and in that time, firearms were banished. There were no wars, no death by bullets, no struggle for power, no prisoners taken, no rape by gunpoint. Not until Japan was threatened by warriors from across the seas did the laws change and progress reassessed and allowed to inch forward.

So Barday's life comes from a past I share with him, our histories repeated often since the age of agriculture and the concept of property.

I have nothing left to say. I do not tell people I am from Nagasaki anymore. I do not tell them about Melody's child. I do not tell anyone about the great bird. These are events I have measured against myself. I need to move slowly, assess the pulse of energy. I need to move slowly as I did that evening on the horse's grave under stars and moon—proceed with the caution of one witnessing revelation. Revelation is change and can arrive in broad painterly sweeps or be witnessed in small increments of time and action. Revelation in any form requires a firm grounding, an understanding of some foundation so that I have a basis from which to act.

The other night I went to Lani's. It was my night off and I brought over flowers, bright red and yellow flowers, daisies and roses. I bought them at Caldonia's. She left me alone in the bathroom while I undressed and ran the bath water. It was a hot evening, hot even for September and the water I ran was only lukewarm. I turned off the water and climbed in the tub, sitting down, holding the flowers against my chest. One by one, I pulled the petals apart. They spun and floated, moving with tiny currents on the surface of the water.

GOING BLIND

Out in the Mojave is a circular grave. Four feet under is the skeleton of a horse, a stainless steel spoon and a streamer of black lace. They lie crowded under dirt on a bed of red clay. The Mojave used to be a frontier, an endless horizon line stretching to nowhere, with an occasional mountain sparring with sky. Now the only true horizons are invisible, and I've crossed over, leaving old terrain. I can't see clearly what I've left behind. Everyone has crossed, splayed out in different directions, no one able to truly follow another. There are links, between Henry and Melody, Bat and Lani, Oxena and Zach, Kinni and Barday. These links are tremulous—like rope bridges swaying between shifting continents, and yet, are woven from hope and therein lies their strength.

The air is humid, heavy, and mosquitoes are starting to bite. Just like in the desert, there is a full moon. I stand on the end of the dock, lake water circling around the pilings, moved in gentle ripples by the moon and fish. There is the languished call of a mourning dove in the evening as night slips between the trees. Across the lake, evergreens grow low, their weight pushing them in down into the sodden earth of the lake bank, some so low heavy black green branches dip and touch the crystal surface of the water. The scent of pine intermingles with the arctic thread of timberline chill. It is different here. The hills and basins are green and full, not in a regimented patchwork of hues, but in lush sprawling swatches. The earth is heavy with water and life. Above, high in the night, are mountain tops always covered in snow. There are seasons all around me. I don't read the Almanac.

There is a picture of Clay in my pocket. He is fat and browned by sun, laughing, with baby food on his face. He is just over a year old. The letter in my pocket is from both Melody and Henry, each writing on one side of a clean white sheet of paper. There is a smudge of food along the bottom of the page and Melody has written on along the margin, this is Clay saying hi with chocolate pudding. I am glad he will grow up next to Henry's trailer, surrounded by bookshelves, a nugget of history.

Eight months ago, I picked up my sliver of bone, packed my trailer, bought an easel, and headed northeast. Right now I'm in Wyoming, listening to whippoorwills in the morning and fiddles in the evening. Thayer is small and not growing. There is a trailer park just outside town, but close enough so I can walk in and get the paper every morning and have a cup of coffee. The job at the gift shop isn't bad either. It's a job. It's between the Tetons and Yellowstone, so I sell a lot of Jack-a-lope postcards and little metal bear banks, mugs with acorns on them and silkscreened T-shirts.

I've sold a couple of paintings too, little watercolors, both inspired by Lani's gray photos. In the first, the checkered tablecloth is now white and red, the poppies a mix of gold and orange, the desert grass is green—the second is a wash of monochrome orange clouds against the horizon of an evening sky. I discovered how the smooth discs of color would blend and run with water.

"So you're going," Henry had said to me when I told him I had to leave.

"Yeah. I think it's time."

"You know I heard from someone someplace that Oxena and Zach were up in Oregon or Washington or someplace like that."

"I'm not headed that way," I said.

"What are you going to do?"

"What?"

"Do? What you going to do? You know, Hattie." His question was swift, urgent, pressing. He seemed anxious about me, leaning forward, intense, shivering, locking his gaze with mine with uncomfortable force. He needed his answer right now.

I pulled out the tin of watercolors from my pocket.

He was standing outside. It was November. It was dark and cold, and he wasn't wearing a coat.

"I'm going to learn how to use these," I said, tapping the rectangular box with my finger.

I left the next day. Henry let me have the Valiant. It's a great car and it can pull my Bullet without too much effort. I went fast. Straight out Rte. 14 to I-40 and then north and didn't stop until I hit Wyoming. No real reason I picked Thayer either. I had a flat. The folks at the gas station were nice. I liked all the space and the way the summer air carried the scent of snow.

And now I'm getting ready to leave again. I've been here a while and I think it's time to move on. This is fine. I think I'll head south and east for a bit. I'm not in such a hurry this time. Tennessee looks good. Or maybe I'll get as far as Virginia. I'm moving now, without much direction, I admit, but at least I'm not lost. Not lost in the past. My days are different and I am learning to revel in that insecurity. And I have my little black box of colors.

From the dock I watch the bats come out one by one, dipping and soaring in their calculated, geometric flight over the water. They are flying blind, moving through air without the assurance of gravity, without sight. Like them, I too, am flying with hidden direction, in the dark. Unlike them, however, I have color.   I watch them flutter and dodge in the air, blacker than the night sky, warmer than my breath.

ABOUT THE AUTHOR

R. A. Morean is a novelist, short story writer, essayist and screenwriter. Her work has appeared in *Salon, Lost Coast Review, Sundial Press, The Tishman Review, Ploughshares, Kalliope*, and more, and her novels are with St. Martin's Press, Escape Publishing, Roundfire Books, and Breese Books. She writes a mystery series under the name Abbey Pen Baker about the daughter of Sherlock Holmes. She grew up in Southern California just miles from Vasquez Rocks and graduated from SUNY Stony Brook. As a *Salon* contributor, her articles and essays have included issues relating to health care, atheism, digital media, parenting and education. She has appeared on radio and television and is president of the Antioch Writers' Workshop. A professor at Sinclair College, she also teaches creative writing workshops throughout Ohio's Miami Valley, focusing on short fiction, the novel, YA novels and screenplays. She is a single mom of four children, two dogs and a cat and has been known to keep goats.

Reading Group Guide: Discussion Questions

1. Much of the novel is told from different points of view and moves from past to present tense. Why? Can time become a character?
2. Which characters wrestle with history? And what histories do they wrestle with?
3. How does the title relate to the stories and characters?
4. Often in literature and film, women's bodies are used to destroy or save men from a purely sexualized perspective. (*The Summer of 42.*) How does Melody's suckling of Bat and Lani's sexual encounter with him differ from this tradition?.
5. Why is the novel set in the desert? What then, is the purpose of all the water imagery?
6. Raceway is not an oval. How are shapes used in the novel and how to they relate to the stories?
7. What sets each character in a position to move forward with their lives?
8. How is color used in the novel?
9. What makes Oxena decide to fall back in love with Zach?
10. How is nudity used in the novel? What are some symbols of fertility?
11. Why is there a supercollider? And a whale?
12. How are caves and subterranean spaces used figuratively and literally?
13. Is the novel a long allegory?
14. How do the relationships between people relate to love?